SILVER SALTS

SILVER SALTS

A NOVEL

Mark Blagrave

Cormorant Books

Canada Council   Conseil des Arts
for the Arts   du Canada

The publisher gratefully acknowledges the support of the
Canada Council for the Arts and the Ontario Arts Council
for its publishing program. We acknowledge the financial support
of the Government of Canada through the Book Publishing
Industry Development Program (BPIDP) for our publishing activities.

Printed and bound in Canada

Library and Archives Canada Cataloguing in Publication

Blagrave, Mark, 1956–
Silver salts / Mark Blagrave.

ISBN 978-1-897151-24-2

1. Title.

PS8603.L39S59 2008   C813'.6   C2007-906473-6

Cover Design: Angel Guerra/Archetype
Text Design: Tannice Goddard,
Soul Oasis Networking
Cover image: Angel Guerra/Archetype
Printer: Friesens

CORMORANT BOOKS INC.
215 SPADINA AVENUE, STUDIO 230, TORONTO, ON CANADA M5T 2C7
www.cormorantbooks.com

ANCIENT FOREST
FRIENDLY

For S, P, and N

REEL ONE

Scenes of
Innocence

1

In the
Looking
Glass

IT BEGINS WITH the shattered mirror I hid beneath the floor-board — my face multiplied and imprisoned on every fragment. My earliest memory? It is the earliest story I remember telling myself. That amounts to the same thing.

I do not feel the cuts on my hands until all the pieces have been cleaned up, but this doesn't surprise me; fear has a way of focusing my mind. What's a little sting beside what my father will do if he finds the broken glass? I would like to stop to admire the new patterns on my palms, red streets on a map made just for me, but I must erase all traces right away. The blood would only lead them back to the glass, and the glass to the mirror. It is the way their minds work. In lines. So I find one of my mother's cloths — the ones only she uses. I am pretty sure she doesn't have them counted out. I know he doesn't.

The maps transfer perfectly onto the cotton. It's just like making a print, so I'm sorry to spoil the patterns as I squeeze the cloth in my hands to put pressure on the cuts. If anybody notices, I will say I fell on the street and landed on my palms. For that I'll need some dirt. Dirt is no problem.

It doesn't take long for the bleeding to slow. I push the cloth into the space between the joists where I have already gathered the shards of glass. The floorboard shrieks a little as I press it back in place. "Quiet," I whisper back.

My mother will miss the mirror. As early as tonight when she goes to brush out her hair, she'll reach for the little hand glass to check the spot in the back she always worries about. The mirror is valuable, and there will be hell to pay — but not for me. Patrick and Mike will be suspected immediately. My brothers are known thieves, though only little things until now — never what my mother calls an heirloom, never anything so bold as a silver-backed, bevelled-glass hand mirror. It's only a matter of time before petty thieving turns to grand larceny, my father will say as he takes out the strap. Unless my mother suspects my father. In that case, she'll say nothing about the missing mirror. I have watched her back down from scenes with him a dozen times. That might be best in this case, even though it hurts to imagine her having to swallow all at once the pain of losing her mirror and the heartache of thinking that her husband has pawned it for liquor or tobacco or another woman.

Had I broken almost any other thing in the whole apartment, I would tell her, even though it might mean a licking. But with the mirror it's different. It's not because it's an heirloom — it was my mother's mother's, which takes it all the way back to Ireland — that's just what makes it sad. And it's not because mirrors are frowned upon for little girls, especially little girls on their own. At school, the nuns made sure there were no mirrors. Even puddles in the schoolyard seemed to dry up unnaturally quickly. The vainer girls were forced to find their faces in the windows when the sun hit just right, or in the brass fittings on the great mahogany doors. I never tried that; vanity was not my sin. You mustn't think that. I haven't been looking in my mother's prized mirror to admire what I see there. It is only to check on what a little boy said to me as I walked home this afternoon. He called me Wednesday.

"Why do you call me that? My name's Lillie."

"Oh," he said, "I thought it must be Wednesday."

"Why?"

"Well, because your eyes are looking both ways for Sunday!" And then he skipped off down Waterloo Street, chasing the rusty barrel hoop he had set to rolling.

A lazy eye, my mother and father call it. Lillie's got a bit of a lazy eye, they say, not minding much whether I am near enough to hear them or not. My brothers never mention it, not even when they're dredging the gutters for insults, so it must be really bad. Whenever I moan about it, my mother hushes me up with a torrent of words. "That's how God made you, my dear, it's not for us to question God's plans for us." Then she tells me how nice my hair is, or my nose.

Had she been home when I came in, I might have told her about the mean boy, been given the sermon on God's will, and everything would have been as always. But only my brothers were there, playing that game of theirs with the ball on the stoop, and I went straight up to the apartment and into my mother's room. I took the mirror out to the sitting-room window. The boy was right. I knew it was wrong to question God, but I did. Then I cried. Then I dropped the mirror and it shattered. From every shard there wept back an image of me, Lillie, my face captured over and over again, lazy eye and all. An awful fairy-tale nightmare. This is what I do not want to explain to anyone, not even my mother.

The floorboard in place, I hurry back into the street. I nod to Patrick and Mike as I race around the corner and into the alley, where I will be able to stash the embossed silver back of the mirror into the rusting bin. And then I will kneel to dirty my blood-sticky hands.

2

The
Burial
Ground

THEN THERE ARE the other memories, flickering shadows on a screen, moving pictures I have watched from a distance a thousand times. They no longer feel like they happened to me, but daughters should know everything about their mothers, so they must be told too.

A cemetery, daylight. In the distance, there's a city skyline arranged around a harbour. St. John, 1913, before the "Saint" was dragged out. Iris-in on the cemetery, the picture starting as a tiny hole in the centre and then growing in a circle until it fills the whole screen. They don't use that much anymore. Cut to a medium close-up of a little girl in the cemetery. She is holding a doll.

THE LITTLE GIRL hears the man long before she sees him, though she is not really aware for some time that she has even heard him. If she has paid any attention to it at all, his sobbing has simply been the *chuff-chuff-chuff* of a gramophone when the music has finished. But she knows there are no gramophones out here. Or thinks she knows. Maybe there is a custom she has not heard about; maybe these people bury their dead with all kinds of things you'd never dream of. Including gramophones. She has heard much stranger stories than that whispered about them. They eat babies, but not pork. They have enormous hordes of money, but would rather die than part with a penny. Their private parts look different from other people's, and work in different ways. These are the things she has heard in the schoolyard, on the back steps, even in catechism. These are the stories that keep her friends away from where she now finds herself, that would have kept her far away, too, if her father had not brought her. He said he has some business here, though what business an Irish-Catholic street-railway worker could have in the Jewish Burying Ground he has not thought it necessary to explain.

The business has something to do with a woman. This little girl, Lillie, is not dumb. She has been on little jaunts with her father enough to know that much and a lot more. She is never supposed to see the women, of course. He always sends her off to play before the woman shows her face. But most times she catches a glimpse, afterwards, when her father and the woman crawl out of the bushes or stumble from the alleyway. Their hair is always a mess, as if there has been a great wind, their mouths like smudges, and they are always tugging at their clothes, something not on quite right. Sometimes she hears noises from the bushes or down the alleyway — grunts, shrieks, once laughter, quite often tears. Bea (that's her doll — a floppy body and a hard head, which is better than the other way around, her mother had said when she gave it to her) sometimes wonders why Lillie's father, who is always so nice and gentle to her and to her mother (except for the yelling and sometimes the back of his hand), would want to fight with these strange women, or why they, so much frailer and younger, would want to fight with such a big, strong man. Maybe when Bea is older, maybe when she is ten, like Lillie, she will understand. Nobody seems to get hurt, she and Bea agree, although once she noticed blood on her father's trousers.

This is the first time for the cemetery. Lillie supposes that the opponent of the day must live somewhere nearby. "Out east," as she and her friends dismiss it, as if it were a hinterland too remote and uncivilized for any more detailed notice. She has walked with her father from where the street railway stops at Haymarket Square out to Kane's Corner, holding her nose against the rotten-eggs-reek of Marsh Creek, and then on into what seems like wilderness. He bought her a bag of candy on the way; there is always a bag of candy on these trips. When she complained that her feet hurt, he hoisted her onto his shoulders and she imagined she was riding an elephant into the jungles of East St. John. About half a mile from the cemetery he put her down. Bea was about to complain, but Lillie quieted her — it was because he had to preserve his strength for the upcoming wrestling. She is proud of her father, whatever he does, and she wishes she could make him know it.

They have climbed the fence a few yards from where the gates stand open. He likes to do things the hard way. Why are there fences around graveyards, she asked as they climbed, and then, before he could come up with an answer she had supplied it. Because people are dying to get in. They both laughed. It felt important to laugh in this place where the trees drooped low in mourning and the birds were silent. Her father, who was by nature a loud and boisterous man, spoke in whispers here.

"What do you think, Lillie? Do you think you and Bea can play here for a little? I won't be long. You won't be frightened, will you?" She felt the stubble on his cheek, rough like sandpaper, against hers.

"No, Dad," she lied. "I won't be ascared." She hoped he was proud of her bravery.

"Good girl," he whispered, patting her head as if it were as hard as Bea's. And then he was gone, just a succession of foot-steps crunching the gravel walk.

Lillie sits beside the path, tugging at the back of her skirt so it keeps the grass from tickling her thighs. It has rained in the night and she knows she will be scolded when she gets home for getting her clothes wet. But she also knows that her father will speak up for her, tell her mother to leave the girl alone, she's just a child, and children get dirty.

Bea is having a sulk because Lillie has eaten the last barley candy without offering her so much as a lick, so Lillie sets her aside, face down on some leaves, to think about her behaviour. She usually finds some such excuse to protect Bea from witnessing her father's business. It isn't for the very small.

Before too many minutes, she can hear voices in the next walk; her father and today's woman. Traces of cigarette smoke waft from the same direction. Sometimes they smoke before, sometimes after; never during, as far as she has been able to tell. Then she hears footsteps retreating, the crack of a distant branch as they push their way into the bushes. She counts to a hundred and then begins to tiptoe in pursuit. She needs to hear close-up the squeaks and moans and tears, different every time but still obvi-ously variations on the same old song. So different from the sounds she hears her parents making on Saturday nights after they think she is asleep. At the same time, she feels it is important to be nearby in case her father needs her, in case the woman conquers him and begins to eat him up. They'd do that, they'd eat a man alive if they got the chance, she heard him complain one night when he came home very late with Frank from upstairs, and their speech was slurred and they kept hugging one another to keep from falling over.

Lillie's mother had bawled, "The two of yous shaddap. Can't you see there's people trying to sleep here? Shaddap or, so help me God, I'll cut your balls off, I will." Whatever that was, it couldn't be worse than being eaten alive, but it seemed to shut the men up.

When she approaches the spot, the rustling of the dry leaves has taken on a regular pattern, the sound of someone raking them in short, sharp strokes. Through the bushes, she catches a glimpse of her father's white shirttail flapping back and forth where his trousers no longer hold it in. Around his waist, a pair of calves sheathed in drooping stockings form a writhing sash. One foot still wears a shoe, but the toes of the other are free, and Lillie is hypnotized by their rhythmic curling and uncurling, five red-lacquered cherries in a sack. Soon the sound of their panting blocks out the gentler scratching of the leaves, and finally the mechanical chant of their voices getting faster and faster drowns out both.

Lillie is alarmed by the hush that follows. Has the woman eaten her father? Will she and Bea have to find their way home by themselves? Then she hears him sigh and laugh, and she knows everything is all right. "What do you think? One more time?" she hears her father say. Lillie uses the renewed noises to cover the sound of her creeping away back to Bea.

This is when she finally registers the sound of the man. The *chuff-chuff-chuff* of his sobbing.

She takes off her shoes and socks. She didn't think this precaution necessary for her father, but it seems more appropriate to sneak up on a stranger in bare feet. She wonders what her nails would look like with red varnish instead of their natural pale pink. She practises curling and uncurling her toes as she has seen the woman do, but her foot quickly cramps and she gives it up. As she moves towards the sound, the gravel sticks to the soles of her feet and lodges between her toes so that she has to stop and brush it off. The showers of gravel are probably as much a giveaway of her presence as her shoed footsteps would have been, she realizes, but the man continues to sob, so she moves forward, confident he has not heard her above the song of his own sadness.

He is dressed in black, except for a brightly coloured shawl around his shoulders. He is a bigger man than her father — not taller, although that could be a trick of his position, but broader, massive on top. His clothes are good, not shiny with wear and ragged at the cuffs the way her father's are. Although his face is half turned from her, she can tell he wears glasses. The thin gold arm presses across his temple, flattening the hair before disappearing behind a pudgy ear. The shape of his head reminds Lillie of Bea, and she is almost at the point of moving close to the man to comfort him as she might comfort her doll when suddenly the sobbing stops. It is as though someone, hidden perhaps in the bushes around the grave, has flipped a switch; as though mourning has been cut off for the day. Does that happen? Lillie drops to her knees behind a low branch and watches as the man pulls an enormous white handkerchief from the pocket of his jacket. It waves in the breeze for a moment, like her father's white shirttail flapping back and forth in the bushes, and then his round face disappears into it. The sound he makes is like a klaxon, and Lillie has to bite her cheeks to keep from laughing out loud. She knows that for him it is the sound of grief, and nobody should laugh at that. She gets up as quietly as she can from her crouched position and creeps back along the path to find Bea. Behind her, she hears the man make a big sigh, and then she smells the fresh cigarette smoke that means that her father and his woman are through with their business too.

Bea's dress is wet from the grass but Lillie does not scold her. "There's a man," she whispers to the doll, "a man who is very sad. I think he might have lost his mum. Did you think you might have lost me? Silly Bea, I wasn't far. Daddy will be back soon. He'll be too tired for a ride, we'll have to walk all that way.

But I think he won again. The wrestling. Shall we go see the man?"

The doll's head nods limply and Lillie clutches her to her breast and sets off for the place where she has watched the man in his mourning ritual.

When she arrives, the white handkerchief is nowhere in evidence. She and Bea see the man bend low to kiss the stone. "I promise, Mama," she thinks she hears him say, "I promise ..."

Just as the man straightens up, Lillie's father comes suddenly around the corner in the path. Attached to his arm, her claws bunching the rough fabric of his jacket, is a woman who looks like something he must have robbed from one of the graves. Her eyes are sunk deep in her face and ringed with purple shadows. Her hair is straw, singed black, so brittle it would break off if you brushed against it. Where her breasts should be, her cheap dress flaps against a cavernous hollow, and her legs, where they show below her hemline, don't look big enough around to hold her up. Bea asks Lillie why Lillie's father should want to fight such a corpse, what possible satisfaction could there be in wrestling so thin and haggard a specimen. But her father is grinning, and the woman is smiling with her red gash of a mouth, so Lillie tells Bea it must all be all right.

They are smiling, at least, until they see the man. The instant they register his presence, their lips go tight and the woman drops her hand from Lillie's father's arm. The man, whose face is still shiny with tears, doesn't seem any more pleased to see them than they are to see him. Lillie wonders whether they have met before. She wonders whether the man knows the lady-corpse, or whether her father owes the man money. He looks like the kind of man you might owe money. As she watches, though, she can detect no clear glimmer of recognition on either side. There is only coldness and the kind of shame she might feel if she were caught sneaking pennies from the jar above the sink.

"Morning," the man says finally.

"Morning to you," Lillie's father replies. The woman makes a sound that might have begun as hello but ends in a coughing fit. "I'm, um, I'm sorry for your loss," Lillie's father continues, nodding at the stone beside the man's foot. Lillie feels proud. Her father always knows just what to say to people.

"My mother," the man says, and Lillie hears a little catch in his throat. "She died in the hospital. All alone. I couldn't be here. I — she ..."

"I'm sorry." Lillie's father lays a hand on the man's shoulder, pats him twice, and turns to go, but before he can take a step, the man has spun on his heel and fled the scene.

"I thought so," Lillie hears the woman say after she has studied the stone for a moment.

"What?" Her father sounds bored, tired.

"That was the Mayer kid. Remember? The junk kid. You must remember the junk kid. Used to ride around on his father's wagon, made people feel so sorry they'd give him a break, give away stuff they never meant to, even? Louis, I think. That's the kid." The woman's voice is deep, a young man's voice more than a woman's, Lillie thinks, and Bea is glad because there must have been more fight to her than it looks.

"That fella? Get away with you."

"No, sure, look, this is the mother's grave, I bet. I heard he was some kind of big shot in the Boston States now. Owns a moving picture house, I heard. Louis Mayer. He was dressed like a big shot, wasn't he?"

"There's lots dresses like big shots. That don't mean nothing."

"And there's lots that don't. And there's some look better underneath their clothes. Which kind do you think you are? We could test that out right now if you like, right on the Jew-boy's mama's grave if you want. She won't care, and he won't be back."

"I've got to get back to town. Another time."

"Don't you like me, sugar? Didn't we have fun?"

"Loads of fun, but I've got me daughter waitin' for me, and I don't like to keep her too long."

"You brought your daughter along? I never heard the beat of that. You left her waiting by a bloody tombstone while you was bangin' away at me! Well, you are the champion. That beats all."

Lillie is proud that Bea can hear the woman admitting defeat so clearly.

"Just a little something to remember me by then?" the woman asks, her voice a little hoarse. Before Lillie turns away, she sees the woman grab her father's hand and guide it up her skirts. Why, she wonders, as she hurries back to the place where her father left her, would the woman want to pee on her father's hand? And why would he let her? It must be some kind of custom. This place is rich in customs, she thinks. It must be some kind of custom, she decides, as she and Bea sit down on the wet grass to wait.

And that is where we can iris-out to a black screen.

3

Lucia/
Light

A NIGHT AT the Opera House is something I would never have dreamed possible, not for us. Sometimes, for a treat around the holidays, my parents would take me and my brothers to the Lyric or the Unique on Charlotte Street to see the pictures. Often, there would be live acts as well — knife-throwing, ventriloquism, even, once, a pair of monkeys who could ride bicycles. Variety acts, they were called. I loved them. Despite its fancy name, the Opera House mainly showed pictures and vaudeville, but it was not the kind of place where families like mine usually went. Every now and then it brought in the big travelling shows you'd never see at the Lyric or the Unique, real live theatre shows that people like us never got to see unless we were very, very lucky.

My father got the tickets for helping load the scenery in. The company manager hired him right off his stool at Cronin's. My mother was furious that he hadn't insisted on cash. I don't think it was really the money, though. I think it was because she didn't know what we would wear or how people would look at us. My father said they were papering the house. That way, the newspapers would report a large crowd, and then other people would know they should go see it for themselves. Besides, he said, why shouldn't we see an opera like anyone else? He was very keen on that kind of argument, that everyone is equal. I heard him apply it to everything from schooling to hours of work. In the end, mother relented, even seemed a little pleased. We all put on our Sunday best, which, as my father pointed out, wasn't doing us any good sitting around in the clothespress.

The man taking the tickets looks at us a little funny, but he doesn't say anything but good evening, just as he does to everyone else. As soon as we are seated — so high up I worry we'll only be able to see the tops of the performers' heads — my mother starts pointing people out, people she knows from the cleaning job she has up on Mount Pleasant, people who visit at the Estabrooks's when she is there. Before long, though, the lights dim and she can't make anyone out anymore.

The national anthem starts the evening, which is funny since the company we have come to see is the Boston Opera Company and I know they have a different national anthem down there. My mother leans over to tell us that the singer is C.B. Pidgeon's boy, Walter. C.B. Pidgeon owns the dry goods store in the north end. My father pronounces the father a pirate. I think the boy's voice is beautiful anyway, though his face is a little long.

When everybody sits down, I forget the seat bottoms are on springs and I almost end up on the floor. My brother Patrick catches my arm and jerks me back up. I think he meant it kindly, but my shoulder burns with the wrench. Michael is the one who can be counted on to hurt me on purpose, being closer in age.

The opera is called *Lucia di Lammermoor*. My mother told us the story at supper before we all got dressed to go out. She read it in a book by Sir Walter Scott. She likes to read books about faraway places. When she tells the story, the characters all have Scottish names, which sound a lot like English names. The people who made the opera, though, had to go and give everybody an Italian name. It's only to make it sound more highfalutin, is what my father whispers when we all have trouble in the first few minutes figuring out exactly who is who. My brother Patrick, who is always reading, says that Lucia means light. He never takes his eyes off the lady singer who plays the lead.

Even with the Italian names and all the singing, I am able to make out the main story before long. Lucia loves Edgardo, but he's her brother's mortal enemy, so the two are forced to sneak around the grounds and sing sad songs about saying goodbye. I wonder whether my parents ever had to sneak around on their families. I know they wouldn't have had all those glorious grounds to get lost in. Of course I am aware it's just a stage with pretend stage settings that my very own father helped lug in, but in my imagination the pasteboard fountain has real water in it and the painted floorcloth is lush, dewy grass. It doesn't hurt to imagine.

When Edgardo goes away to France, Lucia's brother Enrico, which is Italian for Henry, like that famous singer I hear sometimes on the phonograph recordings in Thorne's store, intercepts all their letters. Finally, he forges one announcing Edgardo's marriage. He does all this so Lucia will marry his friend Arturo, who is rich and can save the family from bankruptcy. I suppose it could be nice to have somebody who would swoop in and solve all your money problems forever, but it's not so nice for Lucia, who really wishes she could have Edgardo, even though he seems to be married now.

The wedding day comes, and Edgardo appears, too late to tell Lucia he is not married. Lucia and Arturo exit to their wedding bed. Patrick and Mike snicker and ask our parents if I'm a little young for this.

That is when the power fails. The Opera House is very proud of its electric lighting, although the owners have been shrewd enough to keep the gas laid on too, to guide people out safely in case of emergencies. The truth is that the electricity is still not very reliable. The Street Railway owns it, along with the gas. My father, when he is feeling good about the company, insists they are doing a fine job of managing it.

"It's those damned pirates again, I bet," he grumbles as we find our way out into the street by the light of the gas jets. There has been a rash of electrical failures in the city the past few months. Several of the smaller cinemas have been caught jumping the street railway's cables to steal the power for themselves. When they do it wrong, the whole system goes down.

So it is not until years later that I get to see and hear the end, as the mad Lucia makes her final spine-chilling leap.

4

Voice
Box

IF I TIMED it right, and if I didn't get so underfoot that the salesman could no longer pretend he didn't notice me, I could spend
whole Saturday afternoons at Thorne's showroom among the
gramophones. Their music was glorious. More magical, though,
was knowing that I was listening to sounds from somewhere
else and some other time just as if I was right there in the room
when they were first made. Photographs can't manage that. In
those days before the talkies, not even the moving pictures could.
Pictures, moving or still, are flat. Looking at the things you see in
them, you can't help knowing you're not there in the same space.
It doesn't matter how much you pretend. With the gramophone
on those enchanted Saturdays, though, it was just like being where
the music was first heard.

*A simple fade-in. The picture gradually materializes out of the black-
ness. It stays a little blurry around the edges, dreamy. We are looking*

at an interior: the gramophone showroom at Thorne's on Prince William Street. We spy Lillie as part of the overall establishing shot, a little girl trying hard not to stand out, not to be noticed.

A YOUNG COUPLE is looking at a machine with a prettily scalloped horn that is painted all over with leaves and a flower that Lillie doesn't recognize. It is obviously a decorative piece, meant for show. Lillie prefers the plainer Victrolas and Berliners; she doesn't like her listening to be distracted.

"This one's European," she hears the salesman announce. The young woman jumps, she didn't see him coming. "A real beauty to look at."

"Where's the handle?" asks the young man.

"That's the thing, you see, there isn't one. Doesn't that beat all? It's what they call a hot-air engine."

Lillie would laugh out loud, but she doesn't want to get kicked out of the store; and she likes the salesman, hot air or not.

He opens a door in the front of the engine cabinet. "This here is a spirit lamp. You light that and it heats this chamber, and then the hot air —"

"You light a lamp? That sounds like a magic lantern, Mister. We just want a plain gramophone."

"Oh, it's a gramophone all right ..." But the couple is obviously suspicious of anything that does not draw a clear dividing line between the senses. They move on to a Victrola.

"This is a very fine machine. A spring motor, as you can see." The young man is already winding the crank. "That's right, wind it up and we'll have a listen, shall we?" The salesman carefully slides a disc out of its brown paper wrapper.

"I thought it would be a cylinder," the young woman says. Lillie smiles at her ignorance. She must be from up river somewhere where everybody probably still has the old Edison machines.

"No, this one here's a disc machine. The discs are easier to reproduce, and we pass that saving right along to you."

Lillie has heard the man give a much more technical explanation before, in words she likes the sound of even though she doesn't know what every one means. All about how the expansion and contraction of a membrane helps to etch a zinc disc from side to side in a spiral pattern; then how they electroplate the disc to make a negative that they use to stamp copies. He keeps it simpler for this couple. It is part of what Lillie has noticed — that he always knows his audience.

The salesman lowers the soundbox arm. He doesn't give them the lecture about the perfect angle for the stylus. The recording is a quartet singing "Across the Great Divide (I'll Wait for You)." Lillie knows it by heart and hums along, but quietly so no one can hear her.

As the music plays, she looks at the painting that hangs above her, high on the painted tin-stamped wall. It's a dog with his head in the mouth of a gramophone horn.

"He's called Nipper," the salesman said the first day he saw her standing staring up at the picture. "Did you know that?" Lillie said she didn't. "He used to bite the artist's friends," he said. "Do you have a dog?"

"No," Lillie said.

"Do you have a gramophone?" Same answer. She thinks that might be why he didn't shoo her out of the store. Instead, when there were lulls in his afternoons, which there often were, he would talk to her and tell her things about the machines and how they worked. He told her how sound makes vibrations, like waves, and that if you could find something to react to these vibrations and hook it up to some kind of writing instrument you could record the patterns of the waves. He told her how people had tried attaching a boar's bristle (that's a kind of a big pig he had said) to a diaphragm (like stretched skin that can go in and out) to trace the patterns in some lampblack; and about Edison's scratching in a wax cylinder, and about Berliner, who was a German immigrant — the man made it sound like some kind of bad cheese — who had figured out how to write onto a disc made out of zinc. She listened politely. He was a nice man, kind to her. But she still clung to the idea that it was also magic. To hear something from somewhere else and some other time — that would always be magic.

The young couple leaves the store without buying. Lillie can see the salesman blaming himself. He always blames himself, supposes he tried to go too fast, or he didn't hook them fast enough. It's all about timing, he has told Lillie once, confidentially. Then, still on the subject of timing apparently, he went on to explain to her about how there was a governor in the spring engine that kept the turntable spinning at just about seventy-eight revolutions per minute. Lillie has heard about the American Revolution, and has read a little about the French Revolution in a book her older brothers have, but she said she does not know this kind. The man laughed and tousled her hair. She felt as though she was his little dog. Nipper.

Almost immediately, the young couple is replaced by a much older, much more prosperous-looking pair. Lillie likes how this can happen, how one customer can spring up where another one has only just disappeared. They go straight for the Victrola that has the largest engine box and the biggest horn. Lillie is excited for the salesman, who has told her that he makes his living better or worse according to the price of what he sells. For them, he selects Henry Burr, "When You and I Were Young, Maggie," and then "After the Roses Have Faded Away." This brings tears to the woman's eyes, and her husband counts off the money right then and there. They give an address — Germain Street, the nicest side — and are gone.

Then it's time to close up shop. This, for Lillie, is the most wonderful moment of all, the moment that makes it worth having to listen to her mother's scoldings — "Where were you all afternoon, don't you know how a mother worries?" How? she sometimes itched to ask. It's bad for the machines to be left wound up. It's hard on the springs, on the motors in general. So the salesman has to go around the showroom flicking levers, letting them all run down. The whirr of two-dozen motors is music in itself, but on really good days the salesman puts recordings on every turntable and then starts flicking the levers. This is one of those good days. The cacophony is spectacular. Lillie loves that word, taught to her specially by the salesman. Caruso vies with Henry Burr and the Hayden Quartet, and then the banjo orchestra nearly drowns them all out, and then come the moments when all the machines begin to run down. The governors stop working at a certain point when the springs get too loose to turn the platter at seventy-eight revolutions per minute. Caruso becomes a baritone and then a foghorn, the Hayden Quartet becomes four very old men with mouths full of molasses, and the banjos become, at best, elastic bands stretched over cigar boxes.

The last note fades and Lillie, grinning from ear to ear, is about to leave when the salesman calls after her.

"Little girl?" He has never asked her name, and she knows enough not to tell it to strangers. "Little girl? Would you like a special treat?" Of course Lillie would, who wouldn't? but for some reason she has a bad feeling. "It's okay. It's nothing to be afraid of. And it can be our little secret." What could be wrong with that? Lillie thinks, so she nods. "Wait right here." And the man disappears into the back of the shop, behind a velvet curtain.

Lillie looks up at Nipper, still listening attentively for his master's voice.

When the man comes back, he is carrying something that reminds Lillie of the grindstone she has seen her father sharpen knives on, only this one has pieces of a telephone machine attached on either side. He puts it on the tall mahogany counter, and lifts Lillie onto a stool, hurting her armpits only a little.

"What is it?" she whispers. Although she can't identify it, she instinctively knows it is some kind of sacred object and deserves awed tones.

"A tinfoil phonograph," the man breathes. "Would you like to have a try?"

"How does it work?" Lillie is dying to have a try, whatever that might involve, but she knows how much he likes to explain things.

"I turn the crank here, and the drum goes round." He does all of this in the air with his fingers, not yet wanting to make it work. "When a person talks in here," he points to one piece of telephone, "a diaphragm moves — you remember what a diaphragm is?" She does. "And that makes a needle scratch on the revolving drum. Want to try now?"

"What should I say?"

"Whatever you want." Lillie is surprised to hear a grown-up give that advice, and she squints at the man.

"Maybe your name, to start."

Lillie is not about to be tricked so easily. "Um. Norma," she invents. She has always liked the sound of that name. Then a little more confidently, "Norma."

"Just a minute." The salesman moves the needle and starts turning the crank. "Now speak in there." Lillie does. After saying "Norma" three times and "hello" four, she looks at the man. He tells her to say a secret. She thinks for a moment.

"Sorry, too late. It doesn't hold much. You have to say it all at once. Do you want to hear?"

The man disengages the needle that's next to the mouthpiece, and positions the one on the other end. "Put your ear here," he says. Lillie lifts her hair away. The earpiece feels cold. The man turns the crank and there is Lillie. She sounds like her brothers when they talk through tissue paper wrapped around a comb, but still you can make her out, quite clearly announcing herself as some person called Norma who gets no response to her repeated hello. She wishes now she had used her real name.

"Isn't that amazing?" the man asks.

Lillie nods, but thinks, amazing yes, but not magic. She can hear her own voice any old time. She thanks the man nevertheless, and hurries home, her left hand clamped firmly on the precious scrap of tinfoil that contains the shadow of her voice, but no secrets. If she holds it very close, she can see her face dimly reflected, raked across by the scratches made by the needle of the phonograph machine.

She hides the recording in the ticking of her mattress, along with a pebble from the Jewish Burying Ground and a shard from the broken mirror.

5

Reading the Tea Leaves

Here, we can imagine a montage, the turning pages of a calendar telling us time has passed; or an old-fashioned title card with the simple message: "Some Time Later ..." I can't tell you the exact date, but I'll never forget the day.

LILLIE COMES HOME to find her mother in tears. She has not seen her cry since the day she discovered her hand mirror was missing. And that was the secret kind of crying, shown only to her daughter. This is a far more public display — shoulder-heaving, nose-blowing, hankie-wringing, wailing, the performance of grief that reminds Lillie of the keening at a wake.

Lillie's father is sitting at the deal table in the kitchen, alternately swearing and taking long pulls on a bottle of whisky. It is unusual for him to drink so openly, so Lillie knows things must be serious.

"And you couldn't just say it was a mistake?"

"I think they would have known, don't you?" Lillie's mother manages to choke out. "A gramophone record is a little too large to fall just by accident into a person's reticule."

"What the hell did you want with the thing anyways? What good's a —"

"I don't know. I just wanted ..."

"I mean, if you stole something we could actually use, that'd be something. Like blankets or dishes. God knows they've got plenty of them, their kind, they'd never miss them."

"They've got plenty of gramophone records too."

"Or tea, for God's sake. Why couldn't you just ... They have all the tea in China."

"Ceylon."

"What?"

"Ceylon. Their tea is from Ceylon, blended with Indian tea. It's what makes it special."

"You sound like a bloody advertisement, you do. All about the stinkin' blend of their precious tea."

Lillie's mother cleans house for the Estabrookses on Mount Pleasant. They have some live-in staff, but rich people must make more dirt than a live-in staff can cope with, so her mother works there six mornings a week. Worked there. The house is only ten or twelve years old, but it was built on a grand scale, like something from the last century. Theodore Estabrooks made his fortune in tea. His family had traded in all kinds of groceries, but tea was the one he settled on — eventually the very blend her mother has just described, something he christened Red Rose.

Lillie likes the smell of tea, though she can't see how it's anything like a rose. Well, maybe a dried rose. Sometimes in the summer, she and her mother walk by the Estabrooks's warehouses down on Dock Street. When the doors are open, her mother says, you can smell the far-off lands where the teas come from. On Saturdays, Lillie often visits the back alley behind the Dufferin

Hotel, where the smells are mainly sharper and more local. The Dufferin gets its tea from Estabrooks's in large crates, and every few Saturdays they put an empty crate out for the trash. An almost empty crate; there's always a little that hides behind the shiny paper lining in the bottom or is stubborn in the corners. Lillie will look up and down the alley on those special Saturdays, and, as soon as she is sure nobody is watching, she will stick her head into the crate and breathe in as though it's her first breath ever. It's the smell of walking past the warehouses multiplied by a thousand. Then she will unfold her handkerchief on the stones of the alley. It's more of a rag, really, but Lillie calls it her handkerchief. Finally, she turns the crate over, careful not to cut her hands on the tin strapping that is nailed along every edge. She shakes out whatever tea she can onto the grubby square of cloth. Once she has gathered the corners of her handkerchief together and tied a knot in it, she hurries home without even setting the crate upright. Her mother oohs and aahs about the excellent cup of tea Lillie has waiting for her when she gets back from cleaning on Mount Pleasant. "What a fine cup of tea," she says. "Why, I'll bet the Estabrookses themselves don't have as fine a cup of tea." Lillie is pretty sure her mother recognizes the blend — it's not what they can afford — but she never asks, and Lillie never tells.

But now there will be no more Saturday afternoon cups of scavenged tea to celebrate the end of the working week because Lillie's mother has lost her job — for stealing from the Estabrookses something that she could never use herself.

Lillie's father is still trying to fathom the mystery of the act. "How did you know which one you wanted to take? I mean, they all look alike don't they?"

"It was Caruso."

"The fellow on the island?"

"The singer."

"What do you want with this Caruso? Especially when you've got nothing to play the damn thing on?"

Lillie thinks she knows. There is a story she heard her mother tell one of the neighbour women one day. Lillie was ill and stayed away from school, and her mother must have forgotten that when she got home from cleaning. She and the neighbour woman sat down in the kitchen for a cup of tea. It wasn't that Lillie was trying to overhear, but their voices were quite loud and, once the conversation had started, she wasn't sure how she could let them know she was in the apartment. After the neighbour woman left and her mother came across Lillie, she pretended to be sound asleep, responding only on the third or fourth shake. This seemed to satisfy her mother.

"I'm sorry, Seamus."

"Sorry won't butter the parsnips, will it?"

Lillie hates parsnips and can't remember when there was butter in the place.

"How are we going to live? Those boys of yours eat for four."

They are always Bellinda's boys when things are bad.

"Maybe Lillie will have to leave school and take to work," her father snaps.

"Lillie's not leaving school. Don't pay no attention, Lillie." Impossible advice to follow. "I'll find something else."

"And it's a great character you'll be getting from your last place. Nobody wants to hire a thief, Bellinda."

"They're not bringing any charges. They were decent enough to say that."

"But people ask. People talk. If you try to get a job up Mount Pleasant again they'll all know you took the foolish gramophone record and they'll shut the door in your face."

"I don't want cleaning."

"What else can you do?"

"Do you know what it's like cleaning? You wouldn't, you that can make a mess but never cleans it up. Do you know what it's like emptying chamber pots? They have a water closet right in the house, you know, but they don't like to travel so far at night. Do you know what it's like down on your hands and knees with a knife in the corner, trying to scrape God-knows-what out from between their gleaming floorboards? And then there's the spittoons. You wouldn't think fancy folks like them would have them, but they do."

"So you'd like to try men's work, would you? You'd like to sweat in the shop over a railway wheel that should be replaced, except the owners way the hell and gone up in Montreal are too cheap to do it? You'd like to fix the backs on the crappy wooden benches for the hundredth time because passengers think they have a right to lean back in them and the company thinks they don't? Or maybe ride the damn tram with me, taking money and punching tickets?"

"I might like to try."

"There's no jobs, Bellinda. No jobs. Period. Ask Frank at the newspaper. They've got a word for it, what's happened to all the jobs."

"They don't know everything, you know, down at the newspaper. They can't see the future."

"And you can, I suppose? Well, it won't be by reading tea leaves anymore, that's for sure." The chair scrapes on the floor as he stands up. "I'm off." That means he'll be in Cronin's for the evening. Or, worse, down on Station Street.

"If you used that elbow as much for working as you do for lifting a glass to your mouth, we wouldn't be the way we are." Lillie wishes her mother wouldn't say such things — even if her father is long gone down the stairs before she does.

Lillie offers to make a cup of tea.

"No, child. No tea. I'll just go and have a lie-down. Just be by myself a bit."

Lillie thinks about the story she heard her mother tell that day she was home sick from school. She hears her mother and the neighbour woman talking as if it were right now.

"The parlour is bigger than this entire apartment," she hears her mother say. "And grand, too, with tall ceilings and great windows all bundled in velvets."

"I heard the furniture came from England."

"I heard that too, though it gathers dust just like regular furniture."

"Gold dust, though."

"I wish. The floors is beautiful. All different kinds of woods made in a pattern."

"And you have to keep them polished."

"The housekeeper talks about getting some kind of electrical machine to buff them. They have the electricity in every room up there, even though they still use gas for most of the lighting. They haven't got the machine yet, though, so I'm down on my hands and knees doing a proper job."

"Waving your fanny in the air."

"Oh, you're a terrible one!"

"Don't tell me you don't. Just a little. Has he ever tried to, you know ...?" The neighbour lady was a great reader of novels.

"He's an old man, for God's sake. Besides, he's never home. Always at work, that's what the missus says."

"She tells you that while she sits in the parlour and watches you wax her floors?"

"Of course not. The servants hear her say that to him. And they tell me. I've never seen her use the parlour. Not in the mornings when I'm there."

"I bet it's a grand parlour. Have they a gramophone?"

"O Lord, yes. It sits in the parlour, between the windows.

It's a beautiful thing. I keep it polished too. And sometimes ..."

"What, Bellinda?"

"Nothing."

"No, what? Sometimes?"

"Once only, really ..."

"Yes?"

"I wound it up."

"You didn't."

"The housekeeper was on an errand and the maid was up in the top of the house somewhere. I wound it up, and I played it."

"How did you know how?"

"It's not so complicated. Men like to let on that these machinery things are complicated, but they're not. I've looked through Thorne's window enough to get the drift."

"What did you play?"

"It was on the machine already. I wouldn't have the nerve to go through the stack. It was some singer-fella. Eye-talian from the sound of him."

"I like Henry Burr."

"And I danced."

"You what? You never."

"I danced. On that shiny floor, to the tune of that shiny gramophone with that shiny singer-fella on it. Why shouldn't I? I shined them all."

"Not the singer-fella."

"Oh, I polished him pretty good. It was him I was dancing with, see?"

"Really?"

"No, of course not. But in my mind. He held me real close-like, and I rubbed up against him. It was lovely."

"What about Seamus?" Lillie thought that the neighbour lady, whose husband seemed always to be away, might be looking for her mother's leavings.

"Seamus is good for scratching a certain kind of itch. And he's a good man, and a fine provider. But a real flesh and blood man is nothing beside one you dream up!" And they both howled with laughter.

Lillie wishes that it was only an imaginary gramophone record that her mother had slipped into her reticule. She vows never to listen to Mr. Caruso again.

The picture returns to black — but much less gently than it faded in on the showroom at Thorne's.

6

Strike

"C'MON THEN, LILLIE. We're goin' out."

They are familiar words, but I haven't heard him speak them for almost a year. "Where's mum?"

"Gone already. We'll see her there." That explains it. It is not going to be anything like the old days.

The previous summer we must have visited the Jewish Burying Ground at least once a week, along with three or four other places nearer home. I looked often for the man who was so sad but I never saw him there again. Maybe he was some kind of big shot in the Boston States. Sometimes I visited the man's mother's grave with Bea while I waited for my father. Each time I swear I could hear the man's sobbing, then his nose like a horn that a clown might toot, and finally his "I promise, Mama, I promise." Those remembered sounds became every bit as much a part of the experience of my cemetery visits as the thing I saw by spying on my father and his women.

My father stopped taking me with him when the weather turned. He wanted me to stay home with my mother, to be a comfort to her after she lost her job at the Estabrookses. That's what he said when I protested, though I suspected that it had more to do with my getting older. I think that he was suddenly afraid of my finding out what I had already known for some time.

But the thing was, my mother didn't need me. She had envelopes to lick and meetings to plan. She did not find other paying work. Instead, she was what was coming to be known as "political." I heard the neighbours whisper that word sometimes when they thought I couldn't hear. Or wouldn't understand. Which I didn't really, not completely, to be honest.

I started shadowing my mother, for something to do, following her from door-to-door as she peddled her pamphlets. Mainly it was working-people's places she went to. Often they'd invite her in for a cup of tea and a bit of a chat. I would crouch uncomfortably in a bush, or under the stairs, listening to their conversations. My mother would begin with a lot of strident stuff about bosses and workers and wages and uniting for fair treatment. The people would listen politely. Sometimes they asked a question or two. Didn't she think it had always been this way? Didn't she think things were better now than they had been a few years ago? Sometimes the two questions would be asked by the same person, which would make me smile as I pictured my mother struck by the contradiction but so desperate for the woman's support that she chose not to point it out.

At the end of June, after some duke I had never heard of was assassinated over in Europe, she had all of that to talk about — didn't people see there would be a war? Didn't they know what that would mean for the working person? Once, a woman said, yeah, I know what it will mean, jobs! That struck my mother speechless.

Eventually, the conversation would veer away from being what

I was slowly beginning to understand as "political" and it would turn to other, more familiar, subjects. How it was hot for the time of year. Or cool. How yesterday's mackerel hadn't smelled right but they'd cooked it anyway, and now the old fella was sick and did my mother think there was something in that? How the sister-in-law had been twenty-four hours in labour (the other kind) and then had to be opened up. She died, but the baby lived, and wasn't that some kind of miracle? Almost always, the visits ended with the woman agreeing that she'd talk to her man about what Bellinda had said, show him the flyer, and remind him about the meeting. There were endless meetings, especially in July after four motormen and four conductors were suddenly fired one day, all for failing to stop the tram before crossing the steam railway track. That's what the company said.

It is a meeting we are going to now. A rally, my father calls it, and when I ask what that is he says, "A meeting, dear, it's a kind of meeting." About the street railway. About his job.

My mother is already there when we arrive at the disused warehouse that has been taken over for the rally. She is smiling and joking with the men as they come through the doors, and she is passing them sheets of paper printed with large block type and many exclamation points. More exclamation points than I would ever use to make a point in my diary. My father takes one of the sheets as we pass, just like every one of the other men. My mother smiles at him, just like she does at every other man.

There are no other children there that I can see, which is a shame because at some of the meetings before this there have been others and we have played quietly in a corner while the adults talked and talked and made grand speeches about how the world was changing and St. John would have to change with it.

The smell of tobacco and whisky and skunked beer makes me gag even in that huge space. I wonder how my mother stands it. Then I remember how my father smelled after his wrestling matches, and I decide that grown-ups maybe don't mind strong stinks as much as children do. I stay close to my father who, at the moment, smells, if not good, at least familiar.

He is pushing his way to the far end of the building where there is a kind of makeshift stage. It's made out of several tightly wrapped bales of something that might be cotton, with a half-dozen wooden pallets balanced precariously on top. The whole thing rolls, a ship at sea, when he climbs up to join two other men who are already aboard. They make a funny kind of salute that I have not seen before. And then suddenly the room is silent.

The first man to speak is somebody I do not recognize. I am sure he is not one of my father's co-workers. His eyeglasses are the same as the ones worn by the man in the cemetery last summer, the kind that seem to have no rim, but he is slim and not well-dressed like that man was. His voice is high, and I am surprised that the men don't laugh when they hear it. I picture a loon as he leads them through the litany of their sufferings at the hands of the company, his words rushing out in quavering bursts. There is something about the way he speaks — not the loon thing, something else — that I can't quite place. He doesn't form his words the same way my father and the other men do; there is a kind of hardness to the consonants, and the vowels are more pinched, like he resents letting them out at all. I guess that's how people in other places talk. Every now and then he pauses in his delivery, and, after a silence of a second or two, the men clap or stomp or yell their approval. At first, I wonder whether they are simply responding to the silence, desperate to fill it up, but after the pattern repeats itself several times I come to believe that it must be his words that are moving them after all.

When the man finally finishes, he embraces everybody on the platform, causing it to rock about wildly. I am afraid my father and the others might be tossed off into the crowd, but they manage to keep their feet somehow. I am glad because I am not sure what the crowd might do to them if they were to fall among them. How many times have I overheard my own father say really foul things to my mother about our neighbours Percival and Nathan and what should be done to men like them? And yet here he is hugging an even stranger man, and nobody seems to take the least notice.

Now it is my father's turn to speak. The men go wild as he steps to the front of the platform. When he holds up his hand for silence, the noise grows even more deafening and turns into a rhythmic chant — Seamus! Seamus! Seamus! they cry. I know he won't, though. He won't shame them.

There is no getting around it, he is a very attractive man. Magnetic. People listen to him because he is so good looking. People believe him because he is so good looking. My mother keeps forgiving him because he is so good looking. But today it is the listening and believing parts that matter.

"Gentlemen," he begins. "Gentlemen." There is a little nervous laugh and somebody jeers, "Who ya talkin' to, Seamus? I don't see no gentlemen here." I want to strangle the man.

"Brothers." And there is a roar of approval. The other speaker, the man with the glasses, has called them "comrades," which is something like "brothers," and some of them cheered at that. But when my father says "brothers" the response is ten times louder. "These are trying times." Groans of agreement. "I look around me, and I see it in your faces — the pain, the sufferin'. I see it in the faces of your wives and daughters — the want, the hunger. This is the twentieth century. This is Canada. Yet we're not allowed to live as if that's true." Grumbles of no, no. "Why? Because the wealth, boys, the wealth is all bundled up in the hands of a very few. In the grasping, greedy claws of the very, very few." There is a mounting growl of outrage, punctuated by a slap and a giggle somewhere near me where one man has tried to demonstrate the work of grasping, greedy hands and another has not wanted to play along. "What are we going to do about it, you ask yourselves." Here my father pauses to allow them to do just that, but not long enough to let any of his listeners provide the answer they all know is coming. It is for him to say it. "Unite! Unite! That's what! Alone, we can be held down, exploited, abused. Together, we can take control. It's time to show old Van Horne and his crony McLean who the real boss is." The wife? shouts one wag who is immediately shushed. "We've asked. We've ... we've reasoned. We've waited. They haven't listened. Well, it's time my friends, my brothers, to speak to them in a language that they'll have to listen to. Let our statement be loud and strong."

It is as good as benediction at the end of church. I squint and I can see my father now in the flowing robes of the priest, making the sign of the cross at us all just before we pour out of his care to carry on with whatever sins we have been committing before the service. Only my father is younger, and stronger, and ever so much handsomer than any priest. No priest could ever lift, or run, or hold his liquor like my father could. No priest could ever wrestle all those women.

"You know what we have to do. Be resolute. Stand firm. Together, we will be the victors." He and the other men on the platform make the salute again, the one that I have not seen before today. Then, with the help of several of the other men standing around below the platform, they climb down into the crowd and are swallowed up.

Almost instantly, the mass of men starts to turn itself around, at the same time making an aisle for my father and the other men who were on the platform. As they pass, the warehouse begins to empty after them, those closest to the door waiting for the end of the procession to join on. I am pulled along in the tide. Just before I am washed out the door, I catch a glimpse of my mother who has found a safe purchase beside a post at the front of the building and is a still point in all the rush. Her face wears the flushed, exhilarated look that I recognize immediately from my father's other lady partners.

On the street, I manage to separate myself from the mob by climbing onto a low stone wall, where I crouch until the wave has passed. That is where my mother finds me.

"C'mon, sweetie-pie, you'll miss the fun. Wasn't he grand, your pa? Wasn't he the cat's meow?"

"Where are they going?"

"To find a little justice in this hard world. Weren't you listenin'?"

"Yes, but where are they headed right now?"

"King Street. They're going to show those Montreal bastards who really runs the railway." And she grabs my hand so hard it hurts, and begins running down the street after the vanishing mob.

When we reach the corner of King Street and Prince William, I am surprised by what I see at Market Square. There are two street-railway cars on the tracks, quite close together. I would know car 84 anywhere, and I think the other is one of the 70s. Any other day, their closeness would be strange enough because it would mean that the first car has been held up somehow and the other has caught up to it, which would play bloody old hell with the schedule, as my father would say. But today, the marvel is to see any cars at all. My father and a hundred other men have refused to go in to work. So who can have gotten the trains out of the shop?

"Scabs," my mother nearly spits the word in response to my question. "Scabs, that's who. People with no principles. People who'd do anything for a dollar. Not that they'd pay 'em more than twenty cents an hour."

"But it's Daddy's job. Daddy's and the other men's."

"They'll soon sort them out. Don't you worry."

The sorting out begins almost immediately, as if my mother has willed it, which, in a way, I suppose she has.

The foremost car begins to rock from side to side the same as the makeshift platform that my father and the others stood on in the smelly warehouse just a few minutes ago. Except the car is rocking rhythmically, the swaying getting bigger with each repetition. The people inside are screaming now. I can hear them quite clearly, and I wonder why the men don't let up when they hear it. They are so much closer than I am. Maybe the moan of wrenched metal and twisting wood drowns the cry of human voices when you are right up close. I can also hear my father's voice calling out to the men — "heave there, ho there, heave there, ho there." Then I feel better because I know that this rocking of the car that looks so frightening must actually be a good thing. It must be the thing my father meant at the meeting, the thing that they have to do. I begin to chime in, matching my heaves and my hoes to his in a way that makes it a game. I even shut my eyes and imagine him rocking me back and forth, back and forth, the way I rock Bea the nights it thunders.

The complete overturning of the railway car comes as a shock, although, when I think about it later, I realize that it was the inevitable end of what the men were doing. It was what they wanted all along. At the shriek of splintering wood, the cascade of shattering glass, I open my eyes and stop rocking. For a moment I want to laugh, the thing looks so stupid lying there on its side, a turtle that has been turned, a fat woman who has slipped on the ice and can't get up. Then I see the arms poking out of the broken windows and I remember that there are people trapped inside the overturned beast. Some of the people who have been standing around, not the men who were rocking the car, but people who have just been standing there watching them, begin to move forward to help. I can't understand why the men won't let them through, until I see them reaching through the windows themselves, helping people out of the wreckage. Always be prepared to take responsibility for your actions. How many times has my father told me that? And now he is practising it himself, he and the other men, his brothers. It's the same as when you spill your milk and break the glass, you have to clean it up. Or when you drop a mirror. Only, even then I know that the comparison's all wrong. It isn't until each of the passengers has been rescued that I notice the little knot of men standing by the very front of the car, where the motorman sits. They are not letting him out. That much is plain. They are calling him bad names, names like my mother used for the men who were doing my father's job, and worse. My mother, along with the rest of the crowd looking on, has moved in closer, and I edge in after them. I can see the trapped man's face, white with terror, wet with tears.

It is a face I will see for months to come. I will see it, and then I will see my father's face, the face of an angel, a face that makes the men listen and the women want to wrestle with him. My father's face will appear from nowhere beside the man's face as it did that day. Then my father's strong arms will reach into the overturned tram car and lift the quivering man from it so that another man is prevented from pouring kerosene over the upturned face. That is how I will remember it, even though I blackout the moment I see the man pushing through the crowd with the kerosene can and a box of matches.

The *Globe* the next day is full of the story, of course. Frank Rhodes, who lives in our building, has written it, and I hear my father on the stairs arguing with him about it.

"Who are you calling ruffians, for God's sake, Frank? Can't you see who the villain is here? It's the company has done the only true violence, the violence against the people."

"That man could have been killed."

"And we could all starve to death. What's the one beside the many?"

"You think destroying their property is going to help them afford to pay you better?"

"It's going to wake them up, let them know we mean business."

"Business, is it? You don't know a fart about business. Business is what they know. Business is what they do. And they can't do it if they have to pay you a lot more money and replace that car you destroyed."

"I thought the press was supposed to be neutral."

"Nobody's neutral. I'm being rational."

"It's rational to call us Bolsh — what was that word you used in the paper?"

"Bolsheviks. I didn't exactly call you Bolsheviks. I simply mentioned some likenesses. It's the way we write news stories."

"Well it's a damn stupid way, if you ask me. You should concentrate on what's going on right here under your nose, not trying to put some kind of fancy-pants label on it from God-knows-where. Write about them bloody bosses and what they're doing to us."

"And about how you sabotaged the generators and threw the whole city into the dark?"

"Write about how the dragoons was called out against their own countrymen. Write about his majesty the Mayor reading the Riot Act to his very own neighbours. A cavalry charge down King Street into a crowd of civilians, for God's sake! Can't you write about that? Haven't we got freedom of the press in this country, or what?"

"You're a great fella, Seamus. But sometimes you're a bit of a kid, too. How's Lillie?"

"Fine, Lillie's fine. She got a bit of a bump on the back of the head when she fainted. It's nothin' at all."

"Did the doctor see her?"

"What the Christ does the doctor need to do with it? The girl fainted. Girls do, you know, it's one of the two things they're really good at."

At that moment, my mother comes into my room with a cup of hot water with some lemon squeezed into it, and I don't hear the rest of the men's conversation. But I never forget Frank calling my father a kid.

7

The
Home
Front

MY MOTHER DOESN'T seem to mind working in the shed where they pack the shell casings. My father says it's like playing the devil at dice, going in to work there every day, but she just laughs as she makes a pot of Red Rose tea, the real stuff, bought at Van Wart's, not scrounged from the alley, or when she cuts another nice thick slice of baker-bought bread. It pays better than any job she's ever done; it pays better — and I wonder whether this is part of my father's problem with it — than any job he's ever had. That is the funny thing about the war — for all the loss and suffering over there, things at home are better than they have ever been. Both parents are working, my brothers aren't around to torture me, and people seem to mind less and less what I do or where I go. I know I should probably feel guilty for seeing things this way, but I can't quite manage it somehow.

My mother's job at McAvity's came up in the spring. Many of the men had enlisted and were training to go overseas with the

Canadian Expeditionary Force. They were raising a whole battalion from St. John. It became obvious that companies would have to start hiring women, maybe even children, some people said. My mother was one of the first to line up. There were a few nasty incidents that first day. The wives of some of the men who had enlisted came down to jeer. What did these women lined up on the steps think they were doing taking away men's jobs? It was only temporary, the bosses assured them, but that didn't keep one woman from hurling a lump of coal into the lineup outside McAvity's office. My mother didn't get hit by the coal. She didn't get hired in the first wave, either. My father said it was because of the incident with the Caruso recording — those people all talk to one another, he said. But then, when the munitions contracts started a few months later, my mother was taken on the very first day. The work could be a little dangerous, they told her. She looked the man in the eye and said, do you think starving isn't dangerous, Mister? I heard her telling a neighbour about it. She said she almost told him a woman was as fit to do dangerous work as a man was, but she thought the destitute approach might work better. I guess it did.

When my mother announced she had the job, it was my brothers who were most excited. They had both already enlisted in the 26th Battalion. "Now we're working for the same outfit, Ma," they said. James McAvity, brother of George who ran the foundry, was their colonel. My father choked when she told them the wages, and then he went off to Cronin's for a glass or two. It must have been hard on him, I supposed, that he couldn't work for one of the McAvitys too. That had something to do with his objections; I heard my parents discussing it night after night through the winter of 1914–15, in the months leading up to when my brothers enlisted.

As the new routine takes hold, it gets so that my favourite thing all day is to wait for my mother after her shift. She works from five in the morning until five at night; it's important to have your wits about you doing the work she does. The rest of the operation goes on twenty-four hours a day, turning the brass casings, casting the heads and the bases — work you can do half asleep if necessary. I'm not allowed into the explosives shed where my mother works. I know girls who can visit their mothers right inside the foundry and the brass works down on Water Street, but I don't envy them that. Their mothers aren't doing the dangerous work. They may be making the casings or the heads, but they aren't packing the wallop that will send the Kaiser back where he came from.

It's not because I miss her that I like waiting for her. It's more her costume that I look forward to — that first sight of her and the other women coming out the gates. I have to make my way down Waterloo to Haymarket Square and then out the other end of the square and towards the cluster of sheds that seems to get bigger every day on McAvity's Rothesay Avenue site. There is a guard at the gate, and he seems to enjoy it as much as I do when the women emerge in their coveralls and tight-fitting hats. There is something everyone can find funny in a woman wearing trousers. The joke never gets old. Sometimes one of the women forgets to take off the puffy slippers that they wear to keep the risk of sparks to a minimum, and then the picture is even sillier, more clownish.

My mother and the other women wear their coveralls home. I heard her say once that there's no place at the works where a woman would want to change her clothes, and she and the other women wouldn't put it past the few men who are left there to supervise their work to do a little supervising of their undressing too. So they wear their coveralls through the streets to their own apartments. At first, this caused a fuss. One man even drove his buggy into a fire hydrant on Waterloo Street. It was a McAvity hydrant. Now people seem to have gotten used to the sight of eight or ten pairs of legs attached to female faces walking their coveralls through the public streets. If the women keep their hats down, they can pass as men anyway, though why they are wearing toques in the summer would remain a mystery.

My mother pauses in the same spot in Haymarket Square every day as we make our way home. Just for a moment, she stops on the exact spot where she figures the two boys stood as the 26th Battalion assembled in June last year for the march to Pettingill's Wharf, and the S.S. *Caledonia* and *Flanders*. I know that she is praying for their safety as she stands there. But I am glad she has more than prayers. I am glad she is also packing the powder.

Her work clothes smell like the fields of Belgium must smell. It is a sharp scent that makes your eyes water and leaves the taste of onions in your mouth. "Jesus, Bellinda," my father will say as she carries the balled-up coveralls to hang them on the clothesline outside the kitchen window, "you'll blow us all up one day with them coveralls of yours. Can't you leave them at bloody McAvity's?"

And my mother will laugh and say, "What, would you have me walking home in me shift itself, or have me waving my fanny in some changing room for all those louts at the plant to see?" I hate it when she talks like this, but it always silences my father. Sometimes he'll even pat my mother's behind if he thinks I'm not watching.

My mother won't say much about her work. When you do something for twelve hours a day, six days a week, you don't feel like wasting any of the other hours talking about it. She has told me that they work at long wooden tables that are all held together with pegs rather than nails. It is a giant machine for making death for our enemies. There is a huge system of pulleys and ropes that somehow delivers an empty shell to her place at the table, where she measures a charge into it — that's what she tells me they call it, a charge — and then she passes it along to someone else who positions the head. My mother doesn't know how the head is secured in place. She thinks there's some kind of crimping that's done somewhere else. Once, I asked her whether she was curious to know more about how the whole operation worked, but she just laughed and said, "Why, I get paid the same the way things are, don't I?"

I am curious about all of the stages, though, even if she is not. I ask girls I know from school to take me to visit their mothers who work in the Water Street buildings. These were the places where McAvity's famous valves were made before the war — the valves, and the hydrants that carried the McAvity name to every major Canadian city and some American ones, too. Now, the McAvity foundry mark is stamped only in the heavy discs that become the shell bases, and the lathes that used to turn out valves are given over to spinning brass for shell cylinders. The other girls and I pick up shavings of the metal from the shop floor when nobody is looking. We know these should be saved for the war effort but it's hard to resist taking a few, so shiny and so deadly sharp. We have to wrap them in rags to keep from cutting our-selves, and by the time we get them home, the shavings have often worked their way through the cloth. I keep my shavings safe with my other secret things.

Sometimes my mother gives me money to go to the pictures, at the Imperial. I remember one in particular called *The Blind Fiddler*. In the big scene, a group of blinded soldiers dance around to the healing tunes of a fiddler. The man called Nathan, who lives in our building, stands in the orchestra pit of the Imperial Theatre in St. John, New Brunswick, and plays his violin, while the soldiers on the screen, who I know are only actors filmed somewhere in England, dance to the merry tune. It's strange how it all matches up.

The day the first news comes, I have been visiting the foundry. I know a girl whose mother is big and strong enough to stamp the name and the date on the bases. She also pounds a stamp of an arrow into every one. We think this is funny, to mark a bomb with an arrow, but the girl's mother explains something about it being the King's Broad Arrow, and that goes a long way back in history, and we pretend to be impressed. The date the woman is stamping is July 9, 1916. She remarks that it has been exactly a year since she started at her job. I tell her my mother has been working in the powder shed for fifteen months. The woman looks impressed. She has never met my mother, which seems odd since they are both working to produce the same thing, but she obviously knows the respect that's due to the gals who work in the sheds.

I wait for my mother outside the gate, but when the little comic troupe appears she is not among them. "She got called home early, deary," one of the trousered women tells me. "Got some news."

News only means one thing these days. When I arrive home, out of breath, the telegram is still open on the kitchen table. It's Patrick, the older of my two brothers. He would have been twenty in September.

The shades are down. The shades are down in so many windows these days I wonder how much it can really mean anymore. The war seems to be turning out dead boys much like Mr. Ford turns out motorcars. In the dim light, my mother's wet cheeks seem to sparkle.

"Why would they bury him over there? Why can't we at least have a body to mourn, his poor soldier's body to mourn over?"

"They can't be sending every blessed boy home. There's not ships enough on the sea for that."

"How will they know where he is? What happens if Fritz takes the hill or wherever it is they've put him? What happens if ...?"

"If a shell blasts him right up out of the earth?" It is the cruellest thing I have ever heard my father say. That is how I know how much he is affected by this; I will never see him cry though.

The company allows my mother a day's compassionate leave, which is why she is at home the next day when the second telegram arrives. Mike. Much good it did naming him for the warrior angel. My mother does not even cry. I suppose she has used up all her tears. Or maybe she never liked Michael as well as Paddy.

In the evening, some of the neighbours come by — those who haven't fresh losses of their own to mark. There is a lot of talk about sacrifice and shedding blood for your country. It seems, to hear these comforters talk, that the most noble thing a man could do is shed blood for his country. I begin to feel a little jealous. Nobody made this kind of fuss over me when I started bleeding a month ago. My mother just told me that it was a punishment for Eve's sin. If that's the case, then my brothers' deaths must be punishments for Cain's.

My mother returns to McAvity's without even taking the day she's allowed for Mike. My father begins to boast about his two boys, the war heroes. I rifle the apartment madly for mementoes of them. I never really liked them all that much when they were alive, but I understand about the respect that's due to the dead.

When the official letters come, it is obvious that their captain has lost whatever struggle he may have had with the formula prescribed by the war office. If you believe what he wrote, they both died exactly the same — in a clean fight, killed by a bullet flying straight and true. Both had been respected by the other men in the unit and both were buried with full military honours. The only detail that differs between the letters is that Patrick is described as having "gone to the aid of his platoon mates," while Michael was "helping some of his chums." My parents don't seem to notice the duplication, and they solemnly wrap both letters in a black ribbon and place them on the dresser where the framed photographs of the two boys look defiantly at all passersby, daring them to pity them. They would have been your uncles.

8

I had a little bird
And its name was Enza.
I opened up the window
And In-flew-Enza.

Picture this as a title card — the words of the in-flew-Enza song held on the screen long enough for the slowest of readers to mouth through them twice. Then iris-in on a dark St. John walk-up apartment. And me.

LILLIE IS TOO old for skipping in the summer of 1918, but she hears the littler girls chanting the in-flew-Enza song all day long as they jump rope on the street below her parents' apartment. She wants to stick her head out the open window and yell for them to shut up. It's not because of what they are singing. Who cares about a bunch of Spanish people all getting sick at once? It's the endless repetition of it — the rope brushing the pavement like the rhythmic scratching of dry leaves in a cemetery; the constant return to the beginning of the song like the lurch of a street-railway car rocking back and forth, or the *chuff-chuff-chuff* of a gramophone after the record has ended.

She wants to stick her head out the window and shout, but she never does. She is afraid of what the little girls might yell back. Something about her mother wanting to be a man or why does she dress and talk that way? Something about finding her brothers' bodies over there in Flanders, or haven't they maybe just run away with Fritzie? Something about her eyes that look both ways for Sunday, or her clothes that fit too tight over her swelling breasts and hips — doesn't Manchester's carry that outfit in her size? Never anything about her father. He is immune to criticism; they're afraid to spoil their chances of marrying him when they grow up.

"Fourteen's such an awkward age," she hears her mother tell her father one night when he complains that all Lillie does is sit around the apartment reading books.

"They're all awkward ages. That's the bloody joke, don't you see? That's what nobody tells you beforehand. The boys —"

"The boys weren't a bit easier, God rest 'em. You've just forgotten."

"It's a damn funny thing for the preservation of the race to depend upon, forgetfulness. If you didn't forget what the one baby was like you'd never have another."

"Sometimes there are other forces at work."

"You mean like ..."

And she hears that catch in her mother's breath that means that her father is kissing her somewhere. It is a small apartment, and Lillie is a big girl. She rolls over, torn between disgust at the thought of her parents naked in their bed together and comfort that they still have those feelings for one another.

The day Lillie first starts to feel sick is a Friday. The thirteenth of September. She is too weak to go to school. Even her father, who tends to dismiss all complaints of illness as mere malingering, can see that. Her mother makes her hot water and lemon and comes into her room every hour to feel her forehead.

"She's burning up, Seamus," Lillie hears. "Will I go for the doctor?"

"Leave her another day. A rising fever is bound for breaking, and what do we want the doctor for, only to tell us just that and maybe stand by while it does, and then take some credit and want to be paid."

"One day; that's all. It's not right to fool with these things."

That night, Lillie begins to travel inside her head to places she's never been in the flesh.

To France with her brothers. Not that she sees the Eiffel Tower the way you might at the moving pictures, or hears people speaking French — you could do that some places in St. John anyway. No, she knows that it is France because there is a war, and her brothers are there. Mostly it is mud, and noise and the smell of fear. There are rats, but that doesn't bother Lillie because somewhere deep down she knows it is a dream, even if she can't escape its clutches. Her brothers give her blocks of chocolate and brew tea for her in an old can. One of their friends plays on a harmonica and Lillie thinks that the war is not so bad. Not half so bad as having your first period. But then the gas comes. Chlorine. A familiar smell at first, but a million times stronger almost right away. Your eyes swell up and your breathing is all wet and you sink back in the mud, which drowns you before the gas can. If you are lucky.

To the Boston States with that man, Louis something, from the Jewish Burying Ground, it must be five years ago now. Here, there isn't any mud. It's as though they sweep the street three times a day, everything is so clean and smells so good. The man takes her to a restaurant where they eat lobsters with a knife and fork, and then to a moving picture show where there is a live orchestra just like at the Imperial at home but bigger, and you don't know all the players by name. He calls her princess, and when she puts her hand up to scratch her head there is a real tiara on it — that is the right word, a tiara, she has read that in one of her brothers' books. But then the man is trying to touch her in her secret places, and the tiara gets hot and drips around her temples.

To a beach with palm trees. It is nothing like the red-mud beaches she bicycled to the summer before. There is white sand, and no cool breeze to raise the goosebumps, which is just as well, Lillie thinks, since when she glances down at her body as she lies there on that beach it is stark naked. She would be ashamed, but what it looks like bears so little resemblance to what she sees when she sneaks a peek at herself in the mirror after a bath that she cannot connect it with her own body. It is a stranger's body she sees, an exciting body (why does she think of it that way?) with firm breasts and generous thighs. And it is entirely blue, despite the heat.

"The best thing we know for it is bed rest, good food, salts of quinine and Aspirin. I'll check again tomorrow." It is the doctor's voice, heard from far away. Then from even farther away, Lillie hears her mother thanking him and saying goodbye.

"Good food and Aspirin. What does he think we are, bloody millionaires?" This is her father, but his voice is strange. It has the sound of that tinfoil recording she made at Thorne's that time, the buzz when someone hums through a kazoo like the ones her brothers made when they pretended to be soldiers on parade. Before they actually were soldiers on parade.

"We'll find the money. Maybe Frank would help. He's always had a soft spot for the girl. It's not like she'll eat a lot. And Aspirins can't be all that dear, can they?"

"Don't forget the salts of quinine. Whatever the hell that is."

"What is it, do you think?"

"It sounds expensive, that's all I know."

"Seamus."

"We'll check in at the druggist's on the way back from the meeting."

"You think we can go to the meeting?"

"It's not like we can do anything for her. She's been lying there for two days. She's not going to miss us for two hours."

"What if she wakes up?"

"We'll leave her a note. She likes to read."

"If you think so ..."

"She'll be fine. It's the meeting that won't be all right if we don't get a move on."

He is right. Lillie doesn't really wake up. She goes travelling again instead.

Again, it is the doctor's voice that brings her back.

"Lillie. Lillie, can you hear me?"

She can. She wants to tell him she can, but she can't find her mouth to do it.

"You've got to tell us what you're feeling."

That's a laugh.

"If we don't know what you're feeling, we can't help you."

"Try to tell us, sweetie."

How is she supposed to tell them with her mouth gone missing? How is she supposed to tell them with no breath in her lungs?

The doctor begins to shake her. She can tell because the light begins making wonderful flickering patterns before her eyes. Leaves are scraping. A tram car is rocking. A disc is spinning at seventy-eight revolutions per minute. Little girls are skipping outside her window, the rope making a *chuff-chuff-chuff* on the pavement.

"Jesus!" There is a gush of blood from her nose. Her eyes focus in time to see it splatter across the doctor's face. At the same time, she feels a flood rush between her thighs.

Her mother shows the doctor where he can wash up. After he has gone, she helps Lillie clean up down there, and carries the bloody sheets off to wash them.

"It just may have been what saved her," the doctor says the next day, still talking about Lillie as though she were not conscious there in the room with them. "That nosebleed, and the violence of the menstrual period you are describing." Lillie wishes then that she actually was not conscious to hear this being discussed. "They may just have saved her from the pneumonic complications we are seeing with this illness."

"Thank God. And thank you, doctor."

"You're a very lucky young lady, Lillie," the doctor says to her, finally acknowledging her conscious presence. "The bleeding seems to have saved your life."

She would blush if she had not lost so much blood.

TWO WEEKS LATER, Lillie's parents are stricken. They have just come home from a meeting when her father starts to complain of a splitting headache.

"We've got those Aspirins," says her mother, "the ones we couldn't get Lillie to take."

"I'll try a couple. They can't be getting any better sitting there in the cabinet."

"I might try a few myself," her mother says. "Can't hurt to be careful."

By the next morning they are delirious.

"They knew about this. The bosses knew. That's why they didn't try to do anything to stop the union meetings. Frank told me the city council was all ready to put a ban on public gatherings of any sort, the *Globe* was all set to print it up, but then it got put off for some reason. There's your reason. The bosses wanted us all sick."

"It's the Bosch. They put infected men ashore off them U-boats. Send them round the countryside kissing and coughing till we've all got it. I heard about it from the woman in the grocer's. I thought she was crazy."

Lillie goes for the doctor, but his wife says he is busy and sends her away.

So she goes for Frank.

His apartment is just upstairs from theirs, but Lillie has never been inside it. She passes Frank sometimes on the stairs, and he comes into their apartment often to visit with Lillie's father. She sees him other places from time to time, in the square, outside her school. They seem to have a lot of the same routes, now that she thinks about it.

She has to knock twice before he comes to the door. When he opens up he is fumbling with his belt.

"Sorry. Oh. Lillie. I was just, um, I was just ironing my trousers. What's up?"

She looks past him into the squalor that is apparently both bed and sitting room for him and she judges that he has himself only just gotten up, even though it is eight o'clock.

"It's Seamus and Bellinda." She shocks them both by using her parents' Christian names. "They're sick. Ill. They've taken ill." That was the way people said it properly.

"Have you gone for the doctor?"

"Mrs. Doctor says he's busy."

"Miserable old witch. Let's have a look then." He pulls his door closed behind him, careful to let her see as little of his apartment as possible as he steps into the hall.

Lillie's mother is holding a bloody cloth to her nose when they find her in the kitchen. Her eyes are marbled with red and look as though they would like to pop out of her head. She is wearing only her slip, and Lillie is embarrassed in front of Frank.

"A cold coin on the back of the neck," says Frank automatically. "That stops the nosebleed." But they can't find a coin, so Lillie holds the bowl of a spoon against the flaming skin of her mother's nape. Bellinda's hair, always neatly pulled up on top of her head, has escaped the half-dozen pins that usually hold it and falls in damp tendrils across Lillie's hand. She is surprised by how much grey there is and makes a note to pay more attention.

The bleeding appears to slow. Lillie can tell Frank is surprised although he's trying to hide it.

"Where's Seamus?"

"He went out."

"He went out? Jesus, Bindy, where? Where'd he go?"

"For the doctor."

"No, that was Lillie. Lillie went for the doctor."

"Yes, Lillie."

"Where did Seamus go?"

"Seamus went?"

They help Bellinda into her bed. Lillie thinks it must be wrong for Frank to be handling her mother's body this way, but she could never manage alone, so she decides she can call it extenuating circumstances, a phrase she has read in a book, even when Frank has to tug at her mother's bodice and one breast peeks out as they lift her.

Seamus has indeed gone out; at least he is nowhere to be found in the apartment. It is no use asking Bellinda again.

"You look after your mother, I'll go try and find your pa. Any ideas?"

Five years earlier, when her father still took her with him on his travels, Lillie would have been able to tell Frank exactly which alley to begin with, which graveyard. But now, since she has become one of "us women," she is at a loss. "Try the union hall. Or Station Street."

Frank shoots her a look that says, "What do you know about

Station Street?" but he doesn't speak a word, just nods and shuts the apartment door.

Bellinda has fallen into a deep sleep. Lillie sits beside her bed, not knowing what to do, but not wanting to leave her alone. Frank has told her to look after her mother, so that is what she must do. She begins to stroke Bellinda's hair, which makes her remember Bea. Where is Bea? At what point has she stopped needing Bea? Was there one morning when she awoke and forgot to reach for the doll? She thinks about what she overheard her father say about forgetfulness and its importance to the preservation of the race. Maybe he was right. Which day did her mother start to forget about her?

She looks down at her hand. It is full of her mother's hair. The fever can cause that to happen. She herself was very lucky. What would her father look like without his masses of wavy hair, she wonders, what would his lady friends think of him then?

Still at a loss for what she can do for her mother, she spreads the hairs out on the blanket and begins sorting them. But where she expected to find only two colours — grey and not — there turns out to be an entire spectrum. There is every shade of brown from chestnut to taupe, blacks that are blue, and blacks that have more than a hint of burgundy. There are even some golden hairs in the mix. Only the grey is uniform. She is reminded of a favourite remark of her father's, "All cats are grey in the dark." But she knows that means something else. By the time Frank gets back, she has arranged the clump of her mother's hair by hue, shaft by shaft, across the red blanket. She sees Frank look at it, but he doesn't say anything.

"Where was he?" Lillie asks, nodding at the limp figure of her father leaning on Frank's shoulder.

"About where you said."

"Which place?"

"He'd been at the one and was headed to the other."

"He wanted to warn them," Lillie says simply, some of her old admiration of her father welling up as she ponders the selfless generosity of such an act.

"That's what he said, it was all a plot by the bosses."

"I meant the women."

"I know you did. Let's get him into bed."

"Beside her?"

"Unless you've a third bed you're hiding somewhere around the place."

"I'll take off his boots. He shouldn't have his boots on in bed."

"His hands are grey."

"So's his legs. Look."

As they lay him beside Bellinda, Seamus's chest makes a light burbling sound, the sound you might expect a drain to make when you let out the stopper very slowly.

"The damned doctor can't be that busy," says Frank, and he rushes out the door again.

Alone with her parents, Lillie feels suddenly awkward, inexplicably shy. It does not help that they are in bed together. The fact that her father is fully clothed (except for his boots) while her mother is in her slip does nothing to make things better. If anything, it makes it more obscene because the match is so imperfect. She tucks the sheet up around their necks. This seems cruel given the heat that is coming off them, but it helps cover the imbalance, and even goes a small way towards preserving what is left of Lillie's sense of modesty.

She wonders about reading to them. Would they hear her? She was able to hear the doctor when she was sick, even though she couldn't talk back to him. Then she remembers that her father seemed to object to her reading all the time — wasn't that what he said? She would sing maybe, but she finds the only tune she can remember is the in-flew-Enza skipping song. She can't get it out of her head, can't find another tune to push it out.

Maybe she could urge a little hot water and lemon between their lips. She liked that when she was sick. She goes into the kitchen to boil the kettle. There aren't any lemons. It has not occurred to her that there would be no lemons. She realizes suddenly that she has never thought about how the lemons get there, or how anything else does for that matter. Somebody would have to shop. That somebody would be her. But where would she get the money, and how could she leave them alone? Frank would have to help her. For now, she settles on plain boiled water, which she pours into two chipped cups that she sets on a battered metal tray. It has the look of something rather grand, and she carries it proudly into the bedroom.

Both of their noses have started bleeding at once. They sleep on while the crimson rivers well out over their lips and chins. Already, pools have formed in the hollows at the base of their throats. Lillie is terrified that they will drown. They have to be propped up. She fetches a bolster from the chesterfield, then slides her hands under her mother's shoulders, pushing her up into a half-sitting position. Finally, she steadies her with one arm while she slides the bolster in where her mother's head has lain on the pillow with the other, and lets her mother lie back. The sitting up has allowed Bellinda's blood to run down the front of her slip. She looks more like a stabbing victim, Lillie thinks, than someone with the influenza, like one of Seamus's drunken brawling buddies more than his ailing wife.

She is trying to raise her father up when Frank reappears with the doctor. One look at the blood sends Frank rushing for the kitchen, where Lillie can hear him throwing up in the sink. The doctor helps her prop Seamus up on a rolled-up overcoat, and then he sends Lillie for cloths to clean her parents up. The nosebleeds slow to a trickle, and they are able to wipe most of the blood off before their mouths and chins are covered over again. Lillie begins dabbing at her mother's slip.

"Leave it, child. You won't get it out now. You can try again later, when the bleeding's stopped."

"The bleeding is a good thing, isn't it? With me the bleeding saved my life, you said."

"I think perhaps it did. You are young. We'll hope for them. Every case is a little different."

She looks at her parents' faces. A fresh trickle has given her father a thin moustache. It makes him look dashing, like an actor in one of the pictures. He always was a handsome man. Her mother's lips seem to have been dyed a brighter, bolder red by the blood. Lillie is reminded of the woman in the Jewish Burying Ground.

"Their skin is grey. How come it's grey? They're burning up, but their skin is grey."

The doctor looks at Frank, who has returned from throwing up. Frank nods as if to say that it is all right to answer her question. Lillie wonders what gives him the right.

"It's their lungs. Pneumonia. Their blood isn't getting enough oxygen."

"Then they'll die, won't they?" She blurts it out just like that, as though it were a question about some insects trapped in a jar, or a dog that had been hit by a dray, not her own parents. "Like my brothers. They'll drown inside."

"Her brothers? Her brothers died of this? Why was this not reported?"

"Her brothers died in the trenches. Two, three years ago."

"A gas attack," says Lillie.

"Nobody knows," corrects Frank.

"I know."

The doctor leaves. There is nothing more he can do, he says, and there are others he must see, others for whom he will not be able to do anything either. He doesn't say this last thing, but Lillie hears it in the weariness of his voice.

When the door has closed, Frank takes Lillie's hand and presses it between both of his. "I'm so sorry, Lillie," is all he says.

"Is it true they planned to ban public meetings?"

"What?"

"Dad said. This morning. They were going to forbid public meetings, and then they didn't. He said you were going to print it in the paper and they told you not to. Is that true?"

"It was decided it would be better not to. It was decided it might ... it might hurt the war effort."

"How could it hurt the —?"

"They read our papers, Lillie, the Bosch. They look for signs of weakness. Printing news of an epidemic, even printing anything about precautions for an epidemic, would be like waving a white flag. It was decided to wait till it was really necessary. Unavoidable."

"When will that be? When everybody is already dead?" It is her first truly adult question. They both recognize that. Just like a switch has been thrown. Lillie thinks it is funny because it is also the first question she can remember asking when she has not had the slightest expectation of an answer.

The next day the ban on public assembly is put into effect. The Opera House, the Imperial, the Gem, the Lyric all close their doors. The unions are served notices. Churches are told to hold their services out of doors.

The day after that, Lillie's parents die within minutes of one another. They hack and burble and gasp. At the end, they both reach for her — drowning people. When they are still, she tries to find herself in their features one last time, and then she covers their faces with the sheet. Before the men arrive to take them away, their bodies stiffen and the fluid in their lungs is forced out their noses. The sheet bears two large stains where their faces were, but Lillie can't bring herself to get a fresh one.

The word influenza, Frank would tell me years later, derives from the Italian. Frank had looked it up sometime early in the fall of 1918. He found it referred to the influence of the stars over our lives.

REEL TWO

Scenes of
Experience

1

Armistice

There is no need for an elaborate montage or even a title card to mark the passage of time here, a straight cut will do. Everything happened very fast. It was the way things went those days. The war, the influenza, the phonograph, the moving pictures all changed how time worked.

LILLIE MOVES IN with Frank on the same day her parents are buried, which is the day after they died, which was two days after they got sick. "We could both use the company," is how Frank broaches the subject, as though it would be good for both of them. "And it would save money for you. Seems kind of silly keeping that great big apartment on for one little girl." Lillie has never thought of calling the two-bedroom flat where she has lived her whole life "big." When her brothers joined the army and left home, it seemed larger, but only very briefly. She finally had a real bedroom to herself, but even the novelty of that wore off quickly. And she no longer thinks of herself as a "little girl." The problem is that she knows Frank is right about the money. So she nods silently as she watches her parents' cloth-wrapped bodies lowered into the pit where several identical bundles already lie, the work of the morning.

Frank did not want her to be present at the burial. He urged her to say goodbye at the door of the apartment when the men carried Seamus and Bellinda out. But she insisted. She needed to see the end of the story. People you loved went into the ground. It's what happened in books, and now that it was happening to her she had to see it through. She quickly found herself wishing she had listened to Frank, or that she was simply reading it in a book, or, better still, watching it as a moving picture. There the smells would be the warm smells of the living people all around her — sweat, bad breath, wet feet — and not the sick-sweet perfume of corruption; the sounds would be the music made by people she knew in the orchestra pit, not the dull thud of her parents landing on top of the silent, sleeping bodies of other people's parents.

In the pocket of her frock, her hand squeezes so tight on the tiny shard of mirror that she can feel blood come warm and sticky in her palm.

Frank has already been right about one thing — that she should not have come to watch. So when he suggests, just at the moment when she is most aware of how perceptive he is, that she move in with him, it seems only sensible to agree. Besides, Frank works for the newspaper, he knows how to look at a story from all angles and make the right judgment. That, and she is afraid of being alone.

They do not stay to watch the bodies covered over, though Lillie sees out of the corner of her eye the bags of quicklime propped up, barely hidden, behind the pile of dirt. The whole walk home she feels flushed, prickly on the back of her neck, as she imagines her parents burning in the white powder. Ashes and dust all at once. As if they had never been.

Frank's apartment, which she realizes she has never properly seen until she is actually moving into it, is much smaller than her parents'. Nathan and Percy, who live across the hall from Frank, help carry her things up the stairs. The landlord, a fat man with red lines all over his face whom Lillie has never liked, is there too. He stands in the doorway, watching every article as it goes out. Lillie's parents, he says, were behind in their rent and so he is keeping the furniture. It isn't worth what they owed him, but it is better than nothing; he has to live, he has children of his own. Lillie is glad that her mother long since pawned the hairbrush that had belonged with the mirror, and the plated candlesticks and the clock. The furniture that is left means nothing to her, and, besides, it would never fit into Frank's place. Everybody wins, she thinks.

Nathan and Percy stay for supper that first night, which is a good thing, Lillie thinks, because Frank seems to have become paralyzed the moment they loaded the last of Lillie's things into his place. His lips froze shut after he put the keys to Lillie's old home into the landlord's impatient hand. Nathan, however, keeps up a steady patter of conversation, while Percy, who is deaf, clatters around noisily in Frank's filthy kitchen. It's almost possible not to notice Frank's silence.

Lillie has never known that men can cook, so she watches, wide-eyed, as Percy moves efficiently about the cluttered space. Meanwhile, her ears are all for Nathan and the stories that he tells. Nathan plays in the orchestra at the Imperial, and he can tell the plot of any moving picture that has been screened there since the theatre opened five years ago. Lillie has listened to him before, but every time her father or mother, or one of her brothers, pulled her away long before she was tired of hearing what he had to tell.

Supper is an omelette. Lillie has never seen such a thing before, although she has read the word in books. In her family, eggs were boiled or poached or fried, sometimes scrambled. But never were they made to puff up, and never had they hidden within themselves such a wealth of other things. There is onion and cheese and a little bit of ham, all nestled in the slightly runny centre. There is toast, too, with drippings to spread on it, and mugs of tea. Lillie takes hers without milk or sugar for the first time in her life because she doesn't want to embarrass Frank by asking for some. It seems the adult thing to do.

Frank continues mute throughout the meal, but he appears grateful for Nathan's prattling, so Lillie decides it isn't bad temper that keeps him from talking. Shyness, more likely, she concludes. Or perhaps he is worried that Lillie and his friends won't like one another. Her father never liked Percy and Nathan, whom he called "the boys" with an intonation that made the phrase sound completely different from when he used it for his sons.

After supper, Nathan cleans up the kitchen. "This is unbelievable, Frank. Don't you ever wash anything? Well, kid, you're going to have your work cut out for you with this fella. I seen pigs with cleaner sties than this!"

"Where've you seen pigs, Farber? What do you know about pigs?" It is the first thing Frank has said in hours.

"In the pictures. I see them in the moving pictures. You can see anything in the pictures. Don't you ever throw anything out, Frank?"

"Sure, I throw things out. When I'm really sure I can't use them anymore."

"When they're old enough to rent a place on their own, more like." There is one of those silences that happen when somebody says something that might be taken to mean more than they intended.

Frank produces a half-gone bottle of whisky from beneath a pile of crumpled clothes that lie in one corner. Lillie's father did most of his drinking elsewhere, but on the rare occasions she has seen liquor inside her parents' apartment, it did not come out from under a mountain of laundry. She is even more surprised to see the way Frank pours it. Her father would pour a thimbleful for her mother and one for himself. That's what he called it, a thimbleful, and her mother always said she shouldn't and then did anyway. For the past year, there wasn't even as much as that in the house. Lillie's father could be a stickler for the law when it suited him, and Prohibition suited him, Lillie supposed, because it allowed him to keep his two lives separate. Frank sloshes his whisky out into three tumblers. There must be a couple of inches in each glass.

Percy fetches a fourth glass and performs a pantomime that is obviously meant as "what about Lillie, would she like some?" Lillie blushes and shakes her head no. Not even a thimbleful. Percy is a painter, Lillie reminds herself, and therefore can't be expected to know much about what is and is not right to offer fourteen-year-old girls. Artists, her mother said to her on several occasions, are really just overgrown children; no concept of what's right and wrong. That was why her mother had married her father, Lillie has decided. He was as little like an artist as any man she could think of. More like a piece of art, a beautiful sculpture.

"Seamus and Bellinda," Frank intones solemnly, raising his glass and staring through its amber liquid at the kerosene lamp that is lighting on a dresser. For a second, Lillie wonders whether he is seeing them there, her parents, in the flame through the whisky. But then Nathan and Percy raise their glasses too and clink them together, and she realizes that it is a toast. She has read about toasts. She lifts her mug quickly. There is an inch of lukewarm tea still in the bottom, and she drains it off, murmuring "Seamus and Bellinda," as she hears Nathan do.

"And Lillie," Nathan says after they have all spent a moment in thought.

"Lillie," says Frank, raising his glass too and touching it to Percy's. Lillie knows from her books that she isn't to drink to this, which is just as well, as there is no more tea in her mug.

When the bottle is empty, and the past, the present and the future have all been drunk to, Percy and Nathan help Lillie stretch a length of twine across one corner of the room. They have to try three spots because the plaster pulls away in the first two places they choose. Over the string they sling two bed sheets they carried up earlier from downstairs. They are the last two sheets, but Lillie doesn't mind because they wouldn't have fit properly on the cot that is to be her new bed anyway. They would always be dragging in the dust on the bare floor and getting all wrapped around her legs as she slept. She goes downstairs to use the bathroom. It is the same bathroom she and her parents used from their old apartment, which is kind of reassuring. When she climbs the stairs again, Nathan and Percy are just disappearing through their door.

"G'night, kid," says Nathan, his speech only slightly slurred. Percy grabs her by the shoulders and makes a great show of kissing her on one cheek then the other, just like she has seen it done in the moving pictures. Then his own shoulders jerk up and down in one of his silent laughs, and he is gone and the door is shut.

"I'll go use the bathroom now," says Frank as soon as she steps into the apartment. "Have you got everything you need, Lil? All set?"

"Thanks, Frank." She moves to hug him. It seems the right thing to do, but he dodges around her and is out the door. She hears him miss his footing on the stairs, swear, then continue down to the bathroom.

He has set the lamp behind the makeshift curtains for her. She turns it down to try to subdue any shadows she might cast on the hanging sheets, and then quickly begins taking off her clothes. Her white breasts catch the lamplight, unrecognizable.

When did they become a woman's breasts? She hurries to cover them again with the flannel nightdress, then pulls off her under-pants and folds them neatly, hiding them beneath her tunic on the chair, and finally dives into bed beneath the blanket Frank has left for her. She need not have hurried. Frank takes ages. What could he possibly be doing all that time in the bathroom?

When he finally returns, she asks him if he wants the lamp.

"Naw, I'm about done in. Will you turn it out, Lil?"

She does, and lies there in the dark, listening through the curtain to the unfamiliar sounds of a strange man breathing.

LILLIE WOULD NEVER have believed you could leave people behind so fast. She asks Frank to take her to visit her parents' grave a few days after she watched them put in it. They have trouble being sure of the exact place. There are so many new mounds, none of them yet marked, some of them, Lillie suspects, never to be marked. The tree she leaned against as she watched Seamus and Bellinda go into the ground, the tree she thought at the time she would never forget, is, after all, just like dozens of trees around the cemetery; it might be any of them. The next week, when Frank offers to take her again one evening, she says, "No, thank you," and goes instead to King Square to watch the movie that is being projected on the outside of the Imperial building. This is Mr. Golding's way of getting around the order to close the theatres.

She begins to forget her parents, piece by piece, but she remembers with envy the man in the Jewish Burying Ground — his grief, his penitence, but mostly his certainty that his mother lay just where she had been buried, beneath his feet.

And then it is November. And the war-to-end-all-wars finally ends itself. People forget about the flu. Always a distant runner-up in the race for public attention when there was news of the war, it is defeated outright by news of peace. No city ordinance, no official cautions, not even the threat of certain death itself could have stopped the huge celebrations that pop up spontaneously throughout the city. Prohibition takes a holiday. Liquor flows in such rivers as to make it clear that the Act has never really had any effect on drying things up. It has only diverted their course.

Lillie and Frank join Nathan and Percy and several other tenants of their building at a party that springs up in Queen's Square. Lillie thinks about how clever it was of the city's architects to have laid out the paths like the lines on the Union Jack, as if in anticipation of this very celebration. Nathan and a group of the other musicians from the Imperial bring their instruments, but whether it is the November cold or the fact that they have not been able to play together during the weeks the theatre has been closed for the flu, the music sounds harsh, grating. It is almost like it is ushering in a new day that will have its own sounds, its own grown-up take on the world, rather than celebrating any kind of return to the way things were before the war. That is fine with her. They might as well be dancing, she thinks, to the wails of the klaxons you can hear down Charlotte Street or the hoots of the ships' whistles in the harbour.

But dancing they are, and singing along with the impromptu band. Nobody is talking. There is a dearth of men, of course. Isn't that what the whole thing has been about? Lillie thinks of her brothers. So a number of the women find other women as partners. At first, they dance at arm's length, awkwardly, like strangers forced together at a party. But as the day wears on, they seem to fit more and more fluidly into one another's embrace. By nightfall, no one shows the least surprise to see several of these couples actually kissing as they rock and sway to the endless music.

Lillie dances with Percy. She asks him only after Frank has refused. The moment she does, when he answers only with a vigorous nod, she realizes her stupidity. How can he possibly dance with her? She has read about the ability of some deaf people to sense the rhythm of a bass drum, for instance, but there is no percussion in this band, and no dance floor to carry the vibrations of the other dancers. He will have to rely totally on her. She will have to lead. The problem is, she has never really danced herself, doesn't know how to follow, let alone lead.

They manage. As she grips Percy's left hand in her right, and feels his other hand firm on the small of her back, she imagines they are doing what those hands know best — making a painting together. She lets the music push them through the square, a bold brush stroke here, a stipple there. She feels the music, harsh and discordant as it is, pulsing through her body and into Percy's. It is a new sensation for her, and frightening. It reminds her somehow of her father and his wrestling partners. This must be like sex, she thinks, suddenly remembering the Baptist friend she had the summer she was twelve, and regretting that she did not listen to her more carefully. Soon she might be kneading Percy's buttocks, pushing her mouth onto his, like in the pictures. It is disgraceful. But she doesn't stop dancing. She can't. Nathan and his friends won't stop playing; Percy's hands are so strong. And the war is over.

It is Percy who breaks it off. He drops his hands, shakes his head and makes the thirsty sign. Lillie feels even more ashamed of her longings, her imaginings. They join Frank, who has located what must be his second bottle of whisky for the day. Percy takes a large swig and passes it to Lillie who, before Frank can stop her, takes a large swig too.

She doesn't choke. She once saw a girl about her age do that in a moving picture, and everyone in the theatre laughed. So she doesn't choke, though the whisky burns on her tongue and the roof of her mouth, and rushes at her nose and ears, desperate for a way out. She cries, but she does not choke. And when the bottle passes again, she takes another large drink. And another after that.

The music starts to get sweeter then. She doesn't care anymore about the dancing. Percy goes off to watch Nathan play. She

finds herself nestled in Frank's arms. He doesn't care about dancing either, she thinks. He smells like her father.

And the band plays on while the picture irises-out to black.

2

Neighbours

IT IS ALMOST a month after the armistice when a new family finally moves in downstairs from us. By then I must have stopped thinking about it as my old apartment. It is simply the empty place downstairs. That is easiest. No point living in the past. The war taught people that, I think. The war and, for me, the flu. My new life, the life I have now, is with Frank. He buys the food, he pays the rent. He has even taken to putting his clothes away sometimes, and he might be drinking less. I watch from my window as the new family carries its pitiful few belongings in by the street door. At some point, the landlord must have sold off the odd sticks of my old life that he had held back to cover the arrears in rent. I didn't hear them leave the building. I suspect that was due more to chance than to delicacy.

Apparently, though, the landlord was not all that thorough because one day, not long after the new family moves in, there comes a knock at the door of Frank's apartment — of our apartment.

"Can I see the girl that used to live in our place?" The tiny voice is full of doubt.

"Downstairs?"

A nod. "Yes please, lady."

"Yeah, that's my old place, I guess. I'm the girl," I admit, half afraid that the waif may be looking for playmates, picturing myself being emotionally blackmailed into skipping or hopscotch or some other pastime that I hated even when I might have felt the right age for it.

"Did you leave this? Is this yours? You seem so ..."

It is Bea, her body still soft, but her head not quite so hard as it once was, cracked across one cheek.

"Yeah. I mean, it used to be. Mine. She used to be. Her name is Bea." I take the doll from the girl, but then I think about it and I hold out one of Bea's worn hands towards her.

"Pleased to meet you, Bea," the little girl plays along.

"Where did you find her?"

"You know that little cupboard behind the stove?"

It was where I used to put Bea to discipline her. It was dark and smelled of mouse poo, and Bea was always very good when she came out. Only, I realize now, one time she mustn't have been let out. I must have forgotten she was in there.

"Would you like to have her?" I know I could never make it up to Bea; better to give her away and let her start a new life. Besides, I must be too old for dolls, mustn't I?

"Sure, if you don't — I mean, I'll have to ask my mum, she told me to bring her up here, but if you say it's okay ..."

"Tell your mum I said it's okay. Really. Now, I've got to get supper ready."

I am closing the door when the little girl says, "Lady?" I like the sound of that — lady. "Can I, can I give her a new name?"

"Sure, kid, you call her whatever you like." It comes out in a whisper, the sound you'd hear when someone is kneeling on a punctured inner tube, trying to squeeze the last breath of air out of it.

After that, I do my best to avoid contact with the new family. I realize that it is not so easy, after all, to let go of the old life. It will take work, determination. You have to keep away from the reminders. The building is small and, therefore, avoidance requires planning. I start leaving the door of the flat ajar so I can hear the bathroom downstairs. I begin making a point never to go myself until I have heard the closet flush and I have counted to thirty-five. The flush means that somebody has just gone, so they won't be likely to need it again for a while, and the thirty-five seconds allows time for them to clear out. Mornings and evenings, I get used to listening for three flushes in fairly close succession before I judge the coast to be clear. Baths are more difficult to manage. I get into the habit of simply sponging myself off while standing at the kitchen sink after Frank has gone off to the newspaper. My hair, I dunk under the running tap.

Frank never once mentions the new family, even after they have been living there a month. I am grateful for this care of my feelings, even though it might just be that he has never noticed them. The family, not my feelings. He is only home at night, when they are least in evidence, and he doesn't seem to need the bathroom very much at all. At first, I thought maybe he never went, but after only a few nights, I realized that he would usually get up sometime after two and relieve himself in the kitchen sink. It doesn't seem like a very nice idea, but then, I remind myself, I really have very limited experience of men and their ways.

Nathan and Percy try to make friends with the new neighbours, but every effort seems to go nowhere.

"Just not clubbable," Nathan announces after one such effort. "Some people aren't, you know." I think he might be right, but

I also wonder whether maybe they just don't approve of Nathan and Percy and the way they are. My own father didn't.

Frank and I are seeing a lot of Nathan and Percy, both together and separately. Often we eat together, late, after Nathan finishes playing the final show at the Imperial. The halls of the building have electricity, but the apartments still do not. To save oil, we burn candles that Percy scavenges from the ash bins behind the cathedral, and the grubby flat is transformed into a magical chateau. Percy's genius for cooking and Nathan's witty chatter both feed the illusion. Even Frank's silent brooding can be made to fit the picture. I imagine him as the world-weary count, a little the worse for wine, waiting for the love of a young damsel to wake him from his torpor and start him on a new life. Some nights I even believe that we will make it to the last reel, where the count and the damsel finally embrace, the snow melts from the trees and the little baby birds all begin to twitter.

THE DAY THAT the people from downstairs finally burst into my world is a Monday. I can remember that because we didn't see Nathan and Percy the day before. On Sundays the Imperial was closed, and Nathan had taken advantage of his time off by hopping on the boat to Fredericton for the day, something he did about once a month. Percy never accompanied him on these jaunts, preferring to stay home to paint. That Sunday, I smelled the oils and knew Percy was not to be disturbed.

Frank slept late, and I heard the family downstairs go off to church. I had just worked up my nerve to go take a real bath when I heard the toilet flush. Somebody had not gone to church. I counted to thirty-five, but the sound I was waiting for didn't come. Instead, I heard the door of Nathan and Percy's flat click. That didn't make sense because I had not heard Percy going down to the bathroom. I counted another thirty-five. Silence. I went and had my bath and thought nothing more about it until Monday morning.

Frank has just gone off to work, and I am shivering in front of the kitchen sink, washing my armpits, when the ruckus breaks out. It begins with hammering on a door. I know it isn't my door, though the vibrations are almost as great as if it were. Maybe this is the beginning of some kind of general alarm, those knocks are so urgent. I get dressed quickly and tug at my hair with a brush.

"Ross! Ross! I know you're in there. Answer this door." I know I shouldn't laugh at this, but it is hard not to be amused at the ignorance of some people. Obviously, whoever is knocking doesn't know that "Percival Ross, Artist," as the card just inside the street door so elegantly describes him, is stone deaf. I am about to open our door to tell the man the mistake he is making when I hear Nathan's voice.

"What the hell do you want? It's eight o'clock in the morning."

I hear something hit the door frame, and Nathan groans. Then I hear the man's voice farther off, deeper in, still yelling for Percy. I breathe in deeply and open my door. Nathan is standing on his threshold, holding his nose. There is blood between his fingers. I run to my kitchen for a damp cloth. When I get back, the noise inside Nathan's apartment has gotten louder and more varied. I can hear wood splintering, glass smashing, canvas ripping. And still the shouting, the fruitless act of screaming at a deaf man.

"You bastard. She's a mother. She's carrying another child, did she tell you that? What kind of devil are you? Did you think I wouldn't smell you on her? The turpentine?" Then there are some dull thuds. The sound you might make hitting your pillow. Nathan and I start into the apartment together but we both freeze as a high-pitched shriek slices the air. It is a sound like nothing I have ever heard, a sound that doesn't really belong to the physical world at all. Still, I recognize it right away. It is the sound of a deaf man who believes he is about to die. It is the sound of all the terror and rage, even the love, that Percy has been hoarding all his silent life.

When we reach the room Percy uses as a studio, the man from downstairs has already finished. He pushes past us and thunders downstairs.

Percy is crumpled in a heap against one wall. His right arm sticks out at an odd angle, his head is bowed onto his chest. But he is obviously breathing, his shoulders rising and falling. *Chuff-chuff-chuff*. When Nathan puts his hand on his chin to raise his face, Percy jumps as if he thinks the beating is about to continue. His cheeks are already starting to show a little green, and one of his eyes is shut tight. There is blood around his mouth and nose. Nathan tries to help him to his feet. That's when it becomes obvious his arm is broken. His right arm. His painting arm.

I look around the studio, at the broken easel, the smashed jars, scattered paint tubes and torn canvases. Even in their shredded state, their subjects are obvious. Each is a nude study, its subject unmistakably the woman downstairs. From the front, from the back, full-length, waist-up, there are far too many to be the product of one single stolen sitting during church-time yesterday. More surprising still is how I feel about what I am seeing. I don't feel embarrassed by the woman's nakedness. Maybe that's because she does not seem embarrassed by it herself. Instead, I think I feel a little envious that Percy should have thought her worth reproducing over and over, from so many angles. And I think I can understand what the woman must have felt being lifted out of her squalid apartment, her routine days, made into a piece of art.

The police come. Somebody in the building must have called them. One of them makes a rude sign to another when he sees what is on the torn canvases. Another makes a different rude sign when Nathan explains that he and Percy live together in the flat. When they try to question Percy and discover he is deaf, they make a final sign and leave. I listen at the head of the stairs. They don't even knock on the door of the apartment below, although Nathan and I both told them who assaulted Percy.

A week later, Percy and Nathan are given notice, asked to leave by the end of the month. Nathan is quick to reassure me that we will still see one another, but I think I would feel better about that if he were looking me in the eye as he said it. While Frank and I are helping them move their things down to the street so the cart can pick them up, I look up at the window of my old apartment. I see Bea and the little girl's face low down in the glass. Above them is the mother's face, one eye still puffy from her husband's rage, and her left hand, fingers spread, a water strider on the pane.

3

Domestic
Arrangements

For this, we will have to fade in very slowly. The picture is reluctant to form out of the blackness. Eventually, an interior comes into focus — the apartment that Frank and Lillie are sharing.

IT IS DARK. Lillie cannot be sure whether she has been asleep. Some of the times she has, sometimes she hasn't. Before her parents died she slept like a baby, could always tell when she woke up. But now the two states have become less distinguishable. She has come to accept that this is part of what is meant by "growing up."

The hall light, the electric one, is not on anymore. When she went to bed it was on, she knew by the yellow sliver beneath the apartment door. Does that mean she has slept? Or might she simply have had her eyes shut when it was turned off or the bulb unscrewed? The light is always on when she goes to bed. Some nights it goes off. Some nights she sleeps. Some nights the light stays on all night. Some nights she does not sleep. It is not possible to make a reliable connection.

The sheets that they strung up the very first night she slept here move a little. It could be a draft, but she knows it's not. The wind does not have feet that stick to the floor and make kissing noises as they cross the room. The wind does not smell of drink and tobacco and sadness. Well, sometimes, but not this strong.

He does not speak. She's glad he never speaks. Somehow it makes it easier the next day. She wishes there was something that could make it easier at night.

The first night it happened, she started to speak. She was going to ask him if there was something the matter with his bed. But he had put his hand over her mouth. Not hard, not so it hurt her teeth or stopped her breathing. His hand smelled of leather, like her father, she thought, which was comforting. She could not tell what his other hand smelled of, it was too far away. Down there, fumbling away already with her nightdress. Neither hand was cold. After the first time she knew there was nothing she could say. He must have sensed this because after a few times he stopped covering her mouth, which gave him both hands to work with and got the whole thing over with faster. And that had to be good, didn't it?

She does not try to hold the blankets tight. Once she did that, pretending to be asleep, cocooning herself tighter as she rolled to face the wall. He grabbed her shoulder then, to pull her around. His nails left marks where he had snatched the cover away. He is not a violent man, and she cannot bear to think of him that way. So she does not hold the blankets tight. Besides, they both know she is awake.

He always comes to her with his trousers on. It is something she does not understand. Something, a detail, she thinks she should be able to understand, at least more than the whole act, which she does not even try to understand. She just puts up with it. There is a pattern to what he does, like it's a ritual. That much she knows, and unbuttoning his pants and pulling them off under the covers is part of it. Leaving them by his own bed, hanging over the chair, would not be the same. Perhaps he thinks that would betray forethought, intention. The first few times, when he kept one hand over her mouth, Lillie wondered whether the moment of fumbling with the buttons was a moment when she might put up a sudden struggle and break free. She even wondered whether Frank designed it that way, like the hunters in books who always gave their prey a moment's head start. That was back when she used to think about it during the day, to play it back, a movie in her head, trying to make sense. Anyway, where would she run? This is her home now.

The cot is small. There's no question of his slipping beneath the covers and lying there beside her. She thinks that might make it more bearable, a moment of companionship, a moment of lying cosy together beneath the covers before the other thing begins. But the only way they will both fit is with him on top. She is glad he is not a large man like her father. She wonders how her mother wasn't crushed. Or snapped.

The first night that he stopped covering her mouth, he tried to kiss her. She turned her face away so fast her neck hurt for three days afterward. Now he doesn't try to kiss. She wishes there was as easy a way to tell him about all of the other little things he does. She wishes she could turn her breasts away, close her belly button, sprout spines on her neck and collarbones. She supposes the little things somehow make the big thing better for him. Like unbuttoning his pants in the bed, they must be part of the ritual.

His left hand has found its way up her nightdress to cup her right breast. She wonders if he knows that a real woman's breast wouldn't fit like that in a man's hand. She thinks about her mother's body, then her own, and wonders if Frank knows the difference. He couldn't — this is what she decides every time — or he would go find a real woman.

After the breast, it is only a minute until the big thing. Lillie lets herself go limp. Like Bea, she thinks, like Bea. It hurts a little less each time. She hardly whimpers anymore. Frank probably doesn't hear her anyway under his own groans.

She waits until she hears him breathing evenly in his own bed before she dares to move. Under her mattress she keeps the nightdress from the first time. She uses it to clean herself up.

It doesn't take her as long to go to sleep afterward as it used to. She has a pattern of words she uses to lull herself. It is her ritual. Not quite a lullaby, but almost as reassuring.

Frank is a good man, she tells herself. He looks after me. He is kind. In the daytime he is always kind. This is just the way things are. It's what grown-ups do. It's over in a few minutes. It's just the way things are. I have nobody else. It is a small price to pay for belonging.

She falls asleep to those thoughts two or three nights a week for almost a year.

The fade-out here is very slow. It makes you wonder if it will ever end.

4

Moving
Pictures

IN THE SUMMER of 1920 I am sixteen. I want to find a job when school lets out, but Frank keeps telling me I'm just a kid still, there's time enough, and we're doing okay the way we are. When I complain to Nathan and Percy, whom we see much less often now they are no longer neighbours, Nathan says he thinks Frank is right, while Percy offers, through Nathan, to take me on as a model at fifty cents a day. I laugh, though I am not certain that he is kidding, and that is the end of that idea. They are of no use.

So I sit around the apartment most days, reading, and getting lazier by the hour. Then I discover the back door of the Gem.

I would never have dared at the Imperial, though I know people who have, but the Gem is a much smaller, much humbler theatre, tucked away on Waterloo Street. The people at the ticket office don't seem to care about what goes on inside, and there are no ushers like you'd find at the Imperial. All in all, the set-up is just too tempting to resist. The restrooms are located by the back door. Patrons have to go through a curtain to the left of the screen to get to them. So what you do, a friend told me one day, is sneak in the back door and wait in the bathroom until the picture starts. Then, with the auditorium dim and the picture flickering, you walk in and take your seat as if you've just been to the ladies' to powder your nose.

Doing it becomes an addiction. At first, it is simply the thrill of getting away with it, of getting something for nothing; it wouldn't matter whether it was a freak show or a sermon. But soon I begin to get caught up in the movies themselves. The sneaking-in becomes merely an amusing prelude to an even more exciting event. I like the movies so much I might even consider paying to see them, if it weren't so easy to get in for free.

There is no orchestra at the Gem. Only a piano player. He is someone I met a couple of times with Nathan and Percy. He has a perpetually harried look about him, nervous, as if he lives in terror of being caught with only the hurry sheets on his music stand when the romantic theme should be coming in. But his hands are steady and sure. I think I would look worried too if I had his job. It's an enormous responsibility, even if the cinema he plays in is tiny. He can make or break an entire audience's experience of a movie. The longer I go to the Gem, the more I have to admire what he is capable of doing. I don't know any other men who could do what he does. He can actually use the music to express everything he feels about the images on the screen. I have the feelings deep inside me too, but no way of letting them out.

I have been sneaking into the theatre for over a month, nodding at this man whenever our eyes meet. It's a kind of guarded nod that might as easily mean "I remember meeting you with Nathan and Percy" as "I see you here every day, don't I?" Then one evening he suddenly speaks to me.

"What did you think? Of the picture?"

I have tagged onto the end of a knot of people heading for the exit to the left of the screen, and I am not sure at first that he is addressing me.

"It's Lillie, isn't it? How did you like it?"

"I, uh, I liked it fine."

"I thought it was a little too obvious."

"Me too."

He takes me to a diner down the block. It certainly isn't a date, just a chat with the friend of some friends. Still, I don't mention it to Nathan and Percy when I see them later that week. Or to Frank. They would only want to know what I was doing hanging around the Gem. Frank thinks I am folding bandages at the Red Cross every evening.

Coffee at the diner after the last show becomes a regular thing. I wait for him — his name is Mike — behind the curtain to the left of the screen after all the people have gone. I jump out at him and yell "boo." He pretends to be surprised and we both laugh. It's nice. I feel easy with him, like I do with Nathan and Percy.

One night I jump out and frighten not one man, but two. Mike introduces me to Fred Trifts. He is the manager of the Gem.

"I see you here quite a lot."

Oh God, he's going to ask me to pay for all the times I've snuck in. "Not so much really. I come when I can, I guess."

"Mike tells me you really like the movies."

"I do," I say. "I love them." It feels good to tell the truth.

"Fred's going to have coffee with us," announces Mike without any trace of enthusiasm. Trifts stops to slam the back door behind us and locks it with a large key that reminds me of something out of a fairy tale.

At the diner, we all order coffee and pie. Trifts takes his black — the coffee, not the pie, he jokes to the woman who waits on us. When it arrives, he slips a slim hip flask out of his pocket and adds to the coffee.

"Want some?" he asks Mike and me, in that way that shows he expects us to say no, which Mike does.

"Sure," I say, "a drop might warm me up." It's what my father would sometimes say.

Trifts and I clink cups while Mike looks intently at the grooves worn in the tabletop.

"You don't know what you're missing, Mike," says Trifts, who is obviously not a man who believes in letting well enough alone.

"To each his own," replies Mike, refusing to rise to the bait. Thank God, I think. I could not have stood a sermon on the evils of alcohol at that moment. I am already feeling bad enough, feeling like somehow, in some small but real way, I have betrayed my friend by accepting a drink from his boss.

"But I thought that's just what your people were against, letting everybody make up his own mind."

"What do you mean 'my people'?"

"Baptists."

"Oh, that. We're not a people, Fred. Being Baptist isn't a whole separate race or anything."

"You're just better than the rest of us."

"I've never said that."

"You don't have to. All you have to do is refuse a drink or say no to a dance. That's enough. That says 'I'm better,' doesn't it?"

"The Lord tries to point us on the good path ..."

"See what I mean?"

"C'mon, Fred, lighten up on him. He just doesn't want your rot-gut whisky in his coffee, okay?"

"This doesn't concern you, Lillie," Mike snaps, in a tone that makes me wonder why I have tried defending him.

"Ah, but it does in a way, don't you see?" says Trifts. "Lillie is the audience, after all. She should be the one who decides, don't you think?"

"Not if she chooses wickedness."

"What are we talking about?" I am lost now.

"So you think that people should only be allowed to choose the things that you've already decided will be good for them."

"What the Lord has decided."

"I wonder what the Lord thinks about ..."

"About what?"

"Never mind. Why don't we find out what Lillie thinks?"

"What Lillie thinks about what? Tell me what you two are talking about."

"I don't want any part of it. I've said what I feel and it's final."

"What's final? What's final?"

"Mike here is refusing to play for next week's picture. Says it's immoral. How do you like that?"

"It is immoral."

"What is?"

Very slowly, Mike takes from his breast pocket a sheet of paper that has been folded and re-folded many times, and slides it across the table. As I unfold it, I try to iron it flat with my fingers. Finally, I find I am running my hands over a cartoon figure of an unclothed woman, turned three-quarters away, and looking over her shoulder at a bear. Across the image are printed the words: "DON'T Book *Back to God's Country*, UNLESS You Want to Prove that THE NUDE IS NOT RUDE."

"I don't get it."

"*Back to God's Country* is this movie made by a fellow by the name of Shipman," Trifts says. "Somewhere up north. In Alberta. Based on this story about a girl who can tame all kinds of wild beasts. In the end, she makes friends with this savage sled dog and he rescues her and her husband from certain death. Some places are making trouble about showing it."

"I didn't know anyone made films up north. But that can't be the reason they ..."

"There's a scene where the leading lady swims skinny."

"Like Annette Kellerman?"

"Pretty much. It's this Shipman guy's wife. Nell, her name is. She takes a swim when she thinks nobody's around."

"But the camera is around."

"And the villain is too, as it turns out. It's a very short sequence."

"Not short enough, I bet," says Mike.

"But this Shipman fella's a kind of genius. He's turned it into the big draw for the movie."

"By trying to persuade people it's art?" I think of poor Percy, his face beaten black and blue, his canvases torn almost beyond recognition. "Naw. People won't go for it."

"Thank you, Lillie," Mike practically yells. "Thank you! You see, Fred, the people do know what's right from what's wrong. The audience." For a moment I am a little afraid he is going to put his arms around me. Yesterday, I wouldn't have minded if he had touched me. I have even wondered why he hasn't yet. Today, I concentrate extra hard to will him away. It seems to work.

Trifts is right in there with a response anyway. "She means they absolutely won't go for the art argument, don't you Lillie? And that's exactly the point. That's what this Shipman's got figured out. If people really bought the art argument, they would stay away in droves. Too boring. Art's the kiss of death. It's exactly because they do not buy it that they'll flock to this picture. They want rude. D'you hear me? They'll flock."

"Not the good sheep."

"There are no good sheep and bad sheep. They all follow. That's what sheep are." It is just the kind of thing Frank is fond of saying sometimes. So clever it doesn't matter whether it is right or not.

"It's your responsibility not to lead them into temptation."

"Yeah, but I gotta make my daily bread, too. I have to show this picture."

"Well, you'll be doing it silent. Lillie, can I walk you?"

Why didn't I say yes? So many things might have been different if I simply said yes and went with Mike. But I don't. I just give my head the slightest shake and mutter "G'night Mike," and watch as he slinks away from the table and out into the night.

We finish our pie in silence. I can think of nothing but the way Trifts's calf has come to rest across my shin under the table. Does he even know it is my leg and not the table's he has found? I should shift my leg, let him see his mistake. If it is a mistake. I do not move. My cheeks are burning. Will he notice how red they are? Why won't he speak? He was chatty enough while Mike was here. Does he just think I am too dull to be bothered with? That must be it.

He stands up, crosses to the counter, and pays all three bills — Mike left in too much of a state to think about such mundane things. Then he helps me on with my coat. I can smell the coffee, warm and bitter on his breath. We shake hands at the door of the diner. Later, when I crawl into bed, I can still smell him on my palm.

Of course I go to see *Back to God's Country* the next week. True to his word, Mike does not play. The images flash on the screen in a silence that is broken only by the clatter of the projection machine at the back of the auditorium. It doesn't matter. Inside my head, I make my own soundtrack. I hear high strings rising to a fury as the Chinaman is murdered in the Yukon saloon, leaving his faithful dog to a life of savage vengeance. Then, in come the imaginary woodwinds with their innocent nature-music as Nell Shipman appears in the woods with her tame squirrels and rabbits. There's even a pet bear cub, which, the title card says, is called Cubby. I make falling-in-love music on viola and cello when Nell's character meets her poet boyfriend, then a brassy cacophony for the wicked trader on the run from the Mounties. When Nell takes the swim, there is no music at all; only the sound of my own blood pumping through my veins. As the villain spots the naked Nell, there is a rush of air that must be the intake of every breath in the theatre as a hundred voyeurs are suddenly shocked by the nerve of one. The killing of Nell's father — he is thrown from a cliff as Nell looks on — is accompanied in my mind by a crash of cymbals. And so it goes, reel by reel and set-back after setback, until Nell and her writer-husband are happily ensconced once again in their woodland home, surrounded by Nell's adoring animals and awash in a pastoral symphony that is a pastiche of every soothing tune I can remember.

The final title card flashes on the screen, the house lights come up, and the audience files out, mostly silent. I sit still in my seat. I have actually paid for it this time, which I reckon makes it perfectly legitimate for me to sit as long as I choose. I am not ready to go back to Frank, and there is no Mike to go for coffee with. Maybe Fred Trifts is around somewhere. I shut my eyes, replaying the images of the film in my head.

He is very quiet. I only know he is there when his breath blows at the stray tendrils of hair that hang around my neck. It tickles, but I don't turn around. Neither of us speak. I feel his lips on the back of my neck, the sandpaper of his whiskers. Still, I do not open my eyes. He nibbles at my earlobes just as I have seen Cubby do to Nell in the film. And then his hand is caressing my collar-bones, first one and then the other, and burrowing at the front of my dress to find a way to my breasts. There are buttons, which he finds finally, popping them through their buttonholes with his thumb. When he takes the right nipple between his thumb and finger, I think I hear myself gasp. It grows enormous at his touch, becomes an aching finger itself. He leans farther over the seat and, still kissing my shoulders and caressing my nipples, begins to pull the hem of my dress up towards my waist. I open my eyes to see the tops of my lisle stockings revealed, then the flash of my thighs, startlingly white. I watch as if it's a movie while his hand wriggles through the pile of material that now lies in my lap, finds the top of my underpants and slides inside. His warm palm rests on the crinkly hair. His fingers go to work on the tender parts. My nipples and the secret place between my legs are joined by some kind of cord, the action of one hand and the action of the other perfectly synchronized. I can no longer breathe normally. There is only the rhythm of the fingers. I do my best to keep silent, but there are tiny squeaks coming from somewhere. Maybe he will think it is the seat. In the end, I shut my eyes again and let myself drown. I never knew it could be like this.

5

Glass
Plates

"TRY TO KEEP them still can't you, Lillie." The children are excited, eager to get on the boat. It is their parents who have ordered the photograph, not the two-dozen fidgeting boys and girls who, without meaning to, are pulling the pose hither and yon. I tell them to pretend they are statues.

Mr. Erb disappears under the black hood and I warn the children to be very still, trying to make my voice sharp like the nuns I remember at school. At this point I am still in the pose with them. I imagine myself upside down on the ground-glass focus plane, blurring and sharpening as the photographer fiddles with the lens. Once he has the group in focus and has emerged to insert the plate, I will move quickly out of the camera's gaze.

I have now been working for Mr. Erb for a month, ever since I finished school, and mostly I like it. It's not just the money, although being able to contribute to the housekeeping week by week will, in time, I think, help change the way things are with me and Frank. He objected at first, and was furious with Nathan for arranging it, but I think he is beginning to adapt.

Isaac Erb is kind to me, patient except in the few minutes just before he makes a photograph. Groups make him especially edgy, which is understandable given the importance of having everyone stay absolutely still for about a quarter of a second while he makes the exposure. A quarter of a second never used to seem like a long time to stay still, but I have learned. Trying to keep the subjects from moving is one of my jobs. I also hand him the plates and put them back in the case once they have been exposed. I am learning to develop and fix the images captured on the plates, too, and how to print from them. And he is teaching me to drive. In his business, he has to have a car. The two of us cover the city most days between making group portraits like the one this morning and making pictures of people's new houses and their businesses, their wares, their ships, even sometimes their accidents and tragedies. We are both happiest making photos of buildings. Buildings seldom move.

"When can we see what we look like?" one of the children asks as I move to hand my boss a plate holder.

"You'll never see it if you don't hold still!" I growl. I don't like that part of the job, but it's necessary, so I do it.

Mr. Erb fits the plate holder onto the back of the camera, slides the cover.

"Now everybody breathe in like I told you," I bark at them as though I am Colonel McAvity. "And hold."

Mr. Erb squeezes the rubber bulb to release the shutter.

"You can breathe again."

Mr. Erb slides the cover back in place, removes the plate holder, holding it out for me to take. "One more." I pass him a second plate holder, and the whole process is repeated. He likes to have what he calls an insurance shot, since we will not know for sure until we develop the plate whether anyone moved and blurred the picture.

Released from their stiff postures, the children become a mass of arms and legs scrambling for the boat that will take them upriver on their picnic. I say something to Mr. Erb about their wildness, their bad manners.

"Were you never a child, Lillie?" He does not speak much, which is part of why I like him, but when he does it is almost always something like this.

I decide to answer him honestly. "Yes and no."

He simply nods and motions for me to put the tripod in the car.

The rest of the day is given over to making photographs of things and places. There is none of the tension involved in taking people. He even lets me look at the ground-glass screen before he finalizes the focus. I am learning a lot from him about composition. After only a month by his side I would never again dream of suggesting that a photograph is simply a direct record of the way things actually are. It makes me proud to know this, though I have little chance to show it off. Sometimes, though, as I walk home from the studio at the end of the day, I stop and look at whatever piece of the city happens to be in front of me, and I plan where I would place the camera to make the most effective composition out of it.

Today, we make a portrait of Mr. Estabrooks's new automobile outside his Mount Pleasant house. I try not to think about my mother as I watch a woman in a pinafore and cap passing back and forth in front of the windows, using one of those new electric vacuuming machines. Mr. Erb sends me up to the big front door to ask that the drapes be pulled. I wonder why he doesn't simply ask that the maid stop working for a few minutes. As we pack up the equipment, I say that perhaps one day people will want moving portraits of their vehicles. "It would seem to make more sense, wouldn't it?"

"The spokes on the wheels," is all Mr. Erb says.

I wait. "Sorry?"

"They appear to go backwards on a moving picture. Matching the number of frames per second to the number of revolutions per minute is impossible. The wheels mostly look like they're going backwards." He does not go on to remind me that so-called moving pictures are only a series of stills projected very fast. That's another thing I like about Isaac Erb — he doesn't condescend.

At the City Market, we photograph sides of beef for McArthur's. I have a hard time imagining what use they will make of these photos, I think they would put anyone off meat forever. At first I try to shoo the flies away, but Mr. Erb assures me they won't ruin the exposure. When I look on the focusing plane, I am amazed by how he has somehow managed to set things up so the ribs of the split-open cows and the rafters of the market's lofty ceiling actually seem to complement one another. Upside down, the market's structure looks like the ribs of a ship, which is what it is. The dead meat looks the same either way. Suddenly, I miss my brothers.

My favourite part of the day is when, back in the studio, it is time to develop the plates. Though I do not pretend to understand the exact chemistry involved, I am fascinated by the idea that tiny grains of silver salts dissolved in gelatin and spread on the glass backing of a plate can react with light to capture an image of the world. Mr. Erb has not yet let me handle the newly-exposed glass, but he is happy to have me sit by as he immerses each plate in the chemical bath that will amplify the effect that the light has had. Growing the silver, he calls it. And when that is finished and the plate has been put in the stop bath to arrest the process, large areas of dark appear where the plate received the most light, while the lighter areas represent the shadows. It's called a negative, he says. I love to look at the plates and imagine a world where dark is light and light is dark.

Mr. Erb always keeps the negatives. The client only gets the prints. Most people wouldn't store the glass plates properly, Mr. Erb says, but I think he is reluctant to give up final control over the images he has made. Filing the processed plates into specially made boxes is another of my jobs. Mrs. Erb never tires of telling me how lucky I am. In the old days, when Mrs. Erb still helped out in the studio, the plates were all made by hand, often by her and her husband, from bits of glass that they came by. The variety of sizes made storage a real nightmare. Not to mention the cuts from the rough edges. Now, the plates are prepared in a factory, all to a uniform size and thickness, and the edges are smooth and easy to handle. Mrs. Erb says she envies me the benefits of mass production.

The first day I was asked to file the negatives, I dropped one on the counter and it broke into three pieces. Afraid for my job, I thought immediately of hiding the pieces the way I had hidden the shards of my mother's mirror. But this was someone else's picture, someone else's face. So I worked up my nerve to confess.

"This is why you must be so careful," Mr. Erb reminded me. I braced myself for a blow, but then he simply added, "Look how we fix it." He took two clear sheets of glass the same size as the negative and arranged the three fragments between them. "For storage, you will need a special place, and we will have to bind the glass with string, but for printing it will be just fine like this." And even though he did not need another print of that negative, he made one anyway, to prove to me, I think, that no real harm was done. Even a broken negative could be reproduced an infinite number of times.

Our last subject for the day is a collection of silver spoons. The owner brings them in to the studio and will not let them out of his sight. I can feel the man watching me the whole time I help set up the equipment and check the focus. We make two portraits of each spoon — one front and one back, each from a slight angle. The man packs his treasure back into its walnut case and leaves. Mr. Erb and I both exhale.

As we are developing the plates, I am surprised when an unexpected light spot appears on one of the spoons. Mr. Erb seems unmoved. He prints from that negative first and hands the paper to me. There, on the convex side of the bowl of the spoon, if you look very hard, is my face, a little distorted, my brow wrinkled in concentration as I watch the photographer make the exposure. He must have known it would be there all along. He makes another print for the client, who, we agree, will never notice the miniature portrait of someone he has already forgotten.

6

Jump

Here again, the fade-in is very slow. Another image that does not want to materialize.

STANDING ON THE stairs, Lillie can smell the supper cooking in one of the apartments below. She thinks it may be her old apartment. It isn't a pleasant smell — cabbage mostly — but it's familiar, and reminds her there are still ordinary families, just not for her. She thinks it smells better than her own sweat anyway. Sweeter. She never used to be aware of the smell of her own sweat, thinks perhaps it had no smell at all, until the last few months. Now she can't block it out. She bathes sometimes twice a day at the kitchen sink, so nobody knows, and still the smell overpowers her. She wonders how anyone can stand to stay in a room with her. Did her mother smell like this when she was ...? She has no way of knowing.

The stairs are filthy. Being common area, they are apparently a no man's land when it comes to cleaning. The landlord wouldn't dream of seeing to them, not for the rent they pay. So the balls of dust, the stains of tobacco juice and the trails of mouse droppings accumulate week after week, and everyone just pretends that they aren't there. To notice them would be to volunteer to clean them up.

Lillie counts the stairs. She has counted them before, but that does not stop her. They might have changed. Everything changes. It wouldn't do to be wrong about them right now. On some, there are shards of brittle rubber, the remains of tread guards from the building's better days. If she loses count, she can usually rescue herself by reference to one or another of the patterns of rubber. The stair with the rubber that looks like a horse and buggy is number five, for instance, and she can begin again from there. As long as it hasn't changed. Everything changes. Number eight looks like a woman's silhouette on a cameo brooch. Sometimes she imagines that number eight is her mother. Which makes number nine her father, though it doesn't look a bit like him.

The light bulb in the wall is close to her ear. She can feel the heat. It's meant to stay on all the time, she thinks. Who pays for that, she wonders? Mustn't it burn out? She can't imagine that the landlord replaces it. Maybe Frank does. Frank who used to unscrew it. Or did he turn it off? She has never known for sure. If there's a switch, she doesn't know where it is. She wonders about unscrewing it now, but it would be hot, and she'd have to have something to guard her hands. Maybe if she pulled her dress up over her head, but then she wouldn't be able to see what she was doing. And what if somebody happened up the stairs? How would that look? Even though it might be more believable to say she tripped in the dark, she will have to do without it. People can easily lose their balance in broad daylight, and the pale yellow glow from a single bulb certainly isn't that.

Frank will be home soon, she thinks. She hopes she is guessing right. For weeks she has been marking his arrival times on a calendar she keeps in a drawer, plotting what she hopes is a pattern. It's important he arrive just after. She doesn't want a lot of strangers handling her.

When her periods had stopped, she was terrified. Almost as frightened as when she started for the first time, but back then she had had her mother to calm her and explain to her. Now there is no one. Lillie never missed having girlfriends until the bleeding stopped. If there was anything you would discuss with such a friend, this must be it, she thought. She told herself that maybe her mother had just forgotten to tell her about the end. Maybe it was normal to stop after a few years. It would make a lot more sense that way. All that mess. Who would want more than a few years of that? But then the nausea had started. She couldn't pretend to herself any longer.

It was Nathan who had finally taken her to the doctor. Lillie hadn't said a word to him about all the throwing up, let alone her period, God forbid. Frank would later call it Nathan's women's intuition. Nathan only laughed. Lillie wasn't supposed to have heard. She thought if she were Nathan she might have wanted to hit Frank. More and more, she thought somebody should.

The doctor was the same man who had attended Lillie and her parents during the influenza, though he seemed to have no recollection of her. His manner was abrupt, dismissive. She told him about the nausea, hoping he would diagnose a stomach bug and let her go, but he asked straight away about her monthlies. She was mortified to have to talk to him about that, but she did nod reluctantly when he asked whether her monthlies had stopped. "No need to kill an innocent rabbit over this one," he said to Nathan in the waiting room. Lillie wished he would keep his voice down. "Marry her off if you can," the doctor added, more quietly, as if he had heard Lillie's prayer. Then he took some money from

Nathan, looked at Lillie, shook his head, and disappeared back into his consulting room.

Nathan had taken her for a slice of pie afterwards. "Lil," he had said, "you know what's going on now, right?" Lillie decided to pretend she did not. For both of their sakes. Nathan had a swig of coffee, and, seeing the blank look on Lily's face, plunged on. "It's a kind of a miracle. You're going to ... you're going to have a baby." Oh no I'm not, thought Lillie, though all she let Nathan see was the single tear that welled up and sped down her right cheek.

They had agreed to wait a few days before telling Frank. Nathan never asked if Frank was the father. It only occurred to Lillie later that this might be considered odd, suspicious. A betrayal. That she knew Frank was the father was one thing; that Nathan should know was quite another. In the end, she had decided to let Nathan be the one to talk to Frank, though Nathan had insisted that she at least be in the room.

The timing was important, since they had to be sure that Frank, who was drinking more every day, was sober enough to take in what he was being told. Percy had cooked an early supper for them all, and then slipped away to his studio. While Lillie washed dishes, her back to the men, Nathan began: "You know when I took Lillie to the doc the other day?" Frank did. "Well, the doc thinks, that is, the doc is pretty sure that Lillie's going to ... that Lillie's going to be a mother." Lillie dropped a plate against the side of the sink. It chipped. She had not yet put it that way to herself — Lillie's going to be a mother. She had only thought Lillie's going to have a baby, and, as little as possible, Frank's going to be a father. Because she dropped the plate, she did not hear Frank's immediate response if he made one. What she heard was silence. She was afraid to turn around. Then she heard the scrapes of two chairs, and two sets of footsteps. The men, she thought, have gone to talk about the problem somewhere else. She prayed that Frank would not come back with a marriage proposal. It was too much to hope that he might not come back at all. And she didn't really want that anyway. She would have missed him.

Lillie went to bed. When Frank finally came home, he went straight to his own bed. At least that's over, thought Lillie as she lay in the dark looking at the crack of light under the apartment door.

THE STREET DOOR opens. Too early to be Frank, Lillie hopes. She doesn't want to have to do this again tomorrow. An apartment door clicks below her, and she sighs in relief. It is the rough man from downstairs, home for his cabbage. She wonders if the little girl still has Bea. What was it the little girl wanted to re-name her? It doesn't matter. She will still be Bea. Once you are named, you are named for life. This is probably why she has not allowed herself to think about naming the thing that is growing in her. If she does, she will think of it always by that name. And she does not want to think about it anymore at all.

The cabbage smell is stronger, the door open for a moment long enough to let it escape. The sweat is running down her sides in rivers. Smelling stronger, too. She counts the steps, moves down two. Her hand instinctively goes for the railing. She has to work quite hard to will it off.

She counts to five and launches out into the void in front of her. Before she loses consciousness she is pretty sure she has peed.

A WOMAN HAS to be called in to help with the complications. It's someone Nathan knows. She is ugly, but kind. Lillie watches her closely, looking for signs of judgment, but there are none. Only pity.

"Drink this, dear, it will help you get back your strength."

Lillie is not sure why she should want her strength back, but the woman seems to mean well, so she humours her.

Lillie never asks what became of the thing she had been carrying, the tiny mass of cells made in her image. Nobody ever mentions it again. And nobody asks how she came to fall down the stairs.

REEL THREE

Standing In

1

A Dummy
Off a
Cliff

THE SUMMER OF 1922 is as foggy as any other summer in St. John before or since. Most days, the best we can hope for is that by mid-afternoon the sun will have burned the perennial fog bank out fifty yards into the bay where it will cower for an hour before rolling back in. Maybe Partridge Island will emerge from its shroud, show us its grim monuments to dead immigrants. Living in the city all your life, you grow resigned to the fog. It is simply the way things are, like a lot of other things. The people I know have stopped grumbling about the weather years ago. Some have even turned it into a source of fierce pride, pitying the poor unfortunates in Fredericton who regularly suffer temperatures in the eighties and all that unrelenting sunshine.

So when, suddenly, for four days in late July 1922, the fog subsides — or when the sun proves too strong for it, depending on how you like to see these things — it comes as quite a shock to all of us. Though we are used to putting up with the oppressive qualities of the fog in absolute silence, we have no trouble finding our voices on the subject of the ill effects of the sun. The heat is widely described as utterly killing one day after it has begun. Three days into the wave, it is no longer unusual to see men going into offices in their shirt sleeves. Bosses who are never without stiff collars can be spotted with no collars at all, and the no-collar class unbuttons itself to the second or third hole. Women's silhouettes have been loosening with the new decade, but they appear overnight to shed the last of the body-torturing corsetry of their Victorian and Edwardian mothers.

Isaac Erb declares it too hot to work, and I spend the first three days of the sun's assault dressed only in my slip in the apartment with the blinds all drawn. When Frank comes home in the evenings, I grudgingly shrug on a dress, but I refuse to bother with shoes or stockings.

On the third night of the inferno, Nathan appears just as Frank and I are finishing a cold supper. He invites us to go up the river the next day.

"It's Sunday. I'm off. Percy wants to come. Fredericton can't be any hotter than this. It'll do you good to get out on the water." It is as though he has rehearsed every possible objection before coming over, and has thought of an answer for each. I admire his shrewdness in not pleading that it could be fun. Frank would never agree then.

"I'll need some kind of bonnet," I tell him. "Isn't that what they wear on the steamers?"

"Percy has something in the studio. A real Gibson Girl number. It'll be perfect. Huge."

"And Frank'll need ..."

"Already looked after. Percy and I already made a visit to the man this afternoon."

Frank wipes his dripping forehead with a not very clean

handkerchief. "All right," he says, "that sounds fine." For some reason I feel like a schoolgirl who's been granted a holiday.

As it turns out, Nathan is by no means the only person in the city who has thought that a trip up the river would be a good way to spend an unusually warm summer Sunday. The boat is crowded, "full to the gunwales," Nathan keeps announcing in what he obviously intends to be a jolly-Jack-Tar voice, in poor imitation of the mate who helped us aboard. I find it hard to turn my head, in its enormous bonnet, without rubbing up against the brim of somebody else's equally ridiculous hat. The sound of the water is cooling at first, though.

At Evandale, we decide to disembark. The smell of human sweat and the extra heat generated by all of those bodies packed so close together has become unbearable. The mate assures us there will be another boat headed downriver in an hour. We wave companionably to the boatload of strangers as the steamer pulls away from the wharf and heads up towards Wickham. Then we find a huge oak and settle down in its shade.

That is a good place to iris-in. The scene is very picturesque — a French painting — the four of us under an oak, making a picnic. The image is a little washed out, overexposed in all that sunshine.

NATHAN HAS BROUGHT sandwiches — "Cut with love by my very own hand," he crows — which Lillie is glad to tuck into. The men eat less. They are more intent on the whisky. When the down-steamer arrives, they decide to wait for the next, and after that one, the next. Lillie removes her bonnet and stretches out for a nap. Percy and Nathan remove their shirts and trousers and go for a swim, thinking they are hidden from view by the bank, but Lillie can spy them through the long grass, wading and splashing and finally plunging out into the river in their underwear. Frank watches Lillie as she pretends to sleep. She can feel his gaze, hot even in all the other heat. Every few minutes he takes another pull on the whisky bottle; she hears the glugs. The outing is not, she thinks, such a change from routine after all.

She supposes that Percy and Nathan take as long as they do to return because they have to let their underwear dry before they can dress again. Flies buzz. She can hear Frank's breathing, wonders whether he has fallen asleep but is reluctant to open her own eyes to check. The afternoon grows old. There must be a last boat of the day, she thinks, one that they had better not miss. Nathan and Percy will know.

"You should have come in, Lillie, the water was beautiful."

"Nathan, sometimes you really do go too far." This is Frank, his speech thick with the drink. "How could Lillie possibly go swimming with you two?"

"You'll notice I didn't actually address you," chirps Nathan, but Frank is not to be bantered.

"This is no kind of company for the girl. We should never have come." Sometimes, when Frank is very drunk, he persuades himself that he is actually still Lillie's guardian and has what he calls her "best interests" at heart. Still. But it is only talk, and she never bothers too much about it.

Today, though, whether it's the heat or the company, she feels she needs once and for all to make things clear. And so she decides she will swim after all. There's a second bottle of whisky in Percy's jacket, which he has left in a heap at the base of a tree in his hurry to get into the water. Lillie scoops up the limp cloth with its stiff burden and rushes away.

"Lil, where are you going?"

"Swimming, Frank. I'm going swimming."

"But ..."

"I'm going swimming, Frank. Alone." She takes a swig from the bottle, refuses to choke, drops Percy's jacket, and starts over the bank. "Gentlemen won't peek," she throws back over her shoulder in a way she has seen Nell Shipman do in the pictures.

There is a thin strand of beach, with a dead tree sticking out of the bank. She sits on the tree and has another swig. She doesn't need to go in the water, she thinks. It's enough if Frank believes that she did. As long as none of them looks over the bank, she can just make some splashing noises, have a few more sips of the whisky, get her hair a little wet, and go back to the men, having won her point, asserted her independence. She hears the grass rustle behind her. Are they calling her bluff? She wishes she had left the bonnet on; it would give her something easy to take off, in order to call theirs. As it is, she makes an elaborate show of undoing the knot in the scarf she is wearing over her middy blouse. She could easily pull the band of fabric over her head without untying it, but she thinks the slower way will be more effective. Once the knot is undone, she pulls on one end of the scarf, and it slithers around her neck, brushes her breast, and waves free.

"C'mon fellas, let's go for a walk," says Frank. She hears the grass rustle again. Relieved, she tilts the bottle to her mouth. That's absolutely the last drink, she tells herself. She'll just wait a few minutes and then climb back up the bank.

A breeze has come up — the afternoon puff, she has heard Nathan call it. It feels good in her hair. She takes off her shoes and stockings and steps into the water. Her feet clench around the slippery stones on the riverbed. She can hear Frank and Nathan talking, some distance away now, up the road towards the building that Nathan says is an inn, or used to be. Then, much closer, she hears the grass rustle for a third time. It might be the wind. It might be Percy. There is no way to know from the conversation whether he is with the others. She holds the bottle to her lips for several seconds, steps backwards out of the river, and begins to unbutton her middy. The grass is silent. She stoops and picks up a large rock, the biggest she thinks she can handle, hefts it into

the water. It makes a most unhuman-like plop and sends a vibra-
tion up the beach. When she turns around, the grass seems to
move a little. Percy may be laughing at her. She shrugs out of
the blouse, drapes it carefully on the dead tree. Another mouthful
of whisky. Her skirt slips out of her hands the instant she has the
waistband undone. It falls in a heap about her ankles. The breeze
feels wonderful. She thinks of Nell Shipman and that picture.
She thinks of the seat at the Gem. It's hard to tell whether it is
Percy's breathing or her own that she hears. Her pulse has picked
up, her face is burning. The whisky? She looks down at her cotton
cami and knickers. They'd never dry, she thinks. She sneaks a
look over her shoulder, careful not to take in the spot where she
imagines Percy to be, calculating instead how far out she can
swim before Nathan and Frank might see her from up the road.
It's not possible to figure that out, she realizes, without actually
going into the water. And once she's under the water why would
it matter anyway? She told them she was going swimming. They'll
be far enough away. She thinks about taking a drink, for courage,
but finds she doesn't need it. The cami and knickers are off and
she is walking into the water. She wishes it were deeper, then she
could dive like Nell or Annette Kellerman. She crooks her left
arm up so it shelters her breasts. Her nipples are hardening with
the rising cold of the river. Her right hand is held an inch above
the patch of fur down there, and as she stumbles on the slippery
rocks, it knocks against her from time to time. Then she is up
over her thighs and she doesn't need the right hand anymore.
She winces as the water touches her there. Finally, she is over
her waist and can stretch out to swim. Only after a dozen strokes
— she realizes for the first time how perfect it is that they are
called that — does she look back towards shore. Nathan and Frank
are clearly visible, but tiny; she judges they're about two hundred
yards away. Percy is not with them. She knew it, but she is a
little surprised to find she does not mind that he is watching.

What bothers her is that she can't make out exactly where he is hidden in the long grass at the lip of the bank. If she is going to be watched, she wants to know where the watcher is. Treading water, she tries to calculate the angle from where she can see her clothes on the dead tree. Just at the moment she thinks she has detected an irregularity in the grass, she hears the whistle of the steamer. Jesus.

She whips around. The boat is not in sight from this low in the water. Couldn't be as far away as Wickham, though, she thinks. The others have all waited to blow their whistles until they were within minutes of docking. She might be able to cover the distance between here and the beach before the steamer comes into view, but she could not possibly dress fast enough, even bone dry, which she will not be.

This is when Percy appears out of the grass, responding to motions downward. Stay low, Lillie interprets. What the hell does he think I'm going to do, start jumping up and waving? She takes a few strokes towards shore. Percy motions her not to come any farther. He points to a willow that weeps out over the water from the point the steamer must be about to come around any minute, and then he makes swimming motions. Lillie thinks it is crazy to swim straight for trouble, but she realizes she has no plan of her own, so she heads for the tree. The pounding from the paddles of the steamer is almost as loud as the pumping of her heart. She can see the smokestack over the top of the tree she's swimming towards. At the very moment when she is prepared to give up, to stop swimming and resign herself to the inevitable catcalls from the steamer, she hears a loud crash behind her.

She looks back at the beach. Percy has smashed the whisky bottle on a rock at the very moment the steamer came into view, and is staggering around on the stones, playing drunk. Lillie swims ten more strokes to the fringe of the willow branches, clutching at the ropey curtain as much from exhaustion as modesty. The steamer is not fifteen yards from her, but she sees that all eyes on deck are trained on the fool on the beach. Some of the men start waving and shouting encouragement. Percy's act grows broader, the staggering making his legs look like rubber. The men laugh as if he's Chaplin. She hears some women's voices too. Percy thumbs his nose. Someone throws a bottle at him. Empty. It lands in the water, well away from its target. The beach is a crescent. As the steamer makes its way down river, Percy moves along it, continuing his performance. A moment later, Lillie can't see the boat any longer, only its stack as it rounds the next point and chugs into the Evandale wharf. Percy turns upriver again, shielding his eyes to try to pick Lillie out among the willow branches. She swims out into view, raises her hand out of the water, waves. The air is cold on her breast. Percy blows her an exaggerated kiss and clambers up the bank. As she swims in to the beach, she sees him getting smaller as he hurries towards the spot where Nathan and Frank have stopped in their walk and turned to watch the steamer.

They get on the next boat down. The men ride inside, but Lillie stays at the rail, combing the riverbanks for signs of indiscretions like hers, hoping to see just one person as foolish as she, until it finally gets too dark to see.

Indiantown wharf is bustling when they pull in, even though the sun has set and the steamer is half empty. Lillie has never been here this late; it must be after eleven. She wonders if these people are out here every night. Nathan and Frank have found a friend on the boat — though Lillie thinks friend is an exaggeration since she has never heard of this man. He has invited them all to a party, even has a car waiting. Lillie would much rather walk. The whisky she drank before her Nell Shipman escapade has turned out to be a bad idea in more ways than one.

"It's just around the corner," Frank says, which Lillie thinks would be a strong argument on her side. "C'mon, just hop in, Lil."

So she does. The man who has invited them to the party sits beside her. It's his car apparently, but he doesn't drive it himself. The man's breath smells like rotting earth, and he keeps wafting it her way in foul gusts that make her wish they were riding in an open car. When the driver turns onto Douglas Avenue, all of the passengers roll to the right, and the man's shoulder grinds into Lillie's so hard she thinks she'll have a bruise. Another right follows rapidly. Lillie leans forward quickly to avoid the shoulder crunch, and the man ends up half-lying on the seat behind her. He has to place his hands on her hips to help himself up. Has to, or simply does.

The house isn't at all what she would have expected. It's the last one in the row before the street comes to an abrupt end, beyond which there is a substantial drop and then, not far, the river. She doesn't know all these details when she gets out of the car — they come later — but she recognizes that the house is absolutely ordinary, the exact likeness of the others in the row. Unprepossessing is the word for it — not at all what you would imagine for a man who can afford his own driver.

In the yard behind the house, the party is already well underway, which strikes Lillie as odd, since the man who invited them just got off the same boat they did. She mentions this to Nathan, who tells her, "This party? This party's been going on for almost two years." Of course. That is how Frank and Nathan know this man — he is their bootlegger.

Frank disappears into the house and is back in two minutes with a bottle, already uncorked and the level an inch and a half down. Lillie is growing a biting headache, so she grabs for the bottle as Nathan is passing it on to Percy. Frank looks angry. The hell with him, she thinks. Percy doesn't seem to care. He just smiles at Lillie in a conspiratorial way she imagines will begin to get on her nerves. She would like to go home, and she tells Frank so. "Jus' a little longer," he says in a voice that means at least another half bottle's worth. While he is talking with a handful of men about whether the damned heat will ever let up, she slips away, out the front gate and onto the street. She thinks briefly about walking home, but it's a very long way, and there are streets between here and there that she wouldn't like to walk alone on, even in broad daylight. So she turns the other way. Once she's across the barrier at the street's end, the sounds of the party fade. There's a narrow path through the bushes. If she thought about it, she would never go down it. But she doesn't think about it. She just walks. The path is increasingly disrupted with outcropped rocks. She stubs her toes several times. Then suddenly underfoot it's all rock. She has come to the cliff. Somewhere below, the river lies quiet, though to her left she hears a murmur from the rapids. To her right, she sees the lights of the steamers, settling in for the night but not yet abandoned. She is tired, dizzy, so she sits.

"Lillie?" She can't be sure how long she has been sitting, or whether the man to whom the voice belongs was already there before her. "Lillie?" She knows that voice. Almost. It will only take her a minute. That's it. Fred Trifts. It has been a couple of years. Since before she started working for the photographer; since before she fell down the stairs. A long time. It's Fred Trifts. From the Gem. Only not from the Gem anymore. What is it he does now? She can't remember.

"Fred," she says, without turning around. She is proud of that.

"May I?"

Lillie turns.

"May I sit?"

Lillie nods and moves over a bit, as if space on the cliff's edge is limited but she can let him have a little.

"I thought I saw you up at McKim's."

So the bootlegger has a name.

"It's been a while."

"Yes."

"You stopped going to the movies."

"Yes."

"I ... I missed you."

"The movies were a phase." Her nipples ache with remembering. "I had to get on with real life. You stopped working at the Gem anyway, didn't you?"

"Had to get on with real life too, I guess. I have a garage. You know, cars."

Lillie does know cars. They also both know the weather and the river, so the conversation stumbles on for a minute. Then, after a long silence, he offers her a drink, not from a bottle, but from a hip flask. A little of the whisky dribbles down her chin. He wipes it with a handkerchief that he produces from somewhere, like a magician. She flushes and laughs, and then he is kissing her. It's like swimming; she is Nell Shipman and Annette Kellerman, diving in. His fingers start on the buttons of her middy. "No," she says. The fingers insist. She thinks he must not have heard and grasps his wrists. "No," she says, louder, and tries to pull away. Fred Trifts is not a large man, but he has positioned himself over Lillie in such a way that gravity is working for him.

"What's the matter? I thought you liked me. You used to ..."

She had let his fingers wander amidst the musty seats of the Gem only three times, starting with the afternoon after *Back to God's Country*. That is what this is about, then. To him, those three times mean she likes him, she will want him to do it over and over again. Multiple prints from a negative. Now, even though he is a garage man, and there is no movie, he thinks it can all happen again. Diving into the same river twice.

"It's not the same," she starts to say, wondering why she should have to say anything.

"What's different?" He is sitting beside her now and holding her hand. She is not sure what will happen if she tries to pull it away. She decides not to find out. "Was I going too fast?" he asks. She wishes he would be struck mute, go totally silent.

"A little," she nods. It is true, just not the whole truth. He wouldn't understand the whole truth.

"It's just that I really like you, and I'm so glad to see you." To illustrate, he places the hand that holds Lillie's into his lap. She feels the bulge, and is about to snatch her hand away when she has a better idea. She lets him brush the back of her hand against his trousers, adds a little pressure of her own, gradually lengthening the strokes to be sure he gets the idea that she is co-operating. Then, in the instant when he lets go of her hand, confident that it is doing the job on its own, she makes a fist and slams it down hard.

"Jesus Christ!" Trifts screams and strikes out for Lillie. She is too quick and on the J- of Jesus she is already up and scrambling along the cliff. "You goddamned little teasing bitch! All right. You want rough, I can show you rough." He lunges and catches her ankle, sending her sprawling. Before she can catch her breath he's on top of her, prying her thighs apart. She thinks, I am right, he is not the man he was in the Gem. This is not the movies. This is not even like that first time with Frank. Frank cared about me. In his way. She stops fighting him, though, and puts her hands up over her face while he is tearing at her underpants. Then she feels the hairpins, and she knows what she will do.

The ear canal is not an easy thing to find in the dark, but Lillie does not miss.

Trifts lets out a screech that seems to propel him backwards, up in the air, off her. The direction of the film passing through the gate has suddenly reversed, time has turned back, undoing the last few minutes. But he does not stop when he hits the ground. He keeps going, over the cliff.

He is gone far too quickly for Lillie to do anything to help him, so she should never really ask herself if she would have.

She leans over the cliff edge. He should be moaning, shouldn't he? Or swearing? Or both? Instead, there is silence. Lillie sits back. She starts to put the hairpin back but it's sticky, and she throws it over the cliff. Nobody up at McKim's will notice if her hair is a little out of place. As she picks her way along the cliff and back along the rocky path, she remembers something she read in a magazine one time. Something a director said about how he started to make a movie just by throwing a dummy over a cliff and photographing it. Then he set to work to write the story that led to that body going over that cliff. She thinks how easy life would be if only it could be like making movies.

IT'S NATHAN SHE finds first; it's Nathan she wants to find first.

"There's been an accident," she says.

Nathan, who is obviously much drunker than she has ever seen him, looks down at his pants.

"On the cliff."

"What cliff?"

"At the end of the street."

"What cliff, what street?" Frank has appeared from nowhere. He seems more lucid than Nathan. That worries Lillie.

"It's Trifts."

"Trifts?"

"Fred Trifts. He's ... he's fallen over the cliff."

"What were you doing out there with Fred Trifts?" Frank asks.

"That's not the point. The point is he's fallen over the cliff."

"Good riddance to bad rubbish."

"He might be hurt. I think he must be hurt. We've got to help him. Can we get a lantern?"

Percy has joined them, and Lillie tries to mime a lantern since the other two are just staring at her. Percy nods and heads into the house.

"How high is the cliff?"

Finally, a sign of sensible response. "I can't tell. It's dark. There are lots of bushes."

"Will we need a rope?"

She is glad they are finally catching on.

"A rope's a good idea."

Nathan vanishes into the house.

"What were you doing out there with Fred Trifts? Do you even know Fred Trifts?"

She wishes she could tell him how Fred Trifts saved her life once. Three times. But this isn't the time.

Percy and Nathan are back with rope and lantern.

"It's a good thing I went in," Nathan says, "Percy was in there paying for another bottle. Not that I stopped him, but I got the lantern, too."

Nobody at McKim's even seems to notice as they let themselves out through the front gate, four staggering souls armed with rope, lantern, and a bottle of hooch.

Lillie has trouble finding the exact place where Trifts fell. She felt sure that there would be signs of their struggle, but she can't make any out, which may be just as well.

"Maybe if I was down at the bottom."

"Where is the bottom?" Nathan holds the lantern out into the void, but it is not much help.

"So we're just going to lower you down into whatever, is that it Lil?"

"I'm the lightest, Frank. The rest of you will need to anchor the rope."

"This is completely crazy. Are you sure he's even down there? Maybe he's gotten up and walked away by now."

"He's down there."

By the time the rope is wrapped around the three men, there is not as much left over for dangling as Lillie had hoped. They look around for an alternative, a tree or a rock, something solid to tie the end to instead, but there is nothing. Three drunken men form the most reliable anchor available. Mack Sennett would love this, Lillie thinks.

Her knees and toes scrape rock, push off, bump back against rock, three times as the men pay out the rope.

"That's it, Lil, that's all there is."

Her feet are dancing on air. "Fred!" She calls. "Fred?" There is no answer. She takes a deep breath and lets go of the rope.

Sharp twigs scratch her thighs as she lands in a bush about three feet below. She has to pull her skirt up around her waist to disentangle herself, hoping, foolishly, that Fred Trifts is not right there to see.

"Lil, are you all right?" The lantern flickers over the cliff's edge. Its light doesn't reach her.

"Fine." Smoothing her skirt. "I'm down."

"Any sign?"

"I haven't looked." She starts walking downriver, away from McKim's.

"Do you want us to lower the lantern?"

"I wouldn't be able to reach it. The rope's too short. I had to drop for the last little bit."

"Then how are we going to get you back up?"

"Can we just do one thing at a time?" She keeps walking, counting her steps.

"You're moving. Should we follow you with the light?"

"No. Stay where you are. I need you to stay there so I know what ground I've covered."

Her toe hits a rock. For an instant she thinks it might be Trifts.

At one hundred paces she turns around and walks back towards the lantern's glimmer. When she is directly below them, Nathan calls down, "Should I come down to help? I think Percy and Frank could anchor me, actually."

"Then we'd both be stuck down here."

"I don't mind."

"I'm heading the other way now. You can follow along with the light now if you want, I'll know what I've covered." At twenty paces she finds him. God, was it this close to the end of the path from McKim's? In the dark she can only feel his features. His skin feels like putty, already chilly. His head seems at an odd angle when she gropes around lower and finds his chest. It's not moving. For confirmation she goes back to the face, holding the back of her hand by Trifts's nostrils. Nothing.

"Lillie?"

"He's here."

"Trifts? Trifts? Are you hurt?"

"I told you he's here."

"Why isn't he answering?"

"I think he's dead."

"Shit."

"I didn't mean to ..."

"What, Lillie? You didn't mean to what? What does that mean?"

"He wouldn't stop. I told him no, and he wouldn't stop. I didn't know we were so close to the edge. I would never have ..."

"So what do we do? Nathan? Nathan? Where the hell?"

"What's the matter Frank?"

"Nathan and Percy, they've gone."

"They can't have gone. Where?"

"Back to McKim's? To call the cops? I don't know."

"We're here." It's Nathan's voice, right behind Lillie.

"How ...?"

"There's a set of steps about twenty yards along. And this is a road we're standing on. It was supposed to run all the way along to the falls, but they never finished it. We can get a car in here, move Trifts out that way."

"Nathan, he's dead."

"Well, we're not going to leave him here for the dogs to eat are we? I mean, I hardly knew the man, but nobody deserves to be eaten by dogs."

"Dogs eat people?"

"If they get a chance."

"Jesus. Too bad we don't have a car."

Percy is kneeling down beside Trifts's body now. There is a jingle of metal as he pulls some keys from the dead man's pocket.

"But Trifts does. Nice work, Perce. We just have to find it. Must be parked right outside McKim's somewhere." By now, Frank has joined them. "You and Percy stay here with ... with the body," says Nathan. "Lillie and I will go find Trifts's car."

"I'll go with Lillie."

"Frank, everyone knows you can't drive."

There are five cars parked on the street by McKim's. Nathan has to try the key in three before he finds the right one. Just like the prince trying the slipper on Cinderella, Lillie thinks. Or Goldilocks. When the motor turns over, Lillie jumps into the passenger seat. Nathan has trouble with the clutch, but they manage to lurch away from McKim's — Lillie is thankful that the car is pointing already in the direction of Douglas Avenue — and they lumber up the street.

There are lights along Douglas Avenue and Lillie notices for the first time that Nathan is nearly green. She supposes she is a similar shade. "What will we do, Nathan? We'll call the police, of course. Will I have to tell the whole story?"

"Is there a story, Lil?"

"You know, I mean, how we struggled, how he was ... will anybody believe me?"

"The way I see it, the guy fell over the cliff, and we found him."

"Why were we looking for him?"

"We weren't. We were just out walking."

Nathan has pointed the sedan between two clumps of alders, into a gap that Lillie doubts will be wide enough. The twigs scrape the sides of the car. "Are you sure this is ...?" But a few seconds later the headlights pick up Percy and Frank.

Lillie stays in the car while the men grapple with the corpse, trying to get purchase beneath its armpits and knees. Then she sees them let him down again. Percy is bent right over Fred's chest. Lillie wonders if maybe he has started breathing again. The sudden movement could have restarted his heart, like in one of those miracle cures you see in King Vidor's pictures. But then, in the headlights' beam, she can make out Percy holding a paper package. All three are looking inside. They leave the motionless Trifts and come back to the car.

"What's wrong?"

"Things just got a little more complicated."

"What?"

"Trifts. He had some money on him."

"So?"

"Quite a lot of money, actually."

"So?"

"Three thousand dollars, Lillie. Three thousand dollars."

"That's a lot of money."

"Not going to do him any good now."

"No."

"But somebody maybe knows he had this on him."

"He has it on him still. Or he did. Shouldn't Percy put it back?"

"You see, Lillie, we're thinking that if Trifts is maybe found in his car, maybe like he was robbed, that can't really hurt anybody, right? Dead is dead."

"He fell down a cliff. He's bound to be covered in bruises. His neck is probably broken. How is that going to look like he was robbed in his car?" Lillie can't believe she is having this conversation. She blames the booze.

As if on cue, Percy offers the bottle around. Nobody speaks for two or three minutes. Nathan has cut the car's engine and lights. The night has grown suddenly chillier. Lillie thinks she can sense the fog rolling back in. Even the whisky can't warm her.

"You go on back up to McKim's, Lillie," Nathan says, an arm on her shoulder. "We'll look after this." She climbs the steps in a daze and picks her way back along the path, but when she comes to McKim's she doesn't go into the yard. She stays outside the fence, retching and heaving, unable to bring anything up.

2

Reflection

A series of folded newspapers spins across the screen, one after another. Each successive boldface headline is more lurid than the last. Time passes. We fade in on Lillie in the apartment. She is reading.

LILLIE CANNOT RESIST the newspaper in the days that follow, though she seldom bothered with it before. It is full of the Trifts murder. That is the big story in the summer of 1922 and on through the fall, as larger and larger rewards are posted for information leading to the apprehension of person or persons ... and so on. The police know almost nothing. Mr. Trifts, who left managing the Gem Theatre a year ago in order to run a garage, was apparently bludgeoned to death with a whisky bottle in his car, a McLaughlin sedan. He received a call from someone on Douglas Avenue around ten o'clock one night, according to his wife, and he was not seen again until his body was discovered inside his car in the north end the next morning. Robbery was the expected motive. Trifts had left his house with a substantial amount of money on his person. This is the story they keep printing over and over. Only the phrasing changes, never the details. But Lillie, like everyone else, reads about it every day, religiously. That is how she comes to see the advertisement.

It is two columns wide, and enclosed in a heavy black border. Difficult to miss. At the top is a list of the who's who of St. John society. Lillie is about to turn the page when the word Films catches her eye. These high mucky-mucks are the directors of a new company calling itself N.B. Films Ltd., capitalization ninety-nine thousand dollars. She reads on. The films will be made by Ernest Shipman, a name, the advertisement boasts, that will be well-known to Canadian audiences. Shares in the company are being sold at one hundred dollars per, twenty-five on application, twenty-five on September fifteenth, and fifty on the first of October. A month earlier, before Fred Trifts went over the cliff, Lillie would have automatically passed the ad by at this point, the cost of a single share being well beyond what she and Frank might be able to save in a year. But they have all that money under the mattress in Lillie's room, where she counts it every night. There is more than enough there for ten shares if they want.

She talks to Frank.

"What else are we going to do with it? It's just sitting there."

"I thought you might want it one day, you know, to go to school or something."

"They say in the advertisement that Mr. Shipman's other films have grossed between two hundred and fifty thousand and eight hundred thousand. That means our fifteen hundred could become forty-five hundred, or even twelve thousand. Twelve thousand, Frank. That's a lot of school."

"Or it could become zero. Americans make the movies, Lil. Canadians watch them."

"He's just finished a film in Ottawa. A Ralph Connor story. And then there's *Back to God's Country*."

"Proving the nude is not rude, that one? That only works once."

"There's money in the movies, Frank. Under my mattress there's only dust."

In the end, she has to get Nathan and Percy to help her talk him into it. They all go down to Robinson's together to buy in.

"Ten shares."

The man behind the counter looks from Frank to Lillie and back again. Lillie wants to punch him, wants to say, what, you think because we don't dress like Walter Golding or the archdeacon we can't buy stock in their company?

"That would be two hundred and fifty dollars down, the same on September fifteenth, and five hundred by the first of October." The man pauses to let that sink in, imagining, Lillie thinks, that he will put them off with the enormity of the sum.

"We want to pay it all right now," says Lillie, pulling the bills out of her coat pocket as if she always keeps a thousand dollars there.

The man's eyes widen, then quickly narrow again. "I'll get the paperwork," he says.

Percy and Nathan buy ten shares too. The man refuses to let them sign their names together for all ten, although he has made no such difficulty with Lillie and Frank. They will have to take five each, he says. They shrug and sign separately.

"How does it feel to own two percent of a film company?" Nathan asks Lillie as they leave Robinson's. "Among the four of us that's what we have, you know. I figured it out. It might be more than Golding holds, or the archdeacon. We might be able to vote them down."

"As long as we all stick together," says Frank; and Lillie suggests they all could use a drink.

A week later, an advertisement appears for local talent to fill the minor parts. Nathan and Percy urge Lillie to go to the Dufferin Hotel to meet with Mr. Young, but Frank is lukewarm about the idea and Lillie is reluctant to go without his full blessing. If it weren't that the ad stipulates "minor parts," it might be different. She does happen by the Dufferin on another errand on the appointed day, and when she sees the lineup that stretches out the door and around the corner, she tells herself she has made the right decision.

Shipman and the director, a man named Hartford, along with the rest of their entourage, arrive in early September. Nell is not among them, Lillie is disappointed to learn. She divorced Shipman not long after they finished making *Back to God's Country*.

There is a reception at the Dufferin and all the shareholders are invited. Lillie, Frank, Percy and Nathan go in a block, which is how they have come to think of their interest in the company. Once inside, though, they separate. Percy and Nathan gravitate to Pierre Gendron, the leading man, who is holding forth in remarkably halting English on the hard life of the sea and how he will bring the character of Jimmy Westhaver to life on the screen. Frank finds a corner where prohibition is temporarily and lavishly suspended and he gets talking to the chief cameraman. Lillie has imagined that she might find David Hartford and congratulate him on *Back to God's Country*, ask after Nell Shipman. Instead, she finds herself toe to toe with Ernie Shipman himself.

"Norma, my dear, what the hell are we going to do for fun in this one-horse town? Old Uncle Ernie will have to come up with a few ideas so his leading lady won't get bored, won't he?"

"I'm sorry, I'm not ..." But he isn't listening.

"Is your room okay? I told them something special for the star. Something large with a view of the park. That's why they put you next to mine. Anything you need ..." He trails off as out of the corner of his eye he catches Norma Shearer standing near the grand piano. "Jesus," he says. "Sorry, honey, I ..." and he hurries away across the room.

Lillie doesn't find Mr. Hartford. Somebody tells her he is probably drunk in his room, although Walter Colvin, Shipman's assistant who seems to be everywhere, denies it flatly. She does, though, meet the leading lady.

It is in the ladies' room. Lillie has fled there in desperation, having not found anyone to talk to. She plans to wait ten or fifteen minutes, collect Frank and the boys and leave. The smell of tobacco is overpowering when she enters the bathroom. There are clouds of bluish smoke billowing up from a stall. Lillie wants to cough, but knows this would be an unsophisticated thing to do. She wets her handkerchief and holds it in front of her mouth and nose. She has read about soldiers in the war surviving gas attacks by peeing on their shirttails and breathing through them, and she has wondered whether her brothers knew this trick. Pee is not necessary in these circumstances, she decides; simple tap water will do. It does help somewhat. The smoking stops shortly anyway, and, after a sigh and a flush, Norma Shearer bursts out of the stall, pulling at her skirt to straighten it, and popping a mint in her mouth.

Even with the handkerchief over her mouth and nose there must be enough about Lillie's eyes and forehead to stop Norma dead in her tracks. Reflexively, she holds one hand up to her face, as if checking for a veil of her own. Then she looks around quickly for the sinks and the mirrors she knows should be over them.

Lillie is slower to see the resemblance. At eighteen she is still reluctant to think of herself as worth looking at, so she seldom does. Now, however, standing beside Norma Shearer at the mirrors, she looks long and hard.

Iris-out on the identical faces, framed side by side in the mirror.

3

Telling the Truth in Motion Pictures

BLUE WATER IS nearly ten days into shooting when Lillie is disturbed by an early-morning knock on the apartment door. Frank has gone off to the paper, and she is in the bathtub. It is one of the luxuries she insisted on for their new place when they decided to move. She ignores the pounding as long as she can. When it becomes clear that whoever is there is not going to go away, she swings herself over the side of the tub, blots front and back on a towel and shrugs on a slip, a skirt and a jumper.

David Hartford is a tall man, filling the entire doorway. The pictures she has seen of him in the newspaper do not do him justice. He is impeccably dressed, right down to khaki-coloured spats that match the tone of his suit. Lillie feels instantly conscious of her bare feet with nails in want of cutting.

"Good morning." The melody of his voice has obviously been developed on Broadway, not on the film set, Lillie thinks.

"Good morning." She tries to sound like an actress she heard once at the Imperial.

"Miss Dempster, I think?"

"Yes."

"I'm David Hartford."

"Yes. I mean, I know."

"May I come in?"

"Oh, yes, sorry, of course. Come in." Lillie takes a panicked look around the apartment. Newspapers, books and empty bottles cover nearly every surface. At least there are no dirty clothes lying around; she has always drawn the line at that. It is the one visible impact her four years of living with Frank has had. "Please, sit down," she says, gesturing generally and hoping that he can discover for himself the least-covered surface.

Just as he goes to sit on a Morris chair, she notices the nail scissors and snatches them away. "Sorry."

"Not at all. I've come without warning. I'm sorry."

Lillie sits opposite him, remembering only as she crosses her legs that she has no underpants on. What a disaster.

"I have a proposal for you, Miss Dempster."

For a split second, Lillie pictures him on his knees before her, hat in hand. "Yes," she says decisively, and then realizes it should be a question. "Yes?"

"You won't have missed the ... resemblance that exists between you and Miss Shearer."

"Resemblance?"

"Several people have commented on it. Your friends at least must have remarked."

"I guess it has come up, yes." In fact, Lillie has grown sick of hearing about it.

"We think that resemblance might be useful to us. That it might be ... exploited to our mutual advantage, is what I'm trying to say."

"I don't understand."

"We'd like to hire you to stand-in for Miss Shearer, from time to time."

"Stand-in?"

"Sorry. That is probably not a familiar term. We would like you to stand in front of the camera at times when Miss Shearer isn't there."

"What times?" Lillie is not about to act like Nell Shipman had in that hidden pool, if that is what Hartford is getting at. Her narrow escape at Evandale has taught her something. Percy has been trying for months to persuade her to model for him, but without success; and he is a friend, familiar. There is no way she is taking off her clothes in front of a camera. She wishes she'd taken the time to put on her knickers.

"Oh, times when she's too tired, or when it doesn't make sense to keep her waiting around to shoot some tiny bit. Mr. Shipman is very anxious that she not get worn out. Apparently I've been working her harder than she expected when she signed on."

Or the producer has devised other calls on her time, Lillie thinks, remembering the gossip she heard only the day before from Nathan, who seems to know everything about everybody else's relationships.

"We hoped that as a stockholder in the company — that is right, isn't it, you hold ten common shares with a man by the name of Frank Rhodes? — that you might have an added interest in helping us out. We would pay you the going hourly rate of course."

"And I'm supposed to pretend to be her, to be Miss Shearer, that's all?"

"You don't even have to pretend to be her. Just look like yourself. We'll do the rest. It's a magical world, Miss Dempster, the movies."

"But what will I tell people I'm doing there? Who am I playing? What's my part?"

"Well, Norma is playing Lillian Denton, you know, the heroine, if that's what you mean. She gets rescued off a wreck and
falls in love with Shorty Westhaver. So I guess, in a way, that you
are playing her too. Kind of a funny coincidence, the name."

"When do I start?"

"That's terrific! I can't tell you what a relief this is. You may just
have saved this picture, Lillie. We could use you this morning,
in fact, if you're free. We can draw up a little contract later on
today, if that's all right with you; but if we could get started this
morning, that would be wonderful."

"Can I have five minutes?"

"I'll be downstairs in the car."

The car, Lillie thinks as she pads to the bedroom; imagine
being driven in an automobile! She chooses a fresh pair of underpants, changes her slip, finds her best stockings and her only pair
of shoes, and heads for the door. She stops for an instant. Should
I leave a note for Frank, she wonders. Why? Then she stops again,
just before going out into the hall. There is a mirror on the wall
right beside the door. She looks hard into it. Norma Shearer stares
back.

THEY ARE SHOOTING in the Victoria Rink. Shipman's slogan is
"Telling the Truth in Motion Pictures." It had a wonderful ring
to it, Lillie thought the first time she read it, but she quickly
learns the difference between the Truth and telling the truth.

There is a large tank of water set up in the middle of what,
in winter, would be the skating surface. On a tripod about five
feet from the tank is a camera, its lens trained on a small model
schooner bobbing in the water. All around the outside of the
tank, out of the camera's field of view, stand men with paddles.
It is an absurd sight, as though the men have been cast off a
shrinking ship and left there, paddles in hand, not knowing what
to do next. Then she hears Hartford's voice, tinny, through a

megaphone, not sweet and seductive as it was in the apartment. "Action!" And all the men with paddles begin to agitate the water, gently at first to build the swells, and then more and more furiously. There is a roar as a huge fan run by a gasoline engine springs into life at one end of the tank. Two men with flour scoops toss water in front of the fan blades and send it shooting in sheets at the tiny schooner. The noise of the artificial storm is deafening, far louder than the real thing, Lillie thinks, but above it all she hears Hartford's voice: "Cut! Cut!" The men stop paddling, the fan engine coughs and shudders into silence. For an instant there is nothing but the *lap-lap-lap* of the water against the sides of the tank. "Can't we get some motion into that boat? It looks like a toy that some kid has forgotten, just bobbing up and down there. It has got to look like it's actually sailing, not like some ghost ship that's already been abandoned."

A man named Monte, whom Lillie knows from the Imperial, comes forward with a length of string and an eye screw. "What if we pull it across the tank?"

"How am I supposed to not shoot the string?" This is the cameraman, though his gestures seem to Lillie every bit as theatrical as any she has seen up on the screen.

"That is why you're a genius, Walter, because you will make us believe there is no string."

They try it once without rolling the camera. Lillie can see that Hartford is disappointed. "The wind in the sails is all wrong. They're flapping every which way and the boat is somehow still moving forward in a straight line. It doesn't make sense."

"We haven't got all morning for this, have we David?" It is Shipman. He has appeared without any warning behind Lillie.

"I'd like to get it right, Ernie."

"Get as close as you can. They'll meet you part way. You've got a ship tossing around there with wind and waves, that's all you need to make them believe."

"Twenty more minutes."

"Ten." And Shipman puts his hand on Lillie's shoulder. "And how are we this morning, my little ..."

"Mr. Shipman, I'm Lillie Dempster. I think we met at the Dufferin."

"Jesus," is all Shipman says, and he walks quickly away.

They paint some shellac on the sails to enhance the illusion of purposeful forward motion, and they shoot the little schooner's progress across the tank twice. The men with the paddles and the man operating the fan break into spontaneous applause after the second take.

"That's a keeper," yells Hartford. "Now what? What happens when the storm gets the better of them?"

"They let go of the wheel."

"The sails start to flap like crazy."

"The what?"

"Well, when they let go the wheel and slack off on the lines, everything just kind of goes nuts."

"Why the fuck didn't somebody tell me this before we shellacked those goddamned sails? We could have shot that first."

"What about the take you didn't like before? The one you said looked like a ghost ship? Could we use that?"

"Perfect! Faith, are you getting this?" Hartford turns to a thin woman with a fat notebook. She nods and scribbles. Lillie nods too. How easily one moment of time can be switched with another.

Somebody touches her elbow. "In New York, I worked on a picture once where they started by filming a dummy being thrown off a cliff. Then they sat down to figure out why, and that was the picture. That's the amazing thing of course, isn't it? Nothing has to be shot in order. You're Lillie, right?" Lillie nods. "C'mon and get dressed. I'm Sue."

Lillie follows Sue to the ladies' dressing room, an ornately decorated salon at the front of the building, originally designed so ladies could put on and remove their skates without revealing their ankles to prying eyes. Three or four large wicker hampers stand around, and there are two free-standing coat racks that have been made out of lead pipes.

"The Lillian stuff is over here," says Sue, catching Lillie's gaze in the direction of a line of slickers on one of the racks. Behind a curtain that has been pinned up in a corner is a low wooden vanity with a large oval mirror and another coat rack, laden with half a dozen outfits. "This is the one for the rescue," announces Sue, pushing a lightweight skirt and middy blouse at Lillie. "It fits Norma, so it should be good for you too. You did have a bath this morning, didn't you? Norma's nose is very sensitive. She hates the idea of people wearing her things."

Lillie waits for Sue to retreat to the other side of the curtain. There is a moment of silence.

"Oh. Little Miss Modesty, are we? Sorry." Sue flicks the curtain and disappears. Lillie can hear her muttering, "We'll see how long that lasts around here."

The costume fits very well, although Lillie thinks it is tighter around the breasts than seems quite right. When she has checked the effect in the mirror, she pushes the curtain aside.

"Not yet," says Sue, pushing Lillie into a chair. "Makeup now. It's the eyes, see, they disappear if we're not careful. You'd think somebody would come up with a better kind of film. All this crap can't be good for a person," she chatters, daubing at Lillie's eyes until she feels she must resemble a raccoon. "We'll do the drops just before the take. No need to be walking around half blind before you have to. C'mon, let's see how close they are to being ready for you."

Lillie has to sit for a further ten minutes while the men paddle up waves and blow water at what is left of the schooner. They have torn the sails, which, because they have been shellacked, stick out oddly at all angles; and one of the masts has been snapped clean off. A second schooner, fresh and looking like new, has been added to the tank and is being drawn closer and closer to the first.

"That's your knight in shining armour, on his way to the rescue," breathes Sue. "Funny it don't get rusty with all that salt, isn't it?"

"So I'm supposed to be on the schooner that's getting wrecked?" Lillie asks.

"They'll tell you everything you need to know when it's time."

Hartford sends the woman called Faith to fetch Lillie shortly after.

"Ready?" is all Faith says.

"I guess so," says Lillie, not knowing for what.

The water tank has been rolled off to the side, and in its place is a full-scale replica of a section of schooner deck. Hartford was right. It is a magic world. She is about to ask Faith how they were able to make the changeover so quickly, but when she turns around, it is no longer Faith at her elbow, but Hartford.

"See this X on the floor, Lillie?"

She does.

"And then this other one, over here?"

Yes.

"What I want you to do when I call for action is to walk from this one to that one. Can you do that?"

Of course she can.

"And I want you to hold your head right up, okay, shoulders back. Try it for me."

She tries it, embarrassed at how her breasts push at the front of the middy.

"Just like that, yes. The wind machine will be on. Let it blow your hair, all right?"

"All right," she laughs, as if she'd be able to stop it from blowing her hair.

"Just be yourself."

"I'm about to be shipwrecked?"

"Don't worry about that. Just be yourself. We look after all the rest."

So she stands at the first X, being herself and waiting for the call to action. The lights are hot. She studies them, curious to see the name Ottawa Films Ltd. stenciled boldly on their hoods. Shipman's last project, she guesses. Sue runs up with a bottle of something.

"Lean your head back. There. Perfect." The drops sting, and everything goes blurry.

The fan roars into motion, and Lillie feels her hair fly about her face. "Action," shouts Hartford's voice from far away. She heads for where she remembers the second X to be, holding her head up, her shoulders back. "Great, Lillie, great," she hears Hartford call. Then, "Now, boys. Go ahead."

It is not that the water is particularly cold, or even that it is entirely unwelcome under the hot lights. It is the surprise of it that is so unfair. Being hit in the face with two buckets of water while trying to hold her head up, her shoulders back, and see an X on the floor, all with some kind of drops in her eyes, is a little much to ask of a first-time actress, thinks Lillie.

"I'm sorry," she wails once Hartford has yelled cut and the machinery has been turned off. "I'm sorry, I just wasn't expecting ... I didn't know you were going to ..."

"Don't apologize, my dear. It was excellent. Just what we wanted. A totally natural reaction. Audiences will believe in that look."

Lillie is horrified to think that her grimace of astonishment will be flickering on the screen in movie houses all over the country. Horrified, and a tiny bit excited.

"Sue, clean her up. You'll have to reapply. When you're ready, we'll shoot the next bit."

More goo is dabbed around Lillie's eyes, but new drops aren't necessary. Everything is still blurry, including Pierre Gendron when he appears beside her. Sue does the honours.

"Pierre, this is Lillie. Lillie, Pierre. Pierre plays Jimmy Westhaver. That's your character's beau. He doesn't speak much English, but who cares when he looks this great?"

"'Allô Lillie," croons Pierre, and he offers a large tanned hand. Lillie takes it, embarrassed that her own is so wet, but hoping that he will put it down to the drenching she has just received.

"Pleased to meet you," she says, slowly and deliberately, as if speaking to an idiot. He smiles back, confirming her assessment. As soon as Sue leaves the two of them alone, he immediately begins speaking to her in English so clear that it sounds as though it has been coming from his mouth since he was a baby.

When she asks him about this, he explains: "I just let them go on thinking I don't speak the language. It has no effect on my getting roles, of course, not unless they ever come up with a talking picture. And it saves me from a lot of conversations I don't want to have. It also encourages them to speak a whole lot more freely in front of me. You'd be amazed. I get to hear all kinds of things they would never say so openly if they thought I actually understood them."

Lillie is instantly intrigued. "Like what?"

"Like I knew you would turn up here today."

"That's more than I knew when I woke up."

"Norma made a fuss yesterday when Faith told her what they were going to shoot today. Said she was damned if she was going through all that. She said she'd been hired to play in a sailor romance. She took that to mean that she'd be romancing the sailor, not playing one herself. She hates water. Scared to death of it, apparently."

"But you're shooting out on the bay."

"Doesn't matter. She's afraid of all water, any water. Says a gypsy told her she'd die by drowning."

"A gypsy?"

"That's what she says. Though God knows how a little Presbyterian from Montreal meets them."

"How does she take a bath, then? If she can't stand water?"

"That's what Hartford asked her. She slapped him. Ernie had to spend an hour running back and forth between them trying to patch it up. In the end, Norma offered you as the solution, and here you are."

"Norma offered me?"

"More demanded, I guess. She said that they would have to get you or she'd walk off altogether. At first, the men said no. They said she had a contract and she was damned well going to fulfill it. She told them she didn't give a rat's ass about any contract — I'm sorry to offend your ears, but it is what she said; she is very colourful, our Norma, when she wants to be. So Hartford agreed to go and ask you. And, voila, here you are."

"Here I am."

"Lillie? Pierre? Over here, please," Hartford calls. "Lillie, see this X?" She barely can, but she nods. "You're going to kneel down there, like you've just had your feet knocked out from under you by a wave. Pierre is going to go down on one knee beside you there, like this. You'll look up at him, smile, and go all limp. He's going to scoop you up and carry you across to this railing here; see the X? That's the bit."

They practise it once. Lillie is shy about Pierre's hand slipping in under her armpit and his other arm cradling her thighs, and she jumps like she's been stung.

"Again, please. Just go limp, Lillie, like you're not even in your body. Limp."

She remembers Bea, and it works perfectly.

"Now, let's wet them down."

Two men with hoses pump water from a large barrel until Lillie and Pierre are drenched. She feels her nipples stiffen with the cold, but she doesn't dare cross her arms over her chest. That is not how they have rehearsed it.

"And action."

Lillie kneels on the deck as more buckets of water are sloshed around her knees from off-camera. She hears Pierre clumping across the deck. She looks up, smiles, goes limp. His hands slide to their appointed places, and she feels herself leaving the ground. She is dying to open her eyes to see just how badly all of this is affecting her tight middy blouse, but she is sure Hartford would notice, and then they would just have to do it all over again anyway. Her bent knee smashes against the railing.

"Merde. Sorry," breathes Pierre, as Lillie winces and Hartford yells cut.

"Right, let's move on."

"I eet Lillie's genou against ze railing. We shoot again?"

"Your body was covering it. Couldn't see a thing. Didn't happen. We'll move on."

Lillie isn't as easily persuaded that nothing has happened, and she begins rubbing vigorously at her knee the moment Pierre puts her down.

"Je m'excuse, je m'excuse," Pierre intones, lapsing back into French for the benefit of Sue, who has run over to see what the matter is.

"It's all right. Nothing to worry about," says Lillie, not believing herself.

"Let's have a look." Sue is pulling at the hem of Lillie's skirt.

"I'm fine. Leave it."

"Let's set up for the next shot, people." Hartford is clapping his hands impatiently.

Lillie limps, leaning on Pierre's arm, towards half of a wooden dory set up on sled runners.

"They make it so the boat can rock," says Pierre under his breath, as he catches Lillie looking at the contraption. He helps Lillie onto a thwart and takes his place beside her, waiting for further instructions.

"Lillie, can we have you sitting on the bottom of the boat, leaning up against that seat there?"

"Excuse me, Mr. Hartford."

"What is it, Monte?"

"No gentleman would ever put a lady in the bottom of a dory. It's not a nice place."

"There's a gale on, Monte, he has just rescued her from a near wreck."

"He would find a way to balance her on the thwart."

"Thank you, Monte. It looks better my way, though. Lillie?"

With difficulty, Lillie sits in the bottom of the half-dory. It is tilted at a twenty-degree angle, making for a small battle with gravity. She bends her sore knee to gain purchase with her foot.

"That's perfect, Lillie. Very good."

"But if she's unconscious, would her knee be up like that?"

"Monte, can you just get the fans over here please? Now, Pierre. An arm around her shoulders. Yes, just like that. Lillie, lean in a little more against his thigh, can you? Yes. Now, the idea here is for Lillie to open her eyes after I've counted to five, and look at Pierre. You'll have to arch your back a little and turn your head. Try it."

Lillie tries it. It hurts, feels completely unnatural, but Hartford likes it. Sue leans into the boat to work on Lillie's eyes, painting the lashes so heavily that Lillie doubts whether she'll be able to open her lids on Hartford's cue.

"The top of the blouse, can we loosen that, Sue?"

Lillie goes rigid.

"It's okay, honey, just a little. Nothing too racy," Sue coos as she works around Lillie's shoulders. "Pierre won't look too close, will you, Pierre? The camera's way over there, and the audience doesn't even exist yet."

"Fans please, Monte." The engine starts up. There is a fine spray of water. "And ... action. One-Mississippi, two-Mississippi, three-Mississippi ..."

When he gets to five, Lillie struggles to open her eyes. She blinks twice, terrified that they will glue shut, then turns to look at Pierre.

"And let your lips come apart just a little. Brilliant. And cut."

IT IS ONE of the longest days in Lillie's life. They break for lunch, tea and supper, but this almost makes it worse. The day itself becomes nearly as chopped up as the action they are filming. Shipman appears at regular intervals to see how things are progressing, but Hartford seems to have a very free hand.

"He's a genius," Sue hisses at Lillie during one of the breaks for food. "A genius. Makes Griffith look like an amateur. You'd never know he started out as a stage man. Stage people like long takes. Not David; he goes for the short thrusts. Way more satisfying." Lillie thinks she makes it sound sexual, which, after today, doesn't surprise her at all.

Pierre is far more critical of Hartford's style. "It's like working for a portrait photographer. All the little X's. Move here, count to three, twist this way. It's not acting. It's just modelling."

WHEN LILLIE RETURNS to the apartment that night, Frank is already slumped over the table. The bottle beside him is not quite empty. Lillie picks it up silently, drains the remaining inch. It burns all the way down, which is what she had hoped for. Having spent the whole day dripping wet, she is afraid she will never be warm again. Even her own clothes, when she was finally allowed to put them on again, felt cold and damp. And there was a light mist, fog really, for her walk home. She had waited around for Hartford to offer to drive her, just as he had picked her up that morning, but he managed to disappear out a side door. She would run a warm tub, but the thought of more water, whatever its temperature, makes her shiver. The kitchen is a mess; she was going to clean it up this morning but Hartford showed up. To do it now would also involve water. In the end, she rubs a little dry tooth powder on her front teeth, sheds her clothes in favour of a flannel nightgown and crawls into bed.

The moment her eyes are shut, the events of the day begin replaying themselves in her head. That is, she knows them to be the events of her day, recognizes them as such, but the overall sequence is not so familiar to her. Some incidents are missing altogether, and some she sees from an angle that is not her own. All have been cut to continuity — she thinks that is what the movie people call it when only the salient points of an action are sketched in. The result, though, is still teeming with detail. She should be overwhelmed by the recall of all that has happened to her, but it is somehow more controlled now, more restrained, more focused than when it was actually happening. And it almost makes sense, which it most certainly didn't all day.

4

Dogs
and
Cats

Fade in immediately over the city: dawn.

LILLIE'S SECOND DAY on the picture begins badly.

She is at the rink before seven as she has been told. Monte
nods at her as she arrives. He is trying to keep a pair of dogs
from snapping their leashes and devouring the breakfast buffet
that is set up in one corner. The dogs are Shipman's addition, he
tells her in a growl that nearly matches theirs. "One for the good
guy and one for the bad. Mr. Wallace agreed to it. But why
should they go changing the book? I wouldn't have let them."
She smiles at the thought of Monte ever getting the chance to
make such an important decision. "Here, hold one of these,
would you?" he snaps, and hands Lillie one of the leashes.

It is a white dog, not quite a poodle, but like a poodle. His
coat has been left shaggy, not fussily cut like a poodle. She thinks

it is cute, as far as dogs go, and kneels down to pat it. Sensing its opportunity, the dog suddenly bounds forward. The leash is jerked out of Lillie's hand as the animal tears off straight for the door to the street. She shoots off after it, narrowly missing Pierre, who has just come in.

The dog only beats Lillie through the door by a second or two, but it's enough. Hartford's car pulls up just at that moment, and the dog goes directly under its wheels.

By the time Hartford has climbed out of his car, every member of the cast and crew is on the street. Monte is screaming at Lillie, "Jesus Christ, I told you to hold the dog. What are you, stupid? Look what you did. Where am I going to get another white dog for crying out loud?"

Crying out loud is exactly what Lillie is doing. She has scooped the bundle of white fur up off the road and is hugging it to her chest, rocking back and forth and jostling it gently up and down. She has seen women do this with babies. The other dog, which is every bit as black and sleek as the other is white and fluffy, begins nuzzling around at her crotch the way dogs do when people are watching. She tries to knee it away, but it begins jumping, trying to get at the bundle Lillie is cradling.

"Jet! Down, bad dog!" The voice belongs to a man Lillie had seen yesterday. His whole job seems to be to pick up the film magazines when they are taken off the camera. "Jesus, Monte, can't you control him? What d'you think a leash is for?"

Lillie thinks that the last question might be directed at her. She is about to answer when Monte retorts. "I don't want to choke him. She let Chiu off her leash. And look what happened. Where am I going to find another dog?"

"This is Chiu?" Hartford has joined them now. "This is supposed to be Shorty's dog?"

"Not anymore," says Monte bitterly.

"My God, that's a woman's dog. No hero in one of my pictures is going to have a pussy dog like that. Did you show Pierre that dog?"

"You wanted a white dog. You wanted the exact opposite of Jet. You said —"

"I didn't want some girly lapdog. Get me a terrier. Something with balls, for God's sake." As he sweeps by Lillie, Hartford mutters to her, "Don't worry about it, my dear, you did us all a favour."

The company follows their director into the rink, leaving Lillie alone on the sidewalk with the man who takes the magazines off the camera.

"C'mon, kid, let's bring him inside. He doesn't have to die on the street here."

Lillie follows the man through the door and sharply to the right, into a room that would normally serve as general storage for the rink. For the time being, though, it has, like everything else, been taken over by the movie people. Rows of metal vats and wooden racks remind Lillie of some kind of bizarre laundry.

"It's the lab," says the man, answering Lillie's unasked question. "We brought this all down with us from Ottawa. No more use for it there. The company folded. It's so they can look at the dailies, you know. That's yesterday's takes all over there. All that. Here, put the little fella down here." He swipes a bunch of bottles and jars to one side of a long table. Lillie's mental image of the place changes instantly from laundry to embalming parlour.

She gently lies the dog down on the cleared surface. The blood that has soaked into her blouse feels cold as soon as the air hits it.

"He was a dandy little dog, Chiu. A great little companion."

"He was ... he is your dog? Oh my God, I'm so sorry."

"It wasn't your fault."

"I let go of the leash. I didn't mean to, but I let go of the leash."

"But he ran. You didn't make him run. And you didn't make Hartford's car drive up just at that moment."

"Yes, but ..."

"He chose to run, and Hartford chose to arrive just then. What did you have to do with any of it?"

"I'm just so sorry."

"I know you are. Thanks, kid." The man takes off his jacket. For a moment, Lillie thinks he is going to drape it around her heaving shoulders, but instead, he lays it like a blanket over the panting dog, leaving the little white head bare, and whispers into one cocked ear.

Lillie doesn't want to intrude on his last moments with his pet, but she is by no means ready to go back out into the makeshift studio and face the others either, so she crosses to the far end of the room and turns her back on the man and his dog.

A few inches in front of her face hang yesterday's dailies. There isn't enough light to make out any level of detail, but two things strike her immediately. The first is that far from being the expected range of greys, the strips of film are of several tints. There are blues and greens and even reds there in separate sections. The second is less of a surprise and more of a reinforcement of something she already knows, though, like most people, she has forgotten it with her eyes — the strips are divided into little boxes. Nathan explained it all to her one day long ago — how moving pictures were really just a trick, they were really just a bunch of still pictures that fooled your eye into thinking they were contin-uous. Different still poses that overcame their difference to give the illusion of motion. She has had conversations with Isaac Erb about it too, of course. But actually seeing it here, now, makes much more of an impression. Yesterday the camera stopped what she and Pierre were doing in front of it, stopped it as often as sixteen or eighteen times a second. There was something impos-sible about that. They would never have been able to stop that often; but the camera froze them. Froze them over and over, all for the final purpose of making them appear to move. Which they were doing anyway in the first place.

In that small space, she is aware of the precise moment when the little dog stops breathing. She does not have to turn around and look. The man lets out a short whimper. It might have been the dog, but she knows he is too weak. She hears the buttons of his jacket scrape across the table as he wraps up the dog. Footsteps. The door. She counts to ten and turns around. It is as though neither dog nor man was ever there. There is no trace except the clear spot on the table where the bottles of chemicals have been pushed out of the way.

There is a new dog within an hour. A terrier this time, light in coat, but hardly white. He and the black dog hate one another on sight, as dogs on leashes will do. Hartford is beside himself with glee, yelling to the cameraman to start rolling. Pierre is given the terrier's leash, and then Monte hands the black dog over to Bill Colvin who is playing Morrissey, the archrival of Shorty Westhaver.

"Where is this supposed to fit in?" Lillie hears Faith asking Hartford.

"It'll fit in wherever. All over the place. We'll cut it in all over the place. It'll be great."

Faith closes her large book with a decided snap.

"Now let them off the leads, and let's see what happens."

"Shut those doors," yells Monte.

Off their leashes, the dogs run around the entire rink.

"God, what I wouldn't give for a camera that could actually move around," Lillie hears Hartford say, and then, "All right, cut. There's no point. We'll try it out in the street another day." By then the dogs have become friends anyway. They are rolling over and licking one another in places that enemies would never be allowed to get near.

NORMA SHEARER APPEARS on the set, full of energy, laughing and flirting when she's off camera, and acting with elaborate pantomime when she's on. Lillie, left with nothing to do, begins to wonder why they have called her in. There is no water anywhere in evidence, so it can't be for that.

At the lunch break she asks Sue if she knows what's going on.

"Am I going to be used today?"

"I don't know, honey."

"Then what am I doing here?"

"Insurance, I guess."

"Insurance?"

"Keeping Norma keen."

"I don't understand."

"As long as Norma sees you hanging around waiting, Hartford figures she'll perform better. It's not like they would actually replace her with you. But they could. That's what they'd like her to think anyway. Looks like it's working, I'd say. Wouldn't you?"

Lillie glances over to where Norma is popping grapes into Pierre's mouth, her head tossed back in exaggerated laughter after each one leaves her fingers. Lillie continues to watch as Shipman strides up and begins talking to Norma. Pierre moves off. Norma looks anxious, then annoyed. Shipman starts to walk away, obviously angry, but Norma calls him back, smiles and lowers her head, brushing a hand on his sleeve. This appears to placate him, and he begins gesturing grandly to underline whatever it is he is saying. Lillie reads all of this the way she would the pantomime of any moving picture. She can tell that promises are being made, but she cannot hear any of the actual words. If only there was a title card. Then Hartford calls for the afternoon's work to begin, and Shipman disappears from the scene as magically as he appeared.

For four hours that afternoon, Lillie sits on a folding chair watching the shooting. With nothing else to occupy her, she begins,

without really meaning to, to memorize Norma's rhythms, her
gestures, the way she holds her head, how she stands with one
knee slightly bent and ahead of the other. She begins to realize
that every set-up is carefully contrived to show Norma in right
profile, or, at most, one-quarter on. Not once is the camera placed
to take the left side of her face, and never is she caught straight
on. Sometimes this involves considerable improvisation in the
action as they struggle to stay on Norma's good side. Once, it is
necessary to do several retakes when Faith points out that these
contortions have resulted in a total reversal of screen direction,
so that a door that begins a sequence on Norma's right, ends on
her left.

"You are learning her, aren't you?" Pierre asks Lillie quietly,
late in the afternoon, as they both sit watching Norma play a
series of shots that will be edited together to become a scene
with her father.

"I'm watching how she does what she does, if that's what you
mean. I want to learn this business."

"You could do better than copying her."

"You don't think she's beautiful?"

"You're beautiful. You're both beautiful. You're dead ringers.
That's not the point. There's more to it than —"

"You said yesterday it was a lot like modelling."

"The way that Hartford does it, not the way everyone does."

"You don't think Norma is going to go far?"

"I didn't say that. But she's not an actress, is she? Look at her.
I'll bet you've learned her already in a few hours, haven't you?
She has a handful of gestures, four or five expressions, and that's
it."

"Everyone says she looks great on camera."

"Oh, it's true. The camera loves her. From certain angles. But
that's because she loves herself. And that is why you shouldn't be
trying to learn from her."

"Because she's selfish?"

"Oh God no. Selfish is a basic requirement. You have to be selfish, narcissistic, I would say, just to make it to the starting gate in this business."

"Then why —?"

"Because, if you study Norma for too long, all you're going to end up doing is loving Norma. But loving Norma will only work for Norma. You have got to learn to love Lillie."

"And how do I —?" But just then the bell rings for tea break and Pierre hurries off without elaborating. He likes to be the first at the cake wagon.

That evening, even without further guidance from Pierre, Lillie purposefully embarks on her own idea of a program of learning to love Lillie.

She drops by Percy's studio, as if by pure accident. She knows he will be there. He works most evenings by electric light, while Nathan is busy playing at the Imperial. If it is a day when the movies change over, he might go to the early showing, but he can be relied upon to be back in the studio by nine-thirty at the latest.

She doesn't knock. There would be no point. People always just walk right in. The amazing thing is that Percy never flinches when someone suddenly appears at his side. It is as though some other sense must tell him when somebody is coming. His models, who can easily hear the warning footsteps on the stairs outside, are much more likely to jump when the studio door bursts open. They blush and lower their heads, reaching for the tattered robe they wear during breaks. This always used to make Frank laugh. He would say it was like catching them having sex, which, he never failed to add, was an absurd notion given Percy's obvious leanings in a whole other direction. Lillie has never tried to explain to him the way she sees it. He wouldn't understand.

The model this evening is one of the few unselfconscious ones, and Lillie takes that as an omen. The woman sits on, defiantly and gloriously nude, and Percy motions to Lillie to have a seat while he continues to work. After a quick, despairing survey of possible sitting surfaces, Lillie settles on the floor, a little to Percy's left. This gives her the same view of the model as Percy himself has, though at a lower angle. The slight distortion is fascinating. When she came in, she was struck by the magnificence of the woman's breasts. They appeared full and pendulous, tipped with brown nipples that measure a full two inches across. Her shoulders looked broad and square, easily able to carry her huge breasts. The hips, by contrast, seemed narrow, and her legs faded into obscurity. From this new angle, though, everything is different. Now it is the knees, which Lillie did not even notice before, that have prominence. The light gleams from their chiselled surfaces. Her thighs, as they recede along the throne, are fuller now, their slopes hiding from view all but the top inch of pubic hair. The woman's hips gain definition, and her bottom pools out in a liquid ring around her. Now the once-glorious breasts seem plastered flat to the model's chest, gazing down at Lillie with their wide brown-eyed stare.

After Percy finishes painting, the model dashes behind the screen to get dressed, returning fully clothed and eager to take the money that Percy presses into her hand. After she has left the studio and her footsteps have faded down the stairs to end with a click of the street door, Lillie would like nothing better than to talk to Percy about the new insights she has gained simply by sitting at his feet to observe his model. She knows that it has something to do with perspective, but she is not sure how to express it; and she is afraid that the ideas are too subtle for the broad pantomime communication that is the only language she shares with her deaf friend.

Instead, she puts her hand on his forearm as he is beginning to clean up his brushes and scrape his palette. When he looks up into her eyes, she nods simply and goes behind the screen. As she pulls her jumper off over her head, she can hear Percy walk across the room to lock the door. She is glad she has taken the first step.

NORMA IS ILL the next day. That is the official version when Lillie arrives at the rink. It was to have been a day for shooting out in the open air, but the fog is too thick. Hartford is muttering under his breath about the lucky stiffs in California who can shoot practically any day of the year.

"But fog is a fact of life. It's part of the sea," Lillie says to Sue. "I thought they were all for telling the truth."

"It's the stock, sweetie. The film can't register anything in low light. You need sunlight. Or these things." She gestures at the huge arc lamps that have been brought all the way from Ottawa for the indoor work.

"So what happens today?"

"Probably a lot of sitting around and hoping the fog will lift. They might try to get the tavern setting together for this afternoon and shoot those bits. They'd have to call all the extras for that, though, and Shipman won't be happy about that. He likes to cram all the extra work into a day or two, not an hour here and an hour there. Listen, while we're waiting, can I get you to try on a dress for me?"

They go behind the curtain where Lillie changed on her first day. There is a long white dress draped over the chair in front of the vanity.

"It's Lillian's bridal dress for the end of the picture," Sue announces. "I wanted Norma for a fitting today, but you'll do. C'mon honey, put it on."

Lillie hesitates only for an instant before taking off her own clothes. Sue doesn't look as though she is planning to leave, and it isn't as though she'll be completely naked, after all. The wedding dress is cool and slippery as she pulls it over her head. Sue's hands tremble as she fumbles with the buttons that stud the back of the dress from waist to nape. Her breath is hot and smells bitter.

"Turn around and let's have a look."

Lillie spins around so the hem of the dress makes a graceful swish before hitting the leg of the chair.

"There's not enough room in here. C'mon out in the open." Sue holds the curtain aside for Lillie, who executes an exaggerated bride's walk into the larger space. A few people waiting around catch sight of her and applaud. Lillie curtsies low, her head bowed deeply. The clapping stops abruptly. When she straightens up, she thinks she must have been transported back into the dressing room, looking into the mirror above the low vanity. There in front of her, her face not eighteen inches away, is Norma Shearer.

"What the hell do you think you're doing, you little bitch? Take that off this minute, do you hear me?"

Lillie not only hears her but feels her. A fine spray of spit accompanies the words, a cold fog settling on Lillie's features. Norma's right hand comes up. Lillie turns, flees behind the curtain. Sue does not follow. As Lillie panics about how she is going to undo all those buttons on the back by herself, she can hear Norma sputtering.

"She's the stand-in for God's sake. The stand-in doesn't try on my dresses! Do you get it Sue? Is it clear? Nobody, but nobody, wears my things."

"I thought you were ill, Miss Shearer. I didn't think it would hurt. I needed ..."

"Never. Do you hear? She is here to do the water scenes. The godforsaken water scenes. That's all. Understood? God, I mean, who knows where she's been?"

Lillie blushes a burning crimson and thinks about tearing the wretched wedding dress off by herself. Instead, she sits down and weeps.

Norma's tirade blows itself out eventually, after several flat denials that she and Lillie really look anything at all alike, and the suggestion that Lillie is the kind who would sell her own mother to get ahead. Lillie thinks this last remark particularly unfair since her mother is dead and Norma has no way of knowing what she herself is like, never speaking to her more than a few entirely perfunctory sentences.

Sue slips behind the curtain.

"Jesus, kid, didn't you hear her? Get out of the dress already."

"I can't. The buttons."

"Oh Christ, the buttons." Sue's hands are shaking even more now as she undoes the buttons and helps Lillie pull the dress over her head.

"Norma? On m'a dit que tu étais malade," Lillie hears Pierre crooning on the other side of the curtain.

"Oh, Pierre." Lillie understands that much of the reply. The rest is a gabble of French and English, delivered so fast and urgently as to be incomprehensible to any but a native Montrealer.

Then she hears Hartford. "Ah, Norma, dear, you've recovered, have you? What was the complaint this time? Migraine again?"

"Fuck off, David. You know damn well what the problem is."

"I'm not interested in problems. Solutions, that's what I trade in. I'm trying to make a picture here."

"So tell him."

"Who?"

"Shipman. Uncle Ernie. Tell him."

"What, that every time he tries to get into your knickers we lose another day's shooting? Is that what you want me to say, darling?"

"It might be a start."

"It might also be the end. Ernie's a sensitive guy."

"Ernie's a what?"

"I mean testy, temperamental. He doesn't like to be crossed."

"I'd noticed."

"Think of it from his point of view. When I worked with him on *God's Country* he still had Nell. He got used to — how shall I say? — fucking the star."

"They were married, for Christ's sake."

"Then she divorced him."

"Right. But not till after the picture was made."

"That's what I'm saying."

"What, David, what are you saying?"

"What could be the harm?"

"The harm?"

"You sleep with the guy a little till we finish the bloody picture."

The sound of the slap is loud and sharp, even through the curtain. Lillie silently counts to thirty before pushing the fabric aside. It is a much less grand entrance in her own clothes than the one she made a few minutes earlier in the wedding dress, but the effect on Hartford is nonetheless great. It is as though she has caught him with his trousers down. Good, she thinks, he ought to be ashamed of himself, talking like that to a woman.

"Good morning, Lillie," he murmurs, and rushes away. Norma is nowhere to be seen.

"The man does have a point, though," Sue whispers to Lillie.

Lillie pretends not to hear. She envies Pierre the ruse of his incomprehension.

The fog burns off by noon. Monte, who has been checking out the door every ten minutes or so, whoops with joy as though he is announcing the Second Coming.

"But without Norma ...?" Lillie wonders aloud to Pierre as they share an apple. "That could be a problem."

"Hartford, he is a man of solutions, not of problems." Pierre shoots Lillie a look that says not only has he overheard the conversation between Hartford and Norma but he knows Lillie did too.

"C'mon, kid, time to get dressed." There is a slight hesitation in Sue's voice, which doesn't surprise Lillie at all, given how the last time turned out.

"What?"

"It's okay. Norma's not coming back today. Hartford says for you to get dressed. He's the boss, however it might look sometimes. We're going down the coast a little anyway. She wouldn't find us even if she tried."

"Qu'est-ce qu'on fait?" Pierre asks Sue.

"Faith will explain it all in the car. Hurry up, Lillie."

There is no trace of the wedding dress behind the curtain. In its place is an ordinary calico housedress uncannily like the one Lillie wears on the rare occasion she can force herself to clean the apartment.

"This is it?"

"Is there something wrong?"

"No, it's just ..."

"Not what you would expect for the leading lady?"

"Has Norma seen it?"

"'Telling the Truth in Motion Pictures.' That's Uncle Ernie's slogan, you know."

"I seem to remember something about that. It's all a bit of a swindle, isn't it?"

"It sells, that's all I know."

"How does it look?" Lillie has stepped into the dress and is buttoning it up the front. "No, don't bother. Ordinary, right? It looks ordinary."

"That's what they want."

"Shipman, Hartford, or Norma?"

"Audiences. They want to feel like they're peeping in at you through a keyhole."

"Like they're peeping in at Norma."

"Whichever."

"That's disgusting."

"Why? You're not even there. It's only your picture they're looking at."

There is a deafening klaxon blast. Hartford has driven his car right in through the rink's double doors and is idling loudly just outside the dressing room.

"Jesus."

"Your chariot arrives, Cinderella." Sue pushes her out through the curtain.

Hartford barely waits for Lillie to shut the door behind her before he bumps the car into gear and they begin lurching across the floor towards the patch of sunlight streaming in at the other end of the building. Faith, who is squeezed into the back seat between Lillie and Pierre, lets out a tiny whimper as Hartford points for the doors and guns the engine.

He could not have known that the two dogs were on the sidewalk at that moment. He would never have driven so recklessly had he known, or so Lillie tells herself. She shuts her eyes as soon as she sees them. One dead dog in a week is enough, she thinks. In a year. But then, these movie people seem to have different standards for just about everything.

They miss the dogs. Pierre tells her later about the look on Monte's face when he saw the car bearing down on him and his two charges. He says he would have given anything to have had a camera mounted on the hood — it is the kind of spontaneous reaction you can never fake. Faith says nothing about it. Lillie supposes she must have had her eyes shut too.

The air grows chilly as they approach Chance Harbour. Lillie wishes Sue had provided a sweater, or that she had thought to bring her own.

Faith has explained on the way that they will be shooting the last few moments of the picture.

"Not le bébé and les noces?" Pierre asks. "Pardonnez-moi, I mean, of course the wedding et ensuite le bébé."

Lillie begins to wish that she had read Mr. Wallace's book.

"Are you kidding?" Faith hisses back, obviously trying not to let Hartford hear from the front seat. "Did you see Norma with that goddamned wedding dress? How territorial she was? Anyway, we can shoot those scenes indoors. It's the bits where you make it back home, back to the fish plant in time to save the contract, those are what we're after today. You know, when you find those papers Morrissey hid from you and everything turns out okay."

"And I am 'ugging ma cherie, non?" Pierre laughs as Lillie leans even harder against the side window. "It is okay, Lillie. C'est la simulation seulement. Make-believe."

"The key bit, of course, is where he offers your father the job in the fish plant. That's what really seals the wedding."

"Pour l'histoire, peut être. For the story. The story, it is your business, Faith, la continuité. Mais, l'amour c'est la grande chose, n'est-ce pas, Lillie?"

There is a real fish plant. With real smells. Lillie is afraid she might throw up as soon as the car door opens. She is glad there's a cold edge to the air; it will help her fight the waves of nausea.

"Our Lillie has turned green. A horticultural inversion of some sort," roars Hartford when he sees her. "Telling the Truth in Motion Pictures, my dear."

"But the people watching the picture won't smell the fish," Lillie chokes.

"Oh, if we make the picture right, they will," Hartford shoots right back, and then bustles off to confer with the cameraman.

"It could be worse," Faith says to Lillie before scurrying off after Hartford. "We could be shooting inside the horrid place."

For nearly an hour, the cameraman, Hartford and Faith plan the set-ups and argue about how much mouthed dialogue will be necessary to tell the story, how many title cards will eventually be added to help. Pierre and Lillie are left to their own devices. They find a large rock upwind of the fish plant, from which they can see a broad sweep of the bay. There is a fog bank still sitting a few hundred yards out, a cloud of spun sugar.

"How could anyone hate the water?" Lillie begins.

"You mean Norma?"

"Norma. Anyone."

"It is not the water so much. Not really. That is an excuse. It is l'oncle Ernie she hates."

"Because she doesn't want to sleep with him, that means she hates him?"

"That is how it looks, is it not?"

"No, it is not. Maybe she just doesn't want to sleep with him because she's ..."

"Quoi? Saving herself? I do not think so."

"Just because a woman isn't a virgin doesn't mean she's a whore."

"You have not been very long in this business."

"But what about you?" Lillie takes a deep breath. The air here is tinged with dulse but not directly with fish. She plunges on. "You don't want to sleep with Faith, for example, do you? And that doesn't mean you hate her."

"Who says I don't?"

"You hate Faith?"

"Who says I don't want to sleep with her?"

"Maybe that was a bad example. Think about somebody you don't want to sleep with, okay?"

"C'est impossible."

"Oh my God. Try."

"D'accord. L'oncle Ernie. I do not want to sleep with him. And you are right. I do not hate him."

"All right." Lillie isn't entirely happy with the way this has gone, but she is keen to win the point. "So why does Norma have to hate him?"

"That is what we all want to know. Why cannot she just sleep with him and make life plus tranquille pour nous autres?"

Lillie is glad when Faith appears at this point to collect them. She finds herself watching the way Pierre looks at Faith's narrow bottom as it twitches from side to side during the descent along the stony path. Is he telling the truth? Does he really look at almost everyone as a potential bedmate? Does he look at her like that? She is tempted to skip ahead along the path to block his view of Faith, to force him to focus on her instead, but she realizes that such a move would be useless in telling her what she wants to know.

"We'll start with you, Lillie," Hartford calls out when they are still fifty yards off. "You are worried about Shorty. Will he make it back in time? Will he make it back at all? You are pacing back and forth." He falls in with Lillie's step and begins guiding her into the picture he wants. "Back and forth, here, like this, okay? Maybe you wring your handkerchief a little."

"I ... I haven't got a handkerchief."

"Then your dress, maybe you wring your dress a little. Would she do that, Faith?"

Lillie wonders why Hartford doesn't simply ask her for her opinion, but Faith answers right away. "Sure," she says, "sure she would." Lillie begins tugging at the cheap fabric of the dress.

"That's brilliant!" crows Hartford. Lillie can't tell whether the praise is for her performance or his idea. "Ready and ... action!" Lillie, who has not stopped moving, is not sure how to interpret this command until she hears the rattle of the camera starting up. She keeps pacing and wringing, and the camera keeps rolling, until she is sure it must be enough. Afraid to miss the signal to stop, she turns her eyes directly to Hartford, who is standing right next to the camera. "Magnificent, and ... cut!"

"She looked straight at the camera," Faith snorts. Lillie feels like a complete fool.

"Exactly. It'll be brilliant. Such a pathetic look. Such a look of waiting, of longing for a sign." Lillie decides to take this as a compliment. "Now, Lillie, I need you to notice Pierre, coming over the rise."

"Which rise?"

"There isn't one. Not there. We'll find one later. I need you to imagine there's a rise just behind me here."

"And Pierre — Shorty — is coming over it?"

"You're thrilled to see him. And relieved. Can you do that?"

"I'll try." She does try. Seven times she tries.

The first four, Hartford tells her, she looks like a madwoman. "Don't do that with your face!" he yells. Then they try three where Pierre actually stands behind the camera, grinning and waving. Lillie just giggles.

Finally, Pierre goes quite a way off, far enough that his features are no longer easily visible. Lillie is determined to get it right. She bites her cheeks until she can taste the blood. She imagines her face as a clay mask; only the eyes can register emotion. She tries to pretend that Pierre is someone else, someone dear, returning to her after a painful absence. But no picture comes. She feels a burning in her eye, and a tear dribbles down her right cheek. She is about to walk out of the shot, to walk all the way back to the city if necessary.

"Cut!" yells Hartford. She waits for the bawling out that should follow. He pauses. Lillie begins to sweat, cold as the air around her. He begins moving slowly towards her. Will he try to strangle her? She has heard that artists have vicious tempers. He is stretching out his hands. "That was beautiful," he is cooing, "beautiful. Perfect. A tear of joy, a tear of relief. It will move them; it can't miss." His arms are wrapped around her. Lillie decides this is not the time to tell him it was actually a tear of utter and desperate loneliness.

The next shot they make is an embrace between Pierre and Lillie. Lillie wonders aloud why they don't shoot Pierre running towards her first. "We need a hill for that," is Faith's curt answer. "Here, help me get him wet."

She and Lillie slosh buckets of water over Pierre, who howls like a dog having a bath. He is shivering when they begin to shoot, and Hartford doesn't like it on the first, second or third takes, after which Lillie is shivering too. The front of her dress has become soaked with the repeated contact. Her teeth are chattering, and her cheeks are burning with shame over what the sodden calico reveals about her body beneath it. She has not yet had enough sessions with Percy to feel comfortable with being looked at in that way. She tries to imagine herself as Nell Shipman, but it doesn't work. Finally, Hartford finds something to like in a take and they are able to move on.

The afternoon progresses as a series of emotional outbursts by Hartford. Lillie soon grows used to the fact that one minute he can be screaming like a homicidal maniac and the next he might be weeping like a baby. It takes her a little longer to accept the fact that she is completely unable to predict which reaction will follow what event. At first, she thinks if she hates what she does then he will love it, but it isn't that simple. She decides that this must be what people mean when they talk about genius.

The cold creates a bond between Lillie and Pierre. Their mutual suffering draws them together into a unit. When one begins to laugh, the other can't stop. Under their breath they banter wittily on everything from the reek of the cameraman's armpits to the utter impenetrability of several of Hartford's directions. Lillie tries to remember when she has felt this kind of closeness, and can't. She thinks she would happily sleep with Pierre if he ever asks.

Hartford drops Lillie at her apartment. Faith has pronounced it too late to return to the makeshift studio. Lillie's pleas to be allowed to change back into her own clothes, which she has left at the rink, fall on deaf ears. There is a party. They will be late for it. Her clothes will still be there tomorrow. So she is obliged to go on wearing the make-believe Lillian's wet housedress as she enters the real Lillie's flat.

Frank is home. And drunk. If that is the right term when a person is almost always in that state.

"Is it raining? You're soaked."

"It's a long story." She is touched that he has at least noticed she is wet, even if he hasn't picked up on the fact he has never seen her in that dress before.

"Does the story have a happy ending?"

"A wet one, I guess. Mainly, it's all middle. That's what makes it long."

"Are the movie people in it?"

"Some of them."

"Then I don't want to hear."

"Like I said, it's kind of a long story anyway." Lillie begins to head for the bathroom.

"Lil."

She stops.

"Are you happy?"

Jesus. It is as though he has punched her in the stomach; she can't get any air. Finally, she whispers, "I don't think about it that much, Frank," turns, and hurries into the bathroom.

She hears the hall door close before an inch of water has had time to accumulate in the tub. He is going out. She would feel a tinge of remorse if he didn't go out every night anyway. Besides, what did he expect her to say? How could he even ask?

As she begins unbuttoning the housedress, she catches a glimpse of herself in the mirror. There is a trace of steam around the edges. It softens the focus and makes it even easier to imagine it is Norma Shearer in the glass. Lillie plays along, adopting Norma's mannerisms, the little tricks she has learned from watching her on the set, as she works her way through the rest of the buttons and shrugs the dress off her shoulders. The slip, she tells herself, is not her slip but Norma's, the underwear beneath it, not hers but Norma's. And later, as she lies in the bath, her breasts are Norma's, her nipples, the slick crevice between her legs. Finally, it is Norma's voice that makes the small moaning noises that echo around the empty apartment.

She is asleep the instant she climbs between the covers, which is why she does not hear Frank and his guest come in sometime after midnight. It is also why, as she rattles around the kitchen the next morning, cleaning up week-old messes and putting some coffee on the stove, she has no idea there are two sleeping bodies behind Frank's closed bedroom door. That, and the fact he has never brought another woman home.

The biggest surprise, though, is who it is who emerges sleepy and dishevelled from the bedroom.

It is Faith.

"Oh my God," is all Faith can say, and she disappears behind the door again. Lillie can hear her hissing at Frank to wake up. Good luck, Lillie thinks, as she throws an empty whisky bottle into the bin. Her knees feel funny, so she sits down to wait for the coffee. She is still sitting when Faith reappears.

"Um. Lillie. I'm ... oh my God, I'm really sorry, I had no idea. We ... he ... we're just friends?"

"It's okay, Faith."

"It's not okay. It's horrible. I feel like ... I feel so ..."

"You like him, don't you?"

"Yeah, well of course I like him. I mean, we only just met, but yes, I like him. I don't usually ..."

Lillie can't suppress a smile as she thinks about what kind of a place the world would be if everyone who said they "didn't usually," actually didn't. Empty, she figures.

"It's all right. Relax, Faith. It's not like Frank and I —"

"But it must be so awkward for you. Awful, really. Here's some stranger coming out of his bedroom in the morning."

"Not a stranger, exactly."

"You know what I mean."

"It's not like Frank and I ..." Lillie tries again. "I just live here, he's not my ..."

Lillie says the word lover at exactly the same moment as Faith says father.

"Oh, thank God. Then it's not quite so bad, is it? Is that coffee I smell?"

And that is it. They drink their coffee. Lillie even loans Faith a pair of stockings. And without waking Frank, they set off together for the factory of dreams.

Norma is on the sidewalk outside the rink, leaning against a lamppost, looking furtively around from time to time. A haze of blue smoke hovers in the air behind her. Lillie thinks that Norma is not likely fooling anyone, but it makes her happy to catch Norma doing something she shouldn't. Maybe a shared secret could be a bond between them.

Norma's greeting, though, is so warm that Lillie is instantly on her guard. She knows right away there is more going on here than just a little conspiracy about a guilty pleasure.

"Faith! Lillie! Just the two people I wanted to see. How perfect is that?" The fact that Lillie and Faith are arriving together suddenly seems less about them and the changes that it marks in their lives and more about the leading lady's personal convenience.

Norma grinds her cigarette out vigorously with one shiny black shoe. Lillie reflexively imagines herself in the cigarette's place and takes a step back. "I need to talk to both of you." Norma now has her arms around their necks; the stink of tobacco is sickening. "I need favours." She says it as though she hasn't been treating Lillie as some lower form of life from the day she arrived on the set. "And you are the gals I need them from. It's all so exciting. I don't know where to start."

"Somewhere in the middle, sweetie, we're late," says Faith.

"Oh, don't worry about that. Nothing's going on in there. Nothing can happen till we get a few things ironed out."

"So start wherever you like," says Faith wearily.

"The telegram. That's a good place. The telegram. It's so exciting."

"Norma."

"Okay. So I got a telegram last night. From Hollywood. That's right, Hollywood. It's from Louis Mayer. You know, Louis B ...?"

"We know."

"Well, he wants me for a picture. Maybe lots of pictures. But one right now. He wants me right now."

"As in ..."

"Yes, today, tomorrow at the latest. It starts shooting next week. A real picture."

Faith winces.

"You know what I mean. A studio picture. It's called *Pleasure Mad*. Doesn't that sound wildly sophisticated?"

"So what happens here? They'll never let you go before this is finished shooting."

"That's where you gals come in." Lillie can't remember ever having been called a gal before, certainly not twice in one day. She supposes that Norma must be preparing herself already for her new role in a new country where people talk like that.

"What can we —?"

"Oh thank you, thank you! I knew you'd help out! So, Faith, I need you to give them a list of all the close shots that they absolutely need my face for. You can do that, can't you, I mean from the continuity script? You know everything you need."

"I guess. I'll have to see."

"Great. We can start taking this morning, and I'll be able to make the night train, I bet. And Lillie. I need you to agree to stand in wherever they need you to finish things up."

Lillie can hardly believe her ears. Yesterday, she wasn't allowed to try on her dress. Now, Norma is asking her to try on her whole body.

"What are Hartford and Ernie saying?"

"What can they say? It's not like they haven't been using Lillie already anyway, is it? And it's not like it's going to hurt this picture's chances if they can promote it with the name of a star who is under contract to Louis B. Mayer, is it? *Blue Water*, featuring Norma Shearer of Louis B. Mayer's *Pleasure Mad*. It's money in the bank for them."

"But if I'm the one who's actually going to be on the screen ..." Lillie begins, but she realizes that she is talking to the lamppost. Norma and Faith have already rushed inside.

Hartford is just inside the door, and he whisks Lillie immediately away into the little room where she watched the dog die.

"I know you can do this, Lillie. It is a truly wonderful chance for Norma, even if she is a bit of a bitch. It's a great chance for all of us. Louis B. Mayer. His stars have pull. I want you to stick to her like glue today. I want you to watch everything she does. Try to learn the way she moves, the way she holds herself, everything. We're all depending on you, do you see?"

Lillie supposes she is expected to say thank you. Instead, she murmurs, "I already know Norma inside out." It is the sort of boast she never makes, and she is surprised it gets past her lips. That is when she knows she really is turning into Norma.

"Just stay close, all right?"

"Thank you, Mr. Hartford." But he is gone.

She finds Norma in the alcove they have been using as a dressing room. It is the first time she has seen the other woman not fully dressed, and she is amazed by how far the resemblance extends beyond their faces. Her first minutes of posing for Percy quickly taught her how to understand the body as a constellation of planes and volumes. That is how she fought the embarrassment, controlled it. She concentrated on seeing herself as he was seeing her, memorized her own physique as a piece of art, plotting in space her shoulders, breasts, hips, thighs. The image she sees in the dressing room now is almost exactly what she has already stored in her memory — the curves of Norma's shoulders, rising ivory out of an ecru slip, are already familiar; the slight drooping of the left breast, visible even through the slip; the line of the thighs from buttocks down to knees that are closer together than the classical ideal.

"Are you okay, honey? You look like you've seen a ghost." It is the first time Lillie can remember Norma expressing concern for anyone else.

"Fine. Sorry. I wasn't meaning to stare. It's just ..."

"I know. It is a little spooky, isn't it? Never mind. My father used to say 'all cats are grey in the dark.'"

"Mine too."

"And movie theatres are some of the darkest places."

"I guess they are."

"Can you help me with this damn middy? I don't know how they expect me to breathe."

It is as simple as that, Lillie discovers. Suddenly she has become Norma's friend, because she is the instrument of her salvation.

Faith identifies twenty-three shots for Norma to play, and they take a further ten shots of her face in close-up, displaying the range of emotions from terror to rage. These, Hartford says, they can cut in for reactions as necessary when they edit the film together. Lillie sits about fifteen feet from the camera and mimes extreme concentration on the business of learning Norma whenever she catches the director looking in her direction. In fact, she is bored stiff.

"You can't wait for her to leave, can you?" Pierre whispers as they both watch Norma do "mild disappointment" for the camera.

"Everybody says what a great chance it is for her."

"Most people are just glad to see the back of her. Some people might think it's a great chance for you."

"Some people might. Nobody here."

"Don't get your hopes up too much, that's all."

"What do you mean?"

"You will still be Norma's double. What kind of future is there in that?"

"I'm going to get all kinds of experience doing this."

"You're going to get one kind of experience. They won't run your name in the credits, you know. I heard them talking."

"I don't care."

"You will."

SOME OF THE cast organize an impromptu party for Norma when the day's shooting is finished. Lillie tries not to go, but Norma insists. Now that Lillie has become her shadow, it seems she isn't willing to shed her until the minute she steps on that train for Hollywood.

"But I'm a mess."

"Everybody's a mess, Lillie. We've been working all day."

"You've been working. I've just been watching."

"You can come to my room and get cleaned up. I even have a dress you can wear, if you want to change."

"But will it fit?" They both laugh.

Norma's room does have a view of the park, just as Shipman told Lillie by accident when they first met. It also has two large beds, which strikes Lillie as useless excess, its own sink and a water closet beyond. That is about all you can tell about it since it seems that every other square inch is covered with articles of Norma's clothing. The shock that Lillie would normally suffer on seeing the clutter is easily eclipsed by the awe she feels at any one person owning so many clothes.

"I don't know how I'm ever going to be ready for that train tonight," Norma laughs, following Lillie's gaze around the room. "When I came up from New York, my mother packed my trunk. But now she's back home in Montreal and there isn't time."

"Maybe I could help. After the party. If you want."

"Oh Lillie, you're an angel. Would you really? I would have asked Sue, only I hate the way she looks at me. Like she ... well, you know. I never felt entirely safe taking my things off around her."

As if she wants to illustrate how differently she feels about Lillie, how secure from unwanted advances, Norma begins shedding her clothes, tossing her jacket onto one pile, her skirt onto another and balling up the ecru slip and flinging it across the room where it drapes itself over a table lamp, where it is joined shortly by stockings and suspenders. Reduced to bra and panties, Norma is actually somewhat smaller than Lillie would have expected, which is to say smaller than Lillie herself. Her ribs show, front and back, like a porcelain washboard.

"Come on, we'd better get cleaned up for this party."

Lillie watches Norma fill the sink and begin sloshing water around, an exuberant robin in a bird bath. The ablutions are confined to the upper half of her body, to Lillie's relief. When she is finished, she pats herself dry with a frayed towel she rescues from under a pile of jumpers, and then she begins slapping herself with a large powder puff. The clouds settle under her armpits, between her breasts, on the inner surfaces of her thighs. The whole room smells of lavender.

Not feeling the need of a real wash, and reluctant for Norma to see how much bigger she is under her slip, Lillie contents herself with splashing a little cold water on her face.

"Wear anything you like," Norma chirps, herself wriggling into a drop-waisted cocktail dress made of a silvery material Lillie has never seen before. "There's a couple of real knockouts somewhere over there, I think," she continues, gesturing vaguely in the direction of a large armchair.

Three layers down, Lillie's groping fingers locate a smooth satin dress and, after disentangling it from the clutches of several other, coarser, gowns, she is able to drag it to the surface. It is red.

"Oh," says Lillie. "Oh no, I can't ..."

"Wear red? Why not? What's wrong with red?"

"It's just so ..."

"So what? Cheap? Honey, there's nothing cheap about that dress."

"Grown-up, I was going to say."

Norma dissolves in laughter.

AFTERWARDS, LILLIE WILL wonder whether it was the sting of that laughter or the redness of the dress that made her behave so wildly at the party. It was not as if she didn't know that drinking straight shots in rapid succession on an empty stomach would have regrettable results, or that dancing close with men who have also been drinking usually leads to a single unwanted conclusion. She has been around, she knows the ropes. That may be what stung her so sharply about Norma's laugh. Norma didn't understand. Lillie knows what it is to be grown-up; she just doesn't particularly like it.

Three shots into the party, her focus goes soft. It is as though someone has put vaseline on the lens. Everything, everybody, in the tawdry hotel room looks beautiful, elegant, sophisticated. Norma is a goddess, which must make Lillie herself at least a demigoddess; Pierre, a god. The chipped paint of the windowsill becomes richly veined marble. Even Uncle Ernie Shipman is raised from goat to satyr.

"Wanna dance?" His breath reeks of something that must have died halfway down his throat, but she doesn't care. Maybe he thinks she's Norma. But she doesn't care.

"Enchawnted," she says, and means it, though it has nothing to do with him.

He is a surprisingly good dancer, given the shortness of his legs and the roundness of his belly.

"You move pretty good," he whispers, as though reading her thoughts and mirroring them back. Then he inches his knee between hers, definitely not reading her thoughts. She tries to tip her pelvis back to avoid the advance, but his right hand drops down her back to find her ass — isn't that what he would call it? — and pulls it towards him. She drops her arms to let him know that the dance is over. All that happens is that his left hand joins the right, and he keeps dancing. After a minute, Lillie senses that the people around them are stopping to look. Even people as jaded as the movie people see this kind of dancing as something worth a second glance, apparently.

And that is when Lillie feels her own hands pressed against the bulging fabric of Uncle Ernie's trousers' seat. What is she doing? Her face flushes the colour of her dress, but she keeps dancing, gyrating really, until the music, mercifully, stops. Shipman's grip reflexively loosens in response to the sudden silence. Lillie takes the opportunity to slip away and cross the room to the farthest corner, where she finds Sue beside a bottle of bath-tub gin.

"Norma know you're wearing that dress? Whaddif she sees you ..."

"Relax, Sue," Lillie snaps, sinking into a chair and reaching for the bottle. "She put it on me herself."

"You wanna go easy on that stuff, honey. It's really raw."

But Lillie just throws her head back and lets the gin burn its way down her throat.

"Lillie, are you okay?"

"Who's Lillie? Call me Theda."

"C'mon, kid, it's a dangerous dress, but not that dangerous."

"Who's a kid? I'm Theda Bara. Bad girl." And she takes another long pull on the bottle.

"Forget it. Just don't throw up all over that dress. Norma would never forgive you. Never. No matter what she says."

Lillie, who has not thought of throwing up until that moment, can suddenly think of nothing else. The gentle soft focus of the party is quickly threatening to become a dissolve. She drags herself from the chair and totters for the door, which has assumed an odd angle by the time she reaches it.

The hall smells of cigarettes and damp plaster. Lillie gags, begins to run. That is, her head tells her legs to run. She can't actually feel her legs, but the walls of the hall begin moving rapidly past her, so her legs must have heard the command. When she reaches Norma's room, she stops. Norma, she remembers gratefully, did not want to be bothered with a purse, so she had not locked the door. Lillie tries the knob, and the door seems to fall open, sucking her into the room. She feels her stomach turn over. Please not in Norma's dress, she says out loud.

She leaves the lights off. It is better that way; she does not feel so ill. And she will not have to see her sorry self in the mirror. At first, she thinks she will never be able to get the damned dress off. It clings to her curves, and her fingers slide off the smooth fabric as they try to tug at the shoulders to pull it over her head. Eventually, by bending from the waist, letting her head hang down by her knees, shrugging her shoulders and moving her hips just as she did at the end of her dance with Shipman, she is able to make some progress. It is a slow process, though, because she can only perform the manoeuvre for a few seconds at a time. Then she begins to taste stomach acid and gin, and she has to stand up straight again for several minutes. The first few times, the dress falls right back into place and she swears. Finally, she is able to get it far enough that, when she stands up, the back of the neckline catches on her forehead. On the next try, her head is somewhere halfway down the back seam. She stands for several minutes in the double dark of room and dress, bathed in the mixed scent of her boozy-sweet breath and her drenched armpits. Norma will be livid if any of that smell stays on the fabric. The thought gives her the incentive she needs on the next bend to free herself of this second red skin. The dress lies in a satiny pool at her feet, where she promptly throws up on it.

Getting rid of a vomit-laden dress poses a significant challenge even for the most resourceful person. Drunk, sick, ashamed, Lillie has never felt less resourceful. She turns on the light to help her think. That is when she becomes aware that Norma's things have all disappeared. The piles of dresses, the festooned lingerie, it has all been magically packed up and carted away. How can it be that late? Her own clothes, the ones she changed out of to put on the ill-fated red dress, are the only personal articles left in the room. How long was she at the party? Has she even said goodbye to Norma? She cannot remember. She vows that she will never drink again.

Then she pads into the bathroom, dips the red dress in the toilet and begins flushing. There is a moment when it looks as though the toilet has tried to swallow the dress instead of simply washing it. Lillie has to tug hard to free it, and she falls back on her behind when she succeeds. Soon, though, she gets the rhythm right. It is all in the wrists — pulling the chain and dipping the dress, then pulling up again as the rushing water reaches a certain pitch.

When most of the vomit is gone, she looks at the dripping mass and realizes she has no way of drying it. And Norma is long gone anyway. She carries it out of the bathroom and across the bedroom to the window. Without even checking to see whether anyone is walking below, she pushes the window up and throws the dress as hard as she can. Then she staggers to one of the beds where she falls instantly and soundly to sleep.

Two hours later, whenever that is, she wakes up needing to pee. She is about to get up when she hears someone in the bathroom. For a moment, she is paralyzed. She has not found Norma's room but somebody else's, she thinks. That would explain the swift disappearance of all Norma's things. But then there are her own clothes. They are there on the chair just as she left them in Norma's room. She thinks about creeping off the bed and across the floor, pulling them on and racing for the exit. But just then the water closet door opens and Shipman steps out. Of course.

He has removed his trousers. Lillie remembers with a shudder the feeling of her hands on the back of those trousers. His jacket, shoes and tie are gone too. His socks remain, with the suspenders that hold them up cutting into the puffy white flesh of his calves. The tails of his shirt hang down well over his thighs. Is he still wearing his shorts or not?

"I think you have the wrong room, Mr. Shipman," she tries, pulling the bedspread around her shoulders. "Yours is next door, I think."

"They're all my rooms, every last one of them, as a matter of fact. Who d'you think pays for all this?"

"Norma's gone. Her things are gone. She's caught the train."

"Fuck Norma."

Lillie is at a loss for how to take this; he delivers the words with so little inflection.

"You're a great little dancer, honey."

Lillie's last grim hope, that Shipman has mistaken her for Norma and will go away when he discovers his mistake, falls in a heap about her.

"I don't usually ..."

"Uncle Ernie doesn't care about the usual. The unusual, that's what I trade in." He has started to cross the room towards her. The shirttail flaps aside, and Lillie's earlier question is answered. He isn't.

Shipman's breath smells of licorice. The scent washes over Lillie when he is still three or four feet away. Frank used to smell like that when he was trying to cover up his drinking.

The bed sags dangerously as Ernie sits on the edge, and Lillie, who is balanced on her knees, ready to spring off, finds herself suddenly falling towards him. Her cheekbone hits hard against his shoulder. She is glad he is a fat man; the knock hurts less than it would with another. Then he is pushing her down onto the bed, his hands pinning her shoulders, his hot licorice breath on her neck. When he lets go for a minute to tug at the straps of her slip, Lillie thinks she sees an opportunity and tries to roll out from under him, but his enormous belly comes down hard, knocking the wind out of her. She bites her lip and thinks of Bea. Her body goes limp.

"Good girl. That's it. You and me, we could be good together. I could be very good for you. That Norma was so stupid. She could have had anything, anything. I'll look after you kid. With your looks and my brains ..."

Lillie wants to scream out, to tell him to shut up, to tell him to save the daddy act for someone who hasn't heard it all before. Just do it, she thinks, just do it and get it over with. She turns her head to the side, trying to bury her face in the pillow that she knows must be there somewhere. But Shipman must want to see her face. He holds her chin with one hand while the other fumbles to get his shirttail out of the way. Is he imagining, in the dim light coming from the bathroom, that she is Norma after all? His hips begin to move, like they're dancing. Lillie braces for the inevitable as the dancing keeps up for a minute or two. Then it stops. Now, Lillie thinks, now comes the part, and she bites her lip harder and tries to be even more like Bea.

But Shipman rolls off of her, to sit on the side of the bed, and then, standing unsteadily, turns back to her.

"It's no good," she hears him mutter. "Useless little whore. Pathetic little double." He spits at her. His right hand comes up as if he is going to hit her. The shirttails part and she sees his penis hanging limply between his chubby thighs. "Breathe one word of this to anyone and I'll see that you never work in the business again." He wobbles off to the bathroom to collect his pants before he leaves the room.

Lillie lies for a full minute after the hall door slams, wondering who Shipman thinks she would ever tell about any of this. She sits up and pats herself all over with her hands, trying to find the wet spot. Nothing. There is only the place where Shipman has spit on her. And then she realizes what has happened. Or, rather, what has not.

She gets up to pee, dresses in a hurry, and runs all the way home.

Faith is there, as she should have known she would be. Frank seems to have passed out at the kitchen table, and Faith is making a sandwich.

"I didn't know whether we'd see you tonight or not."

"What's that supposed to mean?"

"Your little dancing display with Shipman. It looked as though you'd made yourself quite a conquest."

"Me? A conquest?" Lillie is dying to tell her what happened less than an hour before in Norma's room. How the fat old goat had tried to rape her. Conquest might be the right word for it, but it had not been hers.

"Uncle Ernie's smitten. I mean, buying that painting off of Percy, and then the dancing ..."

"Painting? What painting?"

"Some study Percy made. Everybody was talking about it at the party. I had no idea you modelled. You are full of surprises. Frank didn't even know. Apparently." She gestures to the huddled form beside them at the table.

"Shipman bought one of the studies? Percy only made a couple."

"They're all the more valuable, then. He was showing it off at the party. It must have been before you and Norma arrived. I guess he put it away before you got there. I think he must have."

"Percy didn't tell me ... I mean, Nathan never mentioned any-thing about selling ..."

"Why should they? It's Percy's art to sell as he likes, isn't it? You were only the model."

"But I was ... it shows me ..."

"Oh, come on, you're not embarrassed, are you? You were a model. Everybody understands about art and all that. Nobody looks at it like it's you naked. It's a painting. A beautiful painting. It's not about you."

Lillie wishes she could believe Faith is right.

5

Continuity

Cut straight to dawn over the city again, then dissolve to the dressing room.

THE FIRST THING they shoot the day after Norma has left is the wedding scene. Sue is silent as she does the buttons on the back of the dress. The whole place feels like it is getting ready for a funeral rather than a wedding. Lillie feels like she should be in mourning for her head. She felt as though it would split open when she woke up. Faith mixed her a drink that she called a Prairie Oyster. It's the first time Lillie has ever met someone who travels with a bottle of Worcestershire sauce in her purse. Although she almost gagged on the raw egg — "You have to swallow it whole," Faith insisted — the remedy did the trick for the trip down to the Victoria Rink, but the headache came back as soon as she entered the dressing area.

Sue helps her with the veil. Lillie winces.

"No surprise, the way you were last night."

"I didn't see you exactly drinking lemonade," Lillie snaps.

They look at one another and laugh. She sounds just like Norma.

"Here." Sue produces a flask. "Hair of the dog."

Lillie shakes her head, remembers Chiu.

"Dutch courage then."

Lillie takes the flask. The neck tastes of Sue's lipstick. She passes it back. Sue takes a swig too. "Can't hurt," she says.

Hartford is late this morning. When he arrives, he is on foot. Lillie learns later that Uncle Ernie started returning the rentals, beginning with Norma's room in the Dufferin Hotel and David Hartford's car.

As if to counteract the obvious drop in status signalled by his pedestrian arrival, Hartford comes out of the gate yelling.

"Monte! Where's the bouquet? Where's the fucking bridal bouquet?"

"That's it, Mr. Hartford, you're looking at it."

"It's nothing but a bunch of weeds."

"Wildflowers. We checked. They all grow in that part of Nova Scotia, too. We thought they'd be realistic."

"Monte," Hartford's voice is low and dangerous. "Monte, you've been working with us now for several weeks, I believe."

"Yes sir, Mr. Hartford."

"And you still appear to have missed the point by several miles."

"The point, Mr. Hartford?"

"About telling the ... Forget it, Monte. Please get me the biggest bunch of roses this town can produce."

"But sir ..."

"Big, Monte, big. Like it's the Vanderbilts getting married. Or William-fucking-Randolph Hearst."

He sees Lillie. She begins to tremble.

"What's that veil? Sue? Lose the veil."

"You approved the veil," Faith whispers, always on guard against spontaneous decisions that could wreak havoc with continuity. "We have a close-up of Norma in the veil."

"All the better. It can be a reminder to the little quitter every time she watches the picture."

"Or we could re-shoot the close-up with Lillie without the veil."

"That's why I love you, Faith."

So that's what they do while they wait for Monte to get back from the market with the roses.

Sue's gin has put some colour back in Lillie's cheeks, not that it will matter much on the film. The eye drops, Lillie finds, sting less each time they are applied, and today they hardly bother her at all. The blurriness, she tries to imagine, is the natural result of a wedding-day weep; and with Hartford's coaching, she is able to manage what the director keeps referring to as the Chekhov Effect — laughing through her tears, tearful through her laughter. This seems to elate him.

"Brilliant work, my dear, brilliant. They will feel what you feel. I am certain of it!" Lillie tries to imagine whole audiences feeling hungover.

With the arrival of the roses, the groom enters the shooting schedule. Pierre looks a little comical in his slightly ill-fitting suit. It is certainly no match in quality for Lillie's wedding dress.

They shoot the sequence in reverse order. This means they have to start with the final kiss. Lillie is sorry for Pierre. Gin, raw egg and Worcestershire sauce can't be the most appealing combination. Hartford insists that they do it without rehearsal. Something about signalling the heroine's purity, he says. Lillie supposes he is hoping for a reaction like the one he got with the buckets of water that first day. Despite the awful consequences of her vampish performance last night, she is tired of them thinking of her as some innocent kid. So as Pierre's face approaches hers, she closes her eyes and lets her lips fall a little apart. She loses track of time. Hartford calls cut two or three times before Pierre's tongue stops exploring hers.

"We can fade that out, of course. Let's move on."

Putting the ring on Lillie's finger is a purely mechanical set-up, but following such a kiss, Lillie feels it more than she probably should. Then there are individual shots where each nods "I do." Lillie hopes that Faith will not insist on dialogue cards; she hates those unnecessary interventions. She also wishes they had tried to shoot both responses in a single take, like they were actually saying it for each other. Finally, she walks down the aisle that is suggested by six rows of pews. When she asked earlier why they were not shooting the wedding in an actual church she was told that they had been turned down flat by everyone. Even the archdeacon wasn't ready to put his piety where his money was. As she reaches the groom and the minister, she finds it hard to pretend that the kiss has not already happened, and Hartford makes her do the bit three or four times before he decides simply to shoot it from the rear and move on.

"Pierre's quite a kisser, I bet," Sue breathes as she releases Lillie's buttons.

"A lady never tells." Sue slips her hand inside the back of the dress and under Lillie's armpit. She squeals.

"I bet you can't wait to make babies with him."

Lillie feels her blood rush all over.

"That's the next bit. Here, put this on."

It is not a negligee, but a simple housedress. The actual making of the baby will be left to the audience to imagine. The last sequence of the film is to show Lillian and Shorty at home, reading by lamplight and gazing lovingly from time to time into a pine cradle where their newborn baby dreams happily, guarded by the terrier that replaced Chiu.

"Doesn't look a bit like us ... or like Norma," Pierre quips as the baby is lowered into place. Lillie keeps stealing looks at the real mother, who stands nervously just off set. The sequence takes some time to shoot — the dog behaves less well than the baby. By the end, Lillie can see small spots forming on the woman's blouse where her milk has started to run. She folds her arms over her own aching breasts.

In the days that follow, they work backwards through the story, picking up several parts they haven't covered yet, all episodes where water is involved. Norma would never have agreed to these anyway, and it was always the plan that Lillie should do them. But Hartford and Faith begin to confer increasingly between takes, and soon they are re-shooting scenes Lillie recognizes as ones they have already done with the star. That's when she begins to dream seriously about her image, nearly a storey high, projected on scores of shining screens across the continent.

Ernie Shipman is nowhere in evidence. Lillie hears that he shows up at nights to watch the dailies. The rest of the time he is reportedly making trunk calls and sending telegrams, lining up his next project, no doubt. She goes from being relieved that she does not see him to wishing she could. She would like to test herself, to prove she could look the old goat in the eye without flinching. She is becoming the star. He needs her.

One evening she has all but made up her mind to happen by the rink, as if by accident, to catch the producer looking at the day's footage, admiring what she has done as Lillian, but Frank comes home early from the newspaper, which is to say that he does not go directly to the speakeasy.

"So what do you know, eh, Lil?"

"About what?" For some reason she is afraid they are about to have a conversation about the painting Shipman has bought. Frank has never mentioned it. She crosses her arms across her chest, and then, thinking it ridiculous, drops them to her sides.

"About them all just packing up and leaving. The movie people."

"What?"

"You didn't know?"

"Nobody said ..." Lillie thinks she may throw up.

"Faith sent me a note at the paper. Swore me to secrecy. They're leaving tonight. Just like that. Going to Florida to finish, she says. Shipman and Hartford decided it's too cold to finish up here, I guess. You must have got wind of it?"

"Not a breath." How could they?

"They can't have just decided, just like that, in one day."

"It's a fast-moving business, Frank." The bastards.

"You'd think they'd have to tell the investors at least. How can they just up sticks and leave? It's not right. So soon."

"It's okay, Frank, I'll be fine without ..." And then Lillie realizes that Frank's concerns are not for her. Nor is he really upset as an investor in N.B. Films. It's Faith; the fact that Faith is leaving. "I'm sorry, Frank. Maybe she can come back for a visit or something after they finish shooting." She has to say it, even if they both know how unlikely it is.

SIX WEEKS LATER, Lillie goes skating at the Victoria Rink. It is as though the place was never a movie studio. Not a single trace of *Blue Water* remains. For one instant, though, Lillie thinks she spies Norma's reflection in the ice. She leans over to look closer, loses her balance and breaks her leg.

And that is why she doesn't get to see *Pleasure Mad* at the Imperial when it opens and launches Norma Shearer's career in the pictures.

Iris-out on Lillie in bed, her leg encased in plaster.

6

Screening

"I'M CALLING THE picture a sweet, edifying story of sailor-love. Does that sound right? Later, I go on a bit about rivalry, intemperance, faithful friends and burly sailors."

"Well ..." I call from the bathroom where I am pinning up my hair, "I guess that sounds fine, but ..."

"Listen, if you'd like to write it, go ahead. You could at least tell me the story."

"You have to see it. That's the way the moving pictures work, Frank. You see what's on the screen. Then you make the story inside your head."

"But I have a deadline. I have to file this piece before eleven."

"You'll just have to wait and see it." I emerge from the bathroom. "You look —"

"Stunning is what I'm going for. Stunning. Is that what you were going to say?" I am still surprised to hear how I sound with him now, but I remind myself this is the modern world. It is

1924, after all. I am certainly not a kid any longer. And things are different.

"You look like an actress in the pictures."

"That'll do too."

"People will never know you're not her."

"Everybody will know. Everybody knows she turned down the invitation."

"She's just too busy to come to a screening in a backwater town. Mayer is keeping her busy out there. It's the price of fame."

"She doesn't even remember we exist."

"You look way better than she ever did. People will think you've come straight from Hollywood as a lovely surprise."

"Are you kidding? All they'll see is the pathetic little double. That's what Ernie Shipman called me that day, did I ever tell you that?"

"Once or twice. He was a bastard. Some producer. Forget him. God, Lillie, you saved his ass with all that standing in."

"But I didn't kiss it. That was my big mistake."

"Norma didn't kiss it either. Or anything else. And look where she is now."

"Kissing ass in Hollywood." We both laugh.

Nathan and Percy are late. My plan was for them to arrive at the exact moment I made my entrance from the bathroom. I suppose I was relying on them to tell me how terrific I look, although Frank has not done too badly, for Frank. Still, it would mean more from someone else. Nathan was supposed to be borrowing an automobile from one of the men in the orchestra, and we are all to arrive in style at the Imperial. How Nathan is going to get the car parked and make it to his seat in the pit in time for the first bars of the overture has been the subject of hours of planning over the past week. We finally worked out an itinerary down to the last half-minute. And already we are falling behind. I carefully lift the clock from the mantel. It usually lies face down.

It keeps better time that way. "What can have happened to them? I wish they had a telephone."

"Or that we did. Or both, ideally, I suppose." Frank is trying to lighten the mood. It's pathetic, but sweet, I guess.

"Maybe Nathan couldn't get the car. Maybe Percy is still getting cleaned up."

"Maybe the clock is fast."

"Not possible. Was that a honk?"

"They're coming up, remember? We're having a toast."

"Not if they're late. We'll have to skip the toast if they're not here in —"

"If you think I'm going to go to this thing without a drink in me —"

"When was the last time you went anywhere without a drink in you?" I might as well have slapped him. I would rather have slapped him; those marks fade.

Percy and Nathan arrive within seconds, bearing a large bouquet of carnations, which they must have stopped to pilfer somewhere. Maybe the Burying Ground.

"For the leading lady," Nathan intones while Percy produces a deep flourished bow and pushes the flowers at me.

"I'm not the ..."

"You finished the picture. Norma didn't. If it was a running race, and not some silly movie, there'd be no question."

It is easier not to go into it again. "Thank you," I say, and I go to the kitchen for something to put the carnations in. As I fill a large Mason jar at the sink, I can hear the clink of bottle on glass.

I try to sweep into the living room the way I meant to sweep out of the bathroom, hoping for a belated delivery of the lines I have scripted in my head for Nathan and Percy. But they are drinking already, and the golden moment goes by again. I pick up the fourth glass, drain it, and, on a whim, throw it at the faux-marble hearth where it shatters into a thousand pieces. The three men gape at me. "We're late," I say. I grab the window curtain I have reworked into a gorgeous wrap, and head for the door.

The three men follow silently, knowing they have somehow failed me, but at least two of them unsure as to how. At the sidewalk, Percy rushes ahead to open the car door for me, brushing against my left breast as he does so. Something makes me think about that first study he made of me, the fall when we were filming the picture, the study Ernie Shipman was so eager to buy but left behind in his hurry to get out of town. What has become of it?

Nathan is a terrible driver. It's hard to believe, as he bumps the clutch and grinds the gears, that anyone so palpably uncoordinated could actually play a musical instrument. Percy has to keep gesturing to him to keep right, even though it must have been a couple of years now since the new rules of the road were adopted. And all the time he is driving he keeps up a constant patter.

"I've always wondered about something, Lillie. Did you really speak actual lines when you were filming? Percy likes to read lips when he watches the pictures, don't you Percy?" He has turned his head so Percy can see what he's saying. The car swerves and we nearly lose a wheel on the tram track. "Percy says that most of the time, in most of what he sees, the actors are just chattering on about any old thing — what they had for dinner, who they would like to ... well, you know. They're not saying anything that has the least bit to do with their situation. Is that how it was with this picture? Percy will be able to tell, you know, so you might as well come clean beforehand."

At the top of King Street, I am convinced that we are going to roll back all the way down into the harbour as Nathan tries to get into gear again after a stop. Finally, with the aid of an extra foot supplied by Percy, he manages the manoeuvre and we swing around the square to the front of the theatre.

Golding, the Imperial's manager, was a primary investor in the movie, so he's arranged for extra lighting at the doors. There

is a tall young man, decked out in a livery that is pure make-
believe, announcing arrivals. Local people who appear in the
film have been sent large cards, which they have been instructed
to present to this functionary. I have given mine to Frank to hold
because my dress has no pockets and I hate carrying a purse.

"Give the man the card, Frank."

"I, um, I can't find it, Lil."

There is a knot forming behind us — in sympathy, I suppose,
with the knot in my stomach.

"Miss Lillian Dempster." Frank says to the man. "Just announce
her, would you?"

"Not without a card. Mr. Golding said —"

"I don't give a good goddamn what Golding said, this is Lillie
Dempster. She's the star of the fucking movie."

"Miss Shearer is in California, Mr. Golding said. She is busy
with —"

"Forget it, Frank. Let's just go in."

"Evening, Mr. Ross," says the young man as Percy follows us
into the theatre.

We are at least able to claim the seats that have been set aside
for us. Percy was in charge of collecting the tickets from the box
office last week, and he pulls them from his pocket and presents
them to the usher. Frank is still patting his suit in pursuit of the
missing presentation card. He only finds the flask that he has
increasingly come to rely upon ever since I fell down the stairs
almost four years ago. He helps himself to a slug the minute we
are seated.

I look around. Many of the faces I have not seen in the
eighteen months since Shipman left St. John to finish the movie
in Florida. Where could they all hide in a city this size? While
the filming was going on they all became part of a very close
community. And then when the thing broke up, it was as though
they couldn't stay far enough away from each other. It's like the

months after the Street Railway strike. The same kind of closeness followed by the same kind of distance. I wish my mother was here to watch the picture with me.

Two girls, they can't be more than sixteen, are arguing with an usher who has caught them trying to sneak in through the fire-escape doors. "We just went out for a breath of air," they are saying. "Our ... our escorts have our ticket stubs. They're in the balcony. We'll go get them if you want." I think about how easy it was to get into the Gem, and I almost wish Fred Trifts were here to watch the picture with me, even though I know how impossible that is. And ironic.

Nathan waves from the pit. Percy beams with pride. He does this every time we go to the pictures together. He has never heard a note, of course, but he knows that what Nathan does here is important, and that being a friend of Nathan makes him, too, somehow an integral part of this whole exciting operation. Frank waves back at Nathan, elbowing the woman next to him and making an awkward apology. My wrap feels a little uncomfortable where it pushes against the seat. I must have managed to miss taking out a curtain hook. But the wrap is part of the overall look, and I wouldn't part with it for the world. Besides, I am beginning to shiver.

The lights dim. A follow spot picks up the orchestra leader as he makes his way into the pit. He shakes hands with Nathan, puts his head down for a moment, then lifts it and his hands together as if they're attached to a single string, and the music begins. It is a medley of sea shanties, from rollicking to mournful, and several people around me are whispering remembered words to several of the tunes. Just as the last notes are dying away, the drop — a Venetian garden by moonlight, for reasons that nobody has ever been able to fathom — flies out of the way, and the screen springs to life with the flickering text of the opening credits.

I can hear people around me, the same ones who have been singing with the shanties, reading the words. "N.B. Films proudly presents *Blue Water*, after a novel by F.W. Wallace, produced by Ernest Shipman, directed by D.W. Hartford, featuring Norma Shearer as Lillian Denton, Pierre Gendron as 'Shorty' Westhaver, Jane Thomas as Carrie Dexter, adaptation by Faith Green. Executive Producer Ernest Shipman." There is a ripple of uneasy laughter at this second appearance of Shipman's name. It is so utterly like him. I wonder how many in the audience have lost their life-savings to the chippy little bastard's scheme.

From the first scene, I know that not only is the film enjoying its first Canadian engagement, as some of the advertisements in the newspaper have boasted, but most likely its last one anywhere. The story isn't clear. Unless you have read the book, the rural school scenes and the shots where the young Jimmy Westhaver and his friend run an illicit pilot service in the Bay of Fundy make no sense. There are little gasps of recognition when the St. John streetscape appears, doubling for Boston, and nervous giggles as several people in the audience spot themselves in the crowds on the streets, but none of this could make any impression beyond these walls. When Norma Shearer appears, soaked to the skin, to be rescued by Shorty Westhaver from her father's sinking vessel, there are a few isolated whistles of approval from the rear of the theatre. I shiver. Percy looks at me and I nod. Everyone else looks at the screen.

We make it a little game from that point on, Percy and I, keeping score between Norma and me — who has more scenes. When we run out of fingers, Percy pulls a small sketchbook from his jacket and begins marking in it with the stub of a pencil. It is about the only thing that saves the picture for us.

The acting is worse than wooden. The continuity is a mess where they've tried to match the scenes authentically shot in the Bay of Fundy with footage they took later on in Florida. The few title cards are awkward and sometimes laughable in their effort to duplicate Maritime speech. I am surprised Faith did not listen more closely. Virtually everybody in the theatre has a stake in this movie being a success, but by the fifth and final reel everyone is restless, shifting in their seats, rustling the commemorative programs that Golding has had printed.

It is not the money that is the big disappointment that night. Not anymore. Most of us have gotten used to the idea that we have lost that. We know that not only is the film not going to return its promised 250 percent, but we will never even see our original investments again. It is not the money, but that the movie is so obviously bad. It hasn't been able to hold our attention for fifty minutes, and if it can't hold ours, whose could it? The puffs in the paper have said that it's only distribution problems that have held up *Blue Water*'s Canadian release. One even reported that the film has already been placed with much acceptance in the larger U.S. centres. Frank, who I know now was paid by Golding to write those words, is, by the end of the evening, by no means the only person in the theatre to know they are a lie.

As I watch, and while Percy and I tally Norma's appearances against mine, I realize how desperately I have wanted to believe the distribution story. I have even elaborated on it. In the version that I tell myself, Louis Mayer is behind the whole thing. He owns Norma now, and he is trying to control her appearance absolutely. The existence of a film that was shot before Norma was associated with his studio could present problems. So maybe he has used his pull with the big chains to keep it out of circulation. It all makes sense. Until you see *Blue Water*. Then you know that the movie simply stinks.

There is a reception after the screening in Trinity Church Hall. The archdeacon is a major shareholder in N.B. Films, spending his money in the not-so-secret hope that one of his own novels will be the next project to be made. It has already been agreed that it will either be one of his novels or one of Charles G.D. Roberts's animal stories. Since nobody we know can see how they could possibly pull off an animal story, the archdeacon looks like a pretty good bet. Golding, the archdeacon and then other members of the company's board all make short speeches about how wonderfully *Blue Water* augurs for the future of film in New Brunswick. That is when I realize that even they have not seen the movie before tonight's screening. They all wrote their speeches in wishful anticipation, and they haven't had the time, the heart or the guts to change them. What else could they possibly say anyway?

There are toasts with grape juice to the local crew and cast. And to the absent Norma, who is doing so well in Hollywood. I sneeze loudly just at that point, and there is a small ripple through the crowd as a few people look at me briefly and almost mistake me for my famous look-alike. Nobody mentions Ernie Shipman's name.

Frank rushes off to file his review. He, too, has decided not to change his tune, despite what he has just seen. As it turns out, he will even add in a lie or two about the remarkably high quality of the continuity. I know he will go straight on from the newspaper to Cronin's to erase his memory. Percy and I wait on Charlotte Street while Nathan goes to fetch the borrowed car for us. He is determined to play the charade out to the end, right down to the candlelit after-theatre supper that I know will be waiting for us in Percy's studio.

In any event, Nathan's friend has decided he needs his car himself. I saw him leaving the reception with one of the extras from the tavern scene and I suspect I know why he needs it. We walk the two blocks to the studio, faster and more smoothly than we could have driven anyway.

I am right, Nathan and Percy have gone all out to make the

evening special. There are candles and oysters and a sparkling wine pretending to be champagne. My eyes fill up.

"You boys, you shouldn't have. You can't afford all this. I feel terrible." Am I crying because they are so generous or because the film is so bad?

"Don't feel terrible, Lil, feel loved," Nathan says, and Percy gives me a big hug. "Besides, Percy's rich right now. He sold some work."

"Percy, that's wonderful," I mouth the words in a highly exaggerated fashion so I can be sure that Percy will understand. "What work?" I ask Nathan.

"An assortment, really. All to one man, which was the odd thing, considering the variety. A fellow from the States."

I look around the room, trying to recall what is missing. In the two years I have been modelling for Percy, I have come to know the contents of his studio almost as intimately as he has come to know the planes and volumes of my body.

"The designs for the *Blue Water* sets are gone." Although Shipman and Hartford liked to shoot on location as much as possible, there was necessarily lots of studio work in the Victoria Rink, and Percy was happy to have the money, though Nathan always said he preferred to paint people.

"Right. He seemed quite interested in those. Asked a lot of questions."

"And, oh my God. Me. I'm missing. All six of me." By this, I mean a series of studies Percy has recently completed of me. They are costume pieces, really, if nude studies can be called costume pieces. In each one I am supposed to represent a different prominent woman in history at her toilette. They seem a lot like the kind of thing that circulates in photographic form among men of a certain age, but Percy assured me, through Nathan, that they are well on the artistic side of the line. And he does pay his models quite well.

"He was taken with those right away. Kept asking for your name, which we wouldn't tell him. I mean, he seemed like a serious collector, but you never know."

I shiver. "Do you remember that study that Shipman bought? The one he left behind when he hightailed it out of town?"

"It was the first one Percy ever did of you. You were, what, seventeen?"

"Eighteen. What ever happened to that?"

"You mean you don't know? You've never seen it? He hasn't ever ...?"

"Who?"

"Frank. Frank bought it off of Percy. Percy tried to persuade him it wasn't really his to sell anymore, but Frank wouldn't pay any attention. Said how he had hated it when Shipman had bought it before he could, before he even knew it existed; and now he had a chance to make things right. Whatever that meant. You know how Frank gets late at night."

"I know."

"Funny he never told you."

"Funny."

The oysters slip down easily, leaving only faint traces of salt to mark their passage. Salt and mud. The wine is followed by whisky. By the time I leave Percy and Nathan curled up asleep in one another's arms on the studio couch and stumble home myself, I have forgotten all about the paintings.

REEL FOUR

Making
Pictures

1

Finding Faith

I AM SICK of New York fifteen minutes after I step off the train. Faith's letter said that her apartment was only ten blocks from Grand Central Station, so I hurried past the ranks of cabs lined up outside, and struck out on foot. The blocks are longer than I am used to, though, and to negotiate the crowds with my suitcase I have to take one step sideways for every three forward. As my feet grow sore and my bag grows heavier, I begin to doubt the crash-course Mr. Golding gave me on New York geography — avenues run north-south and are numbered; streets run east-west, and they're numbered too. It seemed to make sense as he unfolded it all in the familiar room behind the box office at the Imperial. He even produced a tattered map to illustrate. Now, actually on the ground in this strange city, dropped into the middle of that deceptively tidy grid, it is much harder to have faith. It becomes impossible to believe that the block following 48th Street will ever turn into 49th Street.

I have not slept on the trip. The agony of sitting up the whole time, combined with nerves, overrode the hypnotic *clackety-clack* of the train speeding along the track. There was no question about taking a berth. It was all I could do to save up the regular sitting-up fare and a little for food. If only I could have been sure of the outcome, I might have purchased one-way instead of round trip. Then I could have afforded a berth, even a drawing-room. But that would have been foolish. Despite the loud assurances of Nathan, and even of Frank at the very last, I know that it is equally likely that I will not make it. There is every possibility that Al Altman will take one look at me and all my flaws and tell the cameraman to stop rolling and go home.

Faith has been relatively optimistic about my chances, but she was also the one to stress the importance of having a return ticket. "If everything goes great," she wrote, "you can put it towards upgrading your fare to Hollywood. The studio usually pays coach for its new discoveries. It's when you get out there that they treat you like a queen. But if for some reason things don't work out, then you've got your way home, to your old life." Faith herself always takes a berth when she comes to Saint John (as we finally dragged out the Saint in 1925), which she has done for the last four summers in a way that does credit to her name. And of course, she always books round trip. She can afford to do both. I cannot.

At 51st Street, the heel comes off my shoe. I drop my bag to the pavement with a growl, then, instantly self-conscious, look around to see if people are staring. They aren't. The steady stream of walkers continues, oblivious to my setback, even miraculously rerouting around me as I stand in the middle of the sidewalk. Ants. Not one of them looks me in the face. Not one seems to take any notice when I have to go down on one knee to inspect the damage to my shoe, or when I pull both shoes off and stuff them in my bag. The pavement feels dusty through my stockings, dry like talc.

It isn't until I have straightened up and picked up my suitcase once more that I see the man. He is sitting in the window of the coffee shop I have stopped in front of. The reflection off the glass keeps me from seeing what he is eating, if he is eating anything, but I can make out his face and his shoulders clearly enough through the window. His shoulders are twitching up and down in what can only be silent laughter. Is it silent? I can't tell with the glass between us. His face is pointed straight at mine, his gaze riveted on me. I want to bang on the glass, to retrieve the broken shoe from my reticule and hammer it on the window where his face is, break the glass, maybe break his nose. Instead, I simply mouth "You think this is funny?" The man just continues to stare. "You think this is a big joke?" I speak aloud this time. Still no flicker of response from the man, who keeps on looking at me through the glass as though I am his own private moving picture. "Glad I could give you a laugh! Any time!" I shout now at the impassive face, and I make an exaggerated curtsey. Then I stick out my tongue and join the throng of people who do not appear to give me even a first, let alone a second, glance.

Faith's apartment is two flights up. I drop my suitcase on the first landing and sit on a step to put my shoes back on. The stockings are ruined, and there are blisters starting in several places on my feet, but I wedge the whole mess into the shoes and climb the second flight. Faith mustn't see me arrive barefoot. What would she think?

"Lillie! I'd just been starting to worry. Was your train late? Weren't there any cabs? I should have come down to the station, I just had this thing."

"I wanted to walk. All those hours sitting on the train."

"You walked? You poor lamb. It must be ten blocks."

"Twelve."

"You must be dying to take off your shoes. My God, did you break a heel?"

"I'm fine, thank you. I would like to wash my face, though."

"Of course, in here."

There is a lock on the bathroom door, which I turn as quietly as I can after Faith has left me. Then I sit on the closed toilet and begin to cry. The drops hit the tiled floor, beading into perfect lenses. I take off my shoes and stockings, catching in the long mirror on the bathroom door the reflected flash of white thigh. I continue to look in the mirror through the haze of tears as I lift my bleeding foot high in front of me and guide it over the edge of the sink.

The water feels good, the soap stings. I do the other foot and towel them both dry. Then I remember to wash my face, hoping that Faith will interpret the redness around my eyes as irritation from the scrubbing.

Before unlocking the bathroom door, I look around for a place to get rid of the ruined stockings. Maybe I can hide them somewhere, behind the tub, then slip them into my suitcase when Faith's out of the apartment. Or I could just throw them out, tuck them in at the bottom of the garbage. There is a small wicker basket beside the toilet. It must be for garbage. I lift up a few sheets of torn paper that sit on the top, thinking I might even wrap the stockings in them and then scrunch them up into balls. Beneath the sheets of paper, lying like large slugs discovered under an upturned rock, are five used sheepskin condoms. I stuff my stockings down the front of my dress and carefully lay the scraps of paper back on top of the wicker basket.

"How's Frank? He must be so excited for you!"

"He came around to the idea, in the end."

"How's his ...? Is he ...?"

"Like a fish. He's lonely." I can't remember ever having spoken this directly about Frank's drinking to anyone, but those slugs in Faith's bathroom garbage have made me want to hurt her, to blame Faith for a problem we both know goes a lot further back.

"I know. I can't wait for next summer. I have planned a whole month this time. It's going to be wonderful."

"He counts the days, you know."

"Me too."

"How many is it?" I think I can catch Faith out in a lie — she isn't counting the days any more than I counted the exact number of condoms in the garbage.

"Two hundred and sixty-five."

Of course I have no way of checking. "Oh."

"D'you remember that first night, Lillie?"

"The first night?"

"The morning. When I went out to the kitchen at Frank's place, and there you were."

"I remember."

"I thought you were his ..."

"I know."

"I thought we could just cook something here tonight. You must be so tired."

"Is there a shoemaker somewhere near? I'll need to get this heel fixed before tomorrow."

2

Cyclops

I END UP borrowing a pair of shoes from Faith because the shoe-maker snarled at me that he needed at least two days. When I reported this to Faith, she laughed and said you have to know how to deal with those guys. Then she offered me the shoes. They are expensive. I wonder how Faith can afford them. They are also a little too large, so I stuff part of a balled-up stocking in each toe. Luckily, I lie to Faith, I ran a pair on the train seat, so it's not a loss. The result is a slightly halting walk and a periodic shooting pain in my toes. I can just about manage twenty steps without a full grimace. Fortunately, Faith says that walking all the way to Hell's Kitchen is out of the question anyway, and she insists on treating us to a cab.

"I want to take you in and introduce you myself. Al Altman has the best eye in the business, he's a genius, but it doesn't hurt to let him see who you know — you know, how you're connected and everything. Al's an old pal." I think of the slumbering slugs in Faith's garbage, and wonder how old and how close a pal.

The taxi pulls up in front of a building that's hung with a sign clearly identifying it as Fox Studios. I say there must be some mistake.

"It's okay, honey, this is where Al does the tests, that's all. Fox lets him use the first floor sometimes." She makes it sound the same as a friend lending an apartment for a lunchtime tryst.

"Hey, good luck, kid," the cabbie calls as he drives off. The whole drive here, he has not spoken a word to either of us.

The cameraman — Bill, I hear Faith call him — meets us at the door. He holds out a thin hand, yellow with nicotine, then takes my elbow and guides me into the studio. Faith follows behind, gossiping happily to Bill about people they both know and I do not. At intervals, Bill laughs at something Faith says. Then he has to stop walking while he wheezes and coughs and finally gets up part of whatever it is rattling around in his chest, spitting it on the rough pine floor.

"Mr. Altman's going to be a little late," Bill says during a brief break in the gossip. "He had to see a man about a horse or something," he adds, winking at Faith.

I stop listening to them and begin to look around the room. It is bare of furniture except for the battered bentwood chairs the three of us are sitting on. There are banks of lights much the same as the ones they used in the Victoria Rink for *Blue Water*, only they don't have anything about Ottawa stencilled on them. And there is the camera. It is an Akerley, it says in proud lettering, but that doesn't mean anything to me. The only thing that does mean something is its big gleaming eye — like the Cyclops, waiting in its cave to devour me.

"It's amazing," Al Altman keeps repeating as he wrings my hand seconds after he finally arrives. "Uncanny."

"I told you," says Faith.

"Yes, but I never thought ... I mean, they could be ..."

"Twins. That's what I told you. Ernie Shipman —"

"Ernie Shipman, that old son of a — whatever happened to old Ernie, anyway?"

"Ernie Shipman could never tell them apart. In Florida, the last I heard. Thinks everybody's made a mistake with California. Says Florida's the place."

"New York's the place. Everywhere else is just the workshop. This is where the decisions get made. Always will be. Where did you say you were from — Lillie, is it?"

"New Brunswick. The one in Canada," I add. "Saint John, New Brunswick."

"You summer up there, don't you Faith? Are there polar bears?" I can't tell if Altman is joking, so I am glad when he continues. "Let's get this on the road then, shall we?"

Bill begins throwing switches and the dull room springs to life, blindingly bright. Faith shrieks and shades her eyes, and says she'll wait outside.

"Now, Lillie, this is how we do this. It's quite simple. Do you think you can handle it?"

I want to tell him I will need to know what "it" is before I can answer. Instead, I nod. A nod I have learned from Norma.

"My god. Uncanny. Okay. So, the first thing you are going to do is walk toward the camera. From over there. Okay?"

Another, different, Norma nod.

"Amazing. Ready, Bill?"

"Is she going to do the usual schtick, or what?"

"Oh, Jesus. Yes, of course. I forgot you've never done this. So, Lillie, after you've walked toward the camera, that's Bill here, I want you to look right into the lens, right into it, got that? Full face we call it. There's a mark on the floor somewhere, yeah, here it is, for you to stop on before you look, right? Hold the look for fifteen seconds. I'll count out steamboats for you. Then you're going to turn to the left, so we get your right profile, see? Hold. Then turn to the left, I mean right, for your left profile. Can you remember all that?"

"I think so." I try to sound tentative because it seems as though I am supposed to find it all quite difficult and mystifying.

"What's that accent, anyway?"

"Accent?"

"Rolling," says Bill.

"And action," says Altman.

I begin my walk towards the camera. I have already counted off the steps when getting into place. Twelve. The pain in my toes shouldn't be too bad.

"Try to keep your face still, please." I realize that I have been numbering the steps in a whisper. I look down for the X-mark on the floor where I am supposed to stop.

"Head up, keep the head up. That's better. Now stop. Stop! What? Don't you see the mark?"

I can feel the blood rush into my face and a hot tear racing down one cheek.

"One steamboat, two steamboats ..."

It is hard to know what I should be thinking about. If I don't think about anything at all, my face will come across as stupid, won't it? I wish I asked Altman before the test began. All I can find to think about is how humiliated I am, which can't make for a good look.

"Fifteen steamboats. Now right. No, you turn to the left, remember?"

Why should it matter which cheek I show first? Or why hasn't Altman, who has supposedly done this thousands of times, come up with a less confusing set of directions? I turn the other way.

"And fine, now left profile. Good. See, you get used to it. It's all about what you're showing, not what you're doing. And hold, and cut."

I want to show that I am not such a newcomer. I want them to know I have been around this business before, so I turn to Bill and ask whether there will be enough usable footage after he's edited out all the fumbles.

"Edit?" booms Altman. "We don't edit a screen test. Mr. Mayer would never go for that. He wants the genuine article."

"But ..." It seems to me that if a person is never going to be expected to perform in one long take, it makes no sense to ask it of them in an audition. A look from Bill, though, persuades me not to say anything.

I am about to shake Altman's hand and thank him for the opportunity when he says, "Ready for the emotional part?"

"The what?"

"I want you to work your way through some simple feelings."

Oh God. "We aren't finished?"

"Of course not."

"But the camera's stopped. I thought you didn't edit ... never mind. What do I do?"

"It's not what you do; it's what you show, remember."

"Sorry. Of course. What do I show?"

"Sad, mad, questioning, wistful."

"Wistful?"

"Yeah, wistful. You know."

"I guess."

"Then cry, if you can."

That I think I can manage.

"Ready?"

"I guess."

"Rolling."

"And action. I'll talk you through. Sad, first. Whenever you're ready."

"This is it."

"Oh. Right. No, don't turn. Let's try mad. Mad as in angry, I mean, not mad as in Bellevue."

"This is it."

"Fine, now questioning. Oh, fantastic. And wistful."

"I guess I don't really know what wistful is."

"Bill, what's wistful?"

"Something about longing and all that, isn't it? Pining? Something like that."

"Oh."

"That's perfect!"

"But I haven't ..."

"And cut. Now the final thing, Lillie, is the recitation."

"Recitation?"

"Sure, a little bit from a play you've been in, or a poem or something. Just a little bit."

"But they won't be able to hear me talk. He won't. Mr. Mayer. On the film."

"It's what we do."

I have never been in a play, and the only poems I can remember on the spot are limericks. "I'm drawing a blank."

"How about the pledge of allegiance?"

"The what?"

"Maybe the national anthem. A few lines of that."

"God save our gracious —"

"What the hell is that?"

"Our father, who art in heaven ..."

"Sure, that'll do. Stick with that."

So I do, getting a little mixed up with thems and thoses and who trespasses first, but neither of the men seems to notice.

"And cut. There. That wasn't so bad, was it? Not so scary?"

I just hope I can make it out to the street before I throw up. I quickly shake Altman's hand, then Bill's, and make for the door. When I turn to close it behind me, I can see Bill holding his nose and laughing, while Altman tears a page from his notebook, crumples it, and sends it flying across the empty studio.

3

Stills

"DO YOU WANT to talk about it? Lillie? It might be good for you to talk about it."

Faith and I are back at the apartment. When we came through the door, I threw myself on the couch and buried my face in the pillows. I have stayed that way for almost an hour.

"He sure twigged to the likeness to Norma, didn't he? He seemed pretty impressed when I left you."

Is there a reproach in this? If she hadn't left everything would have gone fine?

"The picture business is a crapshoot, Lil. You can't tell how you really did on some dumb screen test until they see it in Hollywood. And then if they don't happen to like it, chances are it's nothing you could have done anything about anyway."

"Mr. Altman and Bill, they hated what I did. No, sorry. Not what I did. What I showed them."

"Screw them. They're nothing. I mean, Al Altman's a nice guy and everything I guess, but he doesn't call the shots. He's not really a player, you know. Half the time, he sends them tests he's crazy about and they don't watch for more than thirty seconds before they give up on them. You can't tell until the phone call comes. Anyway, no point in moping around here."

"No, you're right. Okay if I borrow your shoes again?"

"Lillie, do me a favour. Let me give you a present. Call it a kind of celebration present. Buy yourself a pair of shoes." And she presses a folded five-dollar bill into my palm.

"Faith, I couldn't. It's too ..."

"Think of it as a loan, then. Or better, as payment of a debt. I actually owe Frank five dollars from last summer, see?"

I don't see, but I take the five and leave the apartment.

The phone call came while I was sitting in the shoe store on the corner, below Faith's apartment, trying on a sensible pair of walking shoes that the clerk had to retrieve from deep in the recesses of his back room. Or maybe it came during the following three hours while I sat on a bench in Central Park, watching the pigeons and imagining I was in King Square. I don't like to ask Faith for the exact time. What seems pretty certain to me is that it came at some point while Faith lay naked and sweating in the arms of some man who is not Frank, some man whom I am pretty sure I can smell when I return at dusk to the apartment, some man who has no doubt left behind another slug or two under the papers in Faith's bathroom.

"They want you back for some still photographs. Tomorrow. Not in Hell's Kitchen. You can go to the office on Broadway. Altman will have a photographer there."

"Why would they want stills? It's the movies I want, not modelling." I am remembering Pierre's advice.

"It's got to be a good sign."

"It's got to be a sign they hate the way I moved."

"Lillie, if there was nothing there, they wouldn't bother paying a photographer, and Al Altman wouldn't be wasting another hour of his time. Sorry. I didn't mean wasting."

1540 Broadway is considerably more daunting as an address and as a building than the Fox Studios were yesterday, but Altman seems a whole lot less set on intimidating me here than he was at the screen test.

"Lillie, my dear, this is Bill." Are they all called Bill? "He's going to take some photographs of you. He'll tell you what he would like to see. Just be yourself. There won't be anything to make you uncomfortable. All natural."

Jesus. Natural. I picture myself posing naked with a pony, like that girl I saw on some postcards of Frank's one time.

Bill returns a manilla envelope to Altman. On it, I can see the stamp of Mayer's studio. "I see what you mean," Bill says. "This should be fun." I feel even worse.

"You know where to go," says Altman. "Lillie, look in here again when you're all done, won't you?"

The room, the lights, the camera are all smaller than yesterday at Fox. There is a dressing screen in one corner. When I see that, I am all set to flee. Taking off your clothes for a photographer, it's not the same as doing it for a painter. Especially when the painter is also a friend.

"We'll start with some simple head shots, please miss," the man says. His tone reassures me a little. I try to pretend he is Isaac Erb. He gets me to look straight at the camera, then straight at it with head tilted to one side, then the other. Then lips apart a little. I think of Pierre. He takes profiles, erect and tilted, and gets me to sit in a chair with my knees pointing one way and my face at right angles to them.

"Now, these next few might sound a bit funny to you."

Here it comes. This is where he asks me to take off my clothes. I strain to listen for the whinny of the pony. Can he be tethered behind the screen?

"I'm going to get you to pose with a tire."

"A tire?"

"You know, like on automobiles. An automobile tire. There's a costume behind the screen. I'm just going out for a smoke while you change into it." The photographer leaves the room, effectively forestalling any plans I might have for flight. How can I run away from an empty room? It would seem ridiculous. Even in the *Perils of Pauline*.

The costume is hanging on the back of the screen. There is a large, floppy white hat, a white shawl-collared blouse with scallops and a black and white blazer. A cute outfit. I look for the skirt. In vain. So that is it. I leave the things on their hangers and sit down to wait for the photographer to return.

"You're not changed. Wasn't the fit right? They were sure that —"

"I couldn't find a skirt." I tense the muscles in my right arm, ready to hit the man when he makes the indecent remark that I know must be coming. My knees, safe beneath my own skirt, blush hot red at the thought of what I am sure he is about to suggest.

"Oh, you just keep your own skirt on — it's only from the waist up we're interested in. We put the tire around you like this," he demonstrates on himself with a tire he has brought into the room with him, "and you kind of wave like this. See? You must have seen the campaign."

"Campaign?"

"Miss Lotta Miles. Norma Shearer was Miss Lotta Miles for Kelly Tires."

"Oh." I go behind the screen to change, trying hard not to think about the presence of the photographer, who hasn't offered to go out for a second smoke.

"WHEN DO YOU head back to Canada?" Al Altman asks when I look into his office. It seems as kindly a way as any to let me down.

"I didn't have a firm plan. I left my ticket open. Whenever I can get a booking, I guess."

"Do we know how to get in touch with you? I mean, besides through Faith."

I would like to call his bluff, but instead I write out my address in Saint John, imagining him crumpling the piece of paper into a small ball the moment I have left the office.

"Thank you. There's just one more thing. If you don't mind, Lillie. Miss Johnstone, would you come in here please?" The bespectacled secretary who keeps watch outside Altman's office door brushes past me. "I'm going to turn around now, and Miss Johnstone here is going to help us out with this ... procedure." He swivels in his chair so he is looking out at the city through the large plate-glass window. "Now, Lillie, if you would just raise your skirt." I turn to leave. "Just above the knees, if you please. I'm sorry, I know it's awkward." Awkward is not the word.

"It's okay. Really." Miss Johnstone's voice is so calm, her eye-glasses so serious looking, that I decide to comply after all. It can't really be any worse than bathing in the bay at Seaside Park, or changing in front of Sue. I clutch the hem of my skirt and lift. "Just a little higher, please," says Miss Johnstone. "An inch perhaps." I pull. "Thank you." Miss Johnstone nods and I let go of the hem.

"Well?" asks Altman.

"Yes," is all Miss Johnstone says, and she brushes past me once more.

Altman swivels around in his chair. "That concludes our business for now, Lillie. Thanks for coming in."

As I leave the office, I catch a glimpse of the bald spot at the back of Altman's head, clearly reflected in the window glass. I could swear that it is glowing bright red.

4

Send-off

We iris-in on the apartment, then cut directly to an insert — a close shot of a hand holding an envelope.

THE TELEGRAM ARRIVES in Saint John exactly a week after Lillie does. It comes directly from Louis Mayer in Culver City. At least, it bears his name at the bottom. "Screen test A-1 — Stop," it reads. "Hope you can join us here — Stop. Norma thrilled — Stop. Will wire $ for ticket on confirmation — Stop. Mayer."

Lillie is out when it is delivered, but Frank opens it and reads it. He is to tell Lillie afterwards that he read it so he could throw it out if it was bad news. She tells him to mind his own business, but when she sees his face fall she says she didn't mean it, and it was nice of him to worry about her feelings like that. Then she thinks about how little has really changed in the eight years they have lived together. Really, just one thing.

"So, what do I do now?"

"Well, you're going to go, aren't you?" He makes it sound as though he wants her to say no.

"Of course I'm going to go. It's the chance of a lifetime. I mean, how do I let them know? How do you answer a telegram?"

"We send wires from the newspaper all the time. I can get someone to do it for you tomorrow."

"I'd like to do it now. Myself." Can he hear the mistrust in her voice?

"There's an office on Union Street."

She goes alone. The man behind the counter is snippy at first, as though Frank has maybe gone next door to phone ahead to tell him to give her a hard time.

"I need more than that to go on, young lady. A man's name and California, U.S.A., isn't going to get a telegram to him."

"He's in pictures. You must know him. He used to live here years and years ago. His father was the junk dealer."

"Well, this telegram you want to send him is in the present, isn't it? Might be a damn sight easier if it was in the past. Then you could just run it around the corner to him in person. Or wait for the junk wagon to come by."

Lillie begins to cry. She bites the insides of her cheeks to try to keep it from happening. She doesn't want this man to see he's had this effect on her. But she can't hold out, so she cries and pulls Louis Mayer's telegram out of her pocket and crumples it up and throws it across the office.

"What's that?"

"That's the message he sent me."

"Who?"

"Mr. Mayer. The man I'm trying to reply to."

"He sent you a telegram? When?"

"It came today. It must have come to this office."

"And this is it?" He has picked up the ball of paper.

"Yes."

"Why didn't you say so? Let's have a look." As he smoothes out the paper, Lillie realizes she now has the advantage. She sniffs more loudly.

"Well, here it all is, everything we need. See?" She can't see, but she nods. "His street address. The thing has to get delivered, doesn't it?" The man reaches into his pocket, and Lillie is sure he is about to pull out a handkerchief to dry her tears, but he produces only a pencil. "Write down the message, and we'll get you set up. You can sit here if you like."

When she has finished, Lillie passes the form across the counter.

"Have you never sent a telegram before, young lady?"

Lillie thinks that it should already have been abundantly evident that she has not, but she knows she has to stay on the man's good side. "No, sir."

"Every word costs money. What you've written here would be, let's see ..." The man's lips move silently. "A dollar fifty. Do you have a dollar fifty?"

Lillie says she has not.

"I don't know why I'm doing this," the man mutters as he takes the pencil from Lillie and begins crossing words out on the paper. After a full two minutes, he puts the pencil back in his pocket, obviously pleased with his work.

Lillie reads what he pushes back across the counter. "Happiest — Stop. Travel-ready soonest — Stop. Advise re: passage — Stop. Best Norma — Stop. Lillie."

"But it's so ..."

"It says what you wanted to say, doesn't it?"

"But there's no ..."

"Do you have a dollar fifty?"

"Thank you. Yes, of course, it says what I want to say."

"Sixteen cents. You can wait while I send it or not; it's all the same price."

Lillie hands the man sixteen cents and then runs all the way home.

Here, we can picture a shot of a map of North America, with Saint John picked out on one end and Hollywood on the other. Between the two is a line of telegraph poles that light up one after another as Lillie's acceptance travels to Mayer, and his confirmation travels back. Then dissolve into a sequence of shots where Lillie shops and packs and says tearful goodbyes as she prepares to leave. Finally, iris-in on a painter's studio.

THE PARTY NATHAN and Percy throw for Lillie's going away is on a Sunday night. It is still the only night Nathan doesn't work. It is the first big party any of their friends have had since Prohibition was lifted. The change is evident not so much in the quantity of booze — they have always known how to get that — but in the quality of the food they can now afford to go with it. The bootlegger's loss is the grocer's gain. That's how Nathan puts it when Lillie exclaims over the lavishness of it all.

They use Percy's new studio on Canterbury Street. The one where they celebrated the opening and closing of *Blue Water* was vandalized and then the building burned early last year. Lillie has not seen this studio before. She stopped modelling for Percy shortly after the sobering premiere of *Blue Water*. She said she could not bear the thought of any more images of herself multiplying out there beyond her control. Nathan said that Percy told him it was a waste and very selfish. So Lillie had simply stopped visiting him altogether. It was easier that way.

Percy's work is all leaning, three and four canvases deep, against the pressed-tin walls. Lengths of fabric have been draped over them. Lillie thinks she recognizes the old teasers from the Imperial. Only the sharp corners of the top canvases show in outline, bony shoulder blades through a velvet frock.

"Tell Percy I'm disappointed that we can't see his work."

Nathan makes some signs to Percy, who makes some back.

"He says that tonight is about you, Lillie, not about anybody else."

She is trying to think of the words to say she is sorry for the rift she has let grow between them, but then Walter Golding arrives.

"Lillie, my dear. We are all so excited for you. Of course, I knew the moment I first saw you at the Imperial with your ma and pa, rest them, I knew that something like this would happen. There is a little girl is going to give Mary Pickford a run, I said. Was it Mary Pickford? There's a little girl is going to give her a run, I said. And here you are."

Lillie can't remember seeing Golding anywhere outside of the theatre building before this. Being teetotal, he is not a man for parties, and all of his good works in the community have to do with clubs and societies that have exclusively male member-ships. He is smaller, she thinks, than he appears on his home turf; and some of the glow is missing. She supposes that in his own theatre he knows all the best-lit spots to stand.

"I knew when we sent you off to New York, when I gave you that little geography lesson — remember? — that good things would come of it."

Lillie reflects on how everyone she meets these days rushes to tell her how they have foreseen her success. Everyone is so proud to have played a vital role in securing it.

"Thanks, Mr. Golding. New York was a whole lot larger than I expected."

"But no match for our girl. I bet Al Altman was speechless."

"Not exactly."

Frank rescues her from any further evasions by appearing at that moment with a bottle of rye and three glasses.

"Mr. Golding. Our old partner in N.B. Films Limited — oh, if only we had known how limited! How about a toast to Uncle Ernie Shipman?"

Golding mutters an excuse and flees.

"Was it the crack about N.B. Films or the booze that scared him off, I wonder?" says Frank.

"Both," says Lillie. "Thanks." She takes the tumbler of rye Frank hands her and drains it. Someone she barely knows is waving madly to her from across the room, and she clinks her empty glass against Frank's and sets off to talk to this stranger.

There is dancing, thanks to Nathan and a number of his friends from the Imperial band. They wait until Golding is gone — he only stays a few minutes after his encounter with Frank — and then break out their instruments and start up. Nathan explains that they didn't want Golding to see them playing on their one day off. It might give him ideas. Lillie wonders how naive they think their boss is; the invitation said there would be dancing. Even a Baptist must know that means music.

"Do you remember that party for Norma Shearer at the Dufferin?" The voice comes to Lillie through an alcoholic haze. She turns to see whose it is, and recognizes a woman who did some of the catering on *Blue Water*.

"Vaguely. I expect I was drinking," Lillie hears herself slur.

"That's when I knew. I said, that's the next one to go. I meant you. I said that's the next one to get the call, the call to Hollywood."

"It must have been a pretty long distance call to take all those years."

"When I saw you dancing with that Shipman guy, I said, she's next."

"Well, you were right, weren't you?"

"Hey, I didn't mean nothing bad ..." the woman calls after Lillie.

After midnight, the party begins to fall apart. It is almost always like that, Lillie thinks. There are usually ten or fifteen golden minutes at about eleven or eleven-thirty where everything and everyone comes together, where the music and the dancing and the drinking and the talking are all parts of some larger whole that is "party," and then it always begins to deteriorate. You can hear it, see it, feel it, smell it even. Maybe there is something to the myth about turning into a pumpkin at midnight.

She tries, at twelve-thirty, to find Percy and Nathan to thank them for the evening, but the band is on a break and none of them knows where Nathan has gone; Percy is nowhere in sight. Finally, she finds someone who thinks she has seen them go up the narrow staircase that leads to the roof. "You probably want to leave them alone up there," the woman adds. "You know." Lillie does know.

Frank is sitting on the floor, his legs spread out straight in front of him, his back against the draped canvases that line the walls. His collar is undone, his hair mussed, the classic picture of a drunken bum, Lillie thinks, and then feels horrible for the cruelty.

"C'mon Frank, let's get you home." It isn't the first time they have done this.

"I'm comfy here, Lil. 'Sbeautiful right here. Try it. Siddown."

"I'm tired, Frank, and I want to go home. To bed." She adds this last with a wince. It might sound to anyone in earshot as though she is promising something. Why that should matter, she can't tell; surely, most people thought they ... oh, who gives a damn what most people think, she tells herself.

"Jus' fer a minute."

"All right. Just for a minute." Her dress is new. Bought with some of the remaining money under the mattress. Bought for California. She is terrified of getting it dirty, but she lowers herself to the floor anyway. She does not lean against the velvet curtains — who knows what dust they have collected in their long years of service in the theatre?

"Nice, isn' it?"

"Very." In fact, Lillie is frightened by the perspective — the enormous and threatening feet of those who are still dancing, the crooked stocking seam running up the calf of the woman standing next to them, the tiny heads on almost-as-tiny shoulders. She remembers sitting on the floor of Percy's other studio, looking at the swelling thighs and vanishing breasts of his model, and wonders why she had not been so frightened then.

"It really is time to go home, Frank." Lillie propels herself up onto her knees, being careful not to put any weight on the dress.

"Give us a han' then."

She stands up, smoothes the dress, then bends to take Frank's hand. She has helped him this way many times, has picked him up off sidewalks, let him lean on her as they negotiated stairs, sometimes hefted the dead weight of him from the floor into his bed. Maybe it is because she has done it so many times that she has such trouble that night. Maybe, she thinks much later, a person only has so much helping in them, and she has used hers up. When she tugs at his hand, he does not budge.

"C'mon, Frank, you've got to put a little into this too. One, two, three and ..."

The expected lift does not come. Lillie finds herself leaning over farther, scrabbling for a hold in Frank's armpits, her feet dancing for a position that will not involve her trampling his legs. His breath is hot against her face. Hot and boozy. She fights to bury the memories. "Here we go," she says, "on three."

But he does not move on three, or six, or even nine. Lillie begins to be conscious of the few people who are sober enough still to be looking for entertainment. They have gathered around to watch. With a final groan, she manages to get Frank's behind to clear the floor. She takes advantage by instantly shifting her grip lower. Her shoulder is against his belly, her arms around his lower back. She will carry him, she has decided, the way she saw a fireman once carry a man from a burning building. How apt is that, she thinks, just before she loses her balance and falls on top of Frank.

"That's how the women do it in Hollywood, I bet," she hears a snickering voice from above. Her face burns white hot. If she were standing and had seen who said it, she would have ripped his throat out. But she isn't and hasn't, and if she had been, he wouldn't have said it, she supposes. She rolls off of Frank, who has begun singing. It may be something traditionally Irish and sentimental, or it may just be ramblings and the drink. She pulls her knees together, feeling around for the back of her dress and how it is hanging. Then she runs one hand up the velvet draperies to where the edge of the top canvas makes a right angle with the wall. She is out of energy. It is the only way she will be able to stand unless any of the onlookers offers her a hand, which doesn't seem likely. As she pulls herself to her feet, the curtain she is clutching begins to slide, and as it does, the canvases, which are lined up with their faces to the wall, begin to fall backwards into the room, like a house of cards triggered by a false move. Only the canvases that Frank still leans against stay in place.

The room falls silent. Of course it does, thinks Lillie, after a scene like that. Her face burns hotter and she turns away from the crowd. That is when she sees the paintings. They lie now in oblique stacks on the floor, in rows on either side of the still recumbent Frank. Every one of them is of Lillie. Images of her by the dozen. How? Nathan has told her that all of the studies were lost in the fire. Why?

She stops thinking about who is watching, stops thinking about getting Frank up off the floor, stops thinking about what is going to happen to her dress, and she kneels beside the nearest stack of paintings. There are four canvases. The top one is a portrait of head and shoulders so large that her hand can barely cover one eye when she places it there. She slides the canvas aside. Beneath it is a full-length portrait. She is dressed in an evening gown she has never worn. If she had not broken her leg that December four years earlier, she would recognize it as the gown worn by Norma Shearer in the climactic scene of *Pleasure Mad*. Beneath the first is another just the same. Then, finally, at the bottom of the pile, there is a full-length nude. The face is hers, the hair, the neck, the shoulders. The rest might be any-one. She knows it is not her body — the breasts are not full enough, hips too sharp. It might be anyone, and to anyone who does not know her, it might be her. Or Norma Shearer. Of course. All cats are grey in the dark. The market must be huge.

Nathan and Percy have come down off the roof. She senses them before she sees them skulking in the doorway. She only spots them after she has gotten to her feet once more and walked the length of the canvas, listening with some satisfaction as her heels tear it in two places.

"Percy wants to explain, Lil."

"What could he possibly say, Nathan? What could he possibly say?"

She walks out of Percy's studio. The next day she leaves the city.

Iris-out on a train leaving Union Station.

5

Under
Contract

HE LOOKS MUCH older than I expected. I have tried to age him
in my mind. It's not as though I imagined he would look just
the same as he did in the Burying Ground that summer when
I was ten. But still, I'm not prepared for how much older he
looks. The eyeglasses are the same, the face is still round; but
there are lines around the eyes, and the hair has changed colour.
He is on the telephone when I am shown into his office, which
gives me a little time to examine him and adapt to the unexpected change.

"That's the thing with Nick," he is bellowing into the hand-
set as he rustles through a pile of papers on the desk, "He always
has to be the big I am, the big cheese. All he knows about movies
you could stick in a cat's ass." Then after a moment, and much
more quietly: "See what you can do, Morrie. Yeah. Thanks."

He puts the receiver down very slowly. Only when it has come
fully to rest does he seem to notice that he is not alone in the

room. Still, he does not actually look up. "And you would be?"

"Lillie Dempster, Mr. Mayer."

"Who?" Then he looks up from his desk. "Oh. Oh, whaddaya know? That's quite remarkable, isn't it? Al Altman is a goddamned genius, I don't care what anybody says. Turn that way, please, my dear?" I think about Al Altman's ambiguous directions. There is no confusion with Louis Mayer. You know exactly what he wants you to do, right away. "Yes, yes that will do very nicely. Welcome, Lillie." He does not get up and come around the desk. Instead, he stretches his hand across it, still sitting. I have to reach a very long way to take it and shake it. This must be a ploy to get a look down the front of my dress, to size me up in that department too. Later, I will be told that Mayer has extensions on the legs of his chair to make him seem taller. He does not come out from behind the desk unless the office is empty.

"I have some paperwork somewhere here. Or no, Miss Johnstone has it." He hollers his secretary's name. To hear him, you can easily imagine him crying his trade from his father's junk cart in Saint John.

"Mr. Golding sends you his very best, sir."

"Goldstein?"

"Golding. From the Imperial. In Saint John."

"Of course. Golding."

"I can't tell you how grateful I am, Mr. Mayer, giving a girl like me a chance." I am not sure whether to play the hometown card again or not. He has not seemed all that delighted to be reminded of Golding.

"You just work hard for me and the gratitude will take care of itself, okay Lillie?"

Miss Johnstone sweeps in with a file of papers. I make a note that the secretaries are all called Johnstone and the cameramen all Bill. "You have a three o'clock with Mr. Thalberg, Mr. Mayer," she says as she walks out again.

Mayer slides the file across his desk. Once again, I have to reach across to retrieve it. This time he is checking my behind, I suppose.

"I've been dying to know what pictures you had in mind for me," I gush as I subside again into the chair, opening the file.

"Pictures? Oh right, pictures. All in good time, my dear. At the present, the arrangement we have to offer is a little different."

I feel the burn in my cheeks. My eyes blur so I cannot read the letters on the pages in front of me.

"It's all there, in black and white. You'll want to take some time to read it, I know. Unfortunately, I have a three o'clock," he says, looking at the gold watch he has pulled from his waistcoat pocket.

I take my cue and stuff the papers back inside their cardboard jacket. As I get up and start to leave the room, I hear myself murmur thanks. But thanks for what? Reflexes die hard.

"Think of it as an acting challenge, my dear. Far more interesting than anything the moving pictures have to offer right now. Far more. I'll expect you tomorrow at ten, shall I? Ask Miss Johnstone to write you in for then." He picks up the phone. As I shut the door behind me, I think I can hear him asking the operator to get him Al Altman in New York.

The studio car that met me at the station in Pasadena is still outside, the driver waiting just for me.

"I'm not quite sure where ..." I begin.

"That's okay. I've got instructions. You're with the studio now. You don't ever have to think again," the man grins.

"But I haven't signed."

"Playing hardball, eh? Good idea. They've got it, you know, but they hate to spend it if they don't have to. It's just the way they are, those people."

"What people?"

"You know what I mean."

I am afraid I do.

The man drives me to this dark alley behind a hotel. When he stops the car, I quickly start to calculate my defence. He is not a large man, but he is obviously stronger than I am, and he probably has experience in pinning down struggling women. I could scream, but the alley is deserted and nobody could get here in time, even if they did hear me. As he comes around to open the door, I slip off my right shoe. Perhaps if I can aim one quick blow to his skull, daze him long enough so I can race away ...

He hesitates with his hand on the door handle. Maybe he has seen the shoe. Then he goes around to the trunk and takes out my suitcase, which he carries to a green door. He knocks twice. The door opens immediately and an impeccably dressed middle-aged man appears. He nods at something the driver says, and then flashes me a huge smile. A bellhop materializes and whisks my suitcase inside. I put the shoe back on.

"Welcome to the Ambassador, Miss Shearer," the smiling man says when I join him in the doorway. "This way, please."

"Good luck, kid," the driver whispers as he climbs back behind the wheel.

"You'll find our staff are the model of discretion, Miss Shearer. We value the studio's patronage, and anything we can do to make you comfortable will be done. The rear entrance is at your disposal at any time. We just ask that you ring, and one of us will be glad to guide you."

The room they have for me is the size of our whole apartment in Saint John. The bed is larger than any I have ever seen. There are half a dozen white fluffy towels in the bathroom, which has a separate shower and bath. When I take off my shoes after the smiling man has left, my feet sink an inch deep into the pile of the carpet.

I do not open the file of papers until after I have showered and changed. I know now what they have to say. I wonder whether Louis Mayer has told Norma yet about his plan.

My answer comes the next morning in Mayer's office. There are three people waiting for me when I arrive. Norma looks tired. Louis Mayer looks a little younger than he did the day before. The third person, I take for an office boy, but when he doesn't leave, and as the discussion develops, I am able to identify him as somebody called Thalberg who is a relatively big cheese.

"Seven years seems a very long time for a contract," I begin.

"It's standard practice. And you can understand with a project of this delicacy that the studio needs an assurance of loyalty. Besides, there is the six-month clause."

"Doesn't that let you out if you want? Not me?"

"Perhaps you'd prefer a job in our legal department? The pay isn't as good, but you could exercise your obvious talents for —"

"I'm sorry. I don't mean to sound ungrateful."

"Then don't." Thalberg laughs when he says it, but I can detect a note of threat anyway.

"I could really use the help, Lillie." Norma's voice sounds as if it has been drained of all the energy I remember from her *Blue Water* days. Ernie Shipman may have been a son of a bitch to work for, but Hollywood is obviously taking a much greater toll.

I think about the room in the Ambassador Hotel, and then about what it would be like to get back on the train and return to Saint John. I think about how my face stands to be reproduced in newspapers, on posters, and maybe in time, even on the silver screen. It's not exactly what I planned, but so what if nobody will actually know that it's my face and not Norma's they see cropping up all over. I will know. I pick up the pen that lies on Mayer's desk. I sign the contract.

TUESDAY NIGHT IS dance-contest night at the Cocoanut Grove. It is also the night that I begin to work off my newly contracted servitude to Louis B. Mayer. He calls for me in my room at nine, actually comes right up for me. We go down the service stairs, out through the back door. He seems to know the way. A car from the studio is waiting. It is much finer than the Chrysler I was in before. Mayer tells me it is called a Hispano-Suiza. That doesn't mean anything to me, but it sounds foreign and expensive. He instructs the driver to continue down the alley for several buildings before pulling back out onto the street. What a picture it must make, I think — this glorious shiny motorcar skulking down the dingy back alleyways — but then I am surprised to find that the idea already seems far less odd than it would have a few days before. I guess I am adjusting to Hollywood.

We pull up in front of the Ambassador. It is the first time I have seen the front entrance, which may help to explain my slightly open mouth in the dozens of photographs that are snapped as I am helped out of the car. "Miss Norma Shearer, on the arm of Mr. Louis B. Mayer," the captions will say.

Inside, the Cocoanut Grove is a sea of faces and a wall of noise. It's funny how much noise a room full of silent movie stars can make. The music hasn't started yet, and people are bunched around tables, sipping from flasks and sucking on lavender cigarettes. Mayer and I join Irving Thalberg, who is already sitting with Morrie Stempel. Mayer whispers the name to me a split second before I need to know. Thalberg shoots me a cool smile, but Stempel seems overjoyed to see me.

"Norma, darling, you are looking wonderful. I've been so worried. What have you done? Is it a new diet? Cucumbers? What? Don't you think she looks better, Irving?"

"I feel like a new person," I try. Mayer kicks me under the table. "It's part Madam Sylvia and part inner peace, I think." I haven't actually met Madam Sylvia yet — that is Wednesday — but from the homework I have been doing already, I think it is a safe enough bluff.

"How anyone could find inner peace with that old bitch bashing away at them, I don't know. But it's sure worked for you. I've never seen you look better. So ripe, so delicious. Drinks?" Stempel produces a set of four silver flasks, and four small matching cups. "I have gin, scotch and something they say is rum, although it smells more like rotting pumpkin, and there's another one but I've forgotten what it is. I expect they're all the same anyway when you get right down to it."

"Scotch, please," I say automatically. Mayer shoots me a look. "I mean gin. Gin is what I always drink, of course. I just thought if they were all the same that maybe I wouldn't mind the ..."

"Now, if only I can remember which one is in which flask ..."

But I no longer care what Morrie Stempel pours into the thimble he has plonked in front of me because I have spotted Joan Crawford across the room, and I am trying to get her attention. Miss Crawford — born Lucille LeSueur as everyone who reads knows — is one of Al Altman's finds, too, so I am sure we could have a lot in common. Faith told me how Altman spotted Lucille dancing in some speakeasy and offered her a screen test. Her first two attempts failed miserably. The New York people had refused even to send them on to Mayer. Then Altman got her to act naturally — he called it an "ad lib test" — while the camera rolled. She was signed almost the next day and christened Joan Crawford. Norma must know her.

I wave, but there is no response. So I half stand and wave again. Mayer grabs my elbow and pulls me back into my chair.

"What're you doing?"

"Waving at Joan Crawford. I thought —"

"Norma and Joan hate each other," Mayer hisses. He and Thalberg both look at Stempel, who is still trying to remember which flask contains which flavour of hooch. He has not noticed my faux pas. "Dance with Irving. That should be safe."

Out on the floor, I am surprised at how light on his feet Thalberg can be. He seems such an intense, frigid little man. I would have called him Calvinist if I thought that were technically possible. So his dancing is a revelation.

He does not seem prepared to talk, which at first suits me just fine. Then Joan Crawford dances by with a man that I-as-Norma should probably be able to place. They are laughing and chatting.

"I think we should be talking."

"I hardly know you."

"Otherwise other people will. Talk. You would talk to Norma."

"I might talk to Norma. I don't always talk to Norma. She doesn't always talk to me."

"Then maybe you could manage to laugh every now and again. As if I've said something amusing. As if Norma has."

"Or you could laugh. I'm actually quite witty when I get going."

"I thought you were the office boy the other day in Mayer's office."

He laughs.

"There, that's not so hard, is it?"

"Norma thought the same thing the first time she saw me."

"Your turn."

"What?"

"We can do this by turns. Make each other laugh. So people won't talk."

"This is all L.B.'s idea. This masquerade. I want you to know that. I told him it would never work."

"So now you're determined to see that it doesn't?"

"I'm not going to make goddamned rhubarb like some third-rate Gilbert and Sullivan chorus. That's an expression, 'making rhubarb'," he adds when he sees how I am looking at him; "it means pretending to talk animatedly while really saying nothing at all."

"Then let's really talk. Why do Norma and Joan Crawford hate each other?"

"That's easy. Kind of. Joan is sleeping with one of the producers."

"And Norma likes this producer herself?"

I can feel Thalberg's back tighten. "No."

"Then what?"

"She's telling everybody that she's doing it to land parts."

"And Norma's offended by the honesty?"

"Joan's been telling everybody that she's sleeping with this guy so that she doesn't have to hang around for the rest of her life and watch Norma Shearer make the most of her three expressions. That's what she says. Her three expressions."

This is unfair. I know that there are at least twenty Norma expressions. I can do them all. But something in Thalberg's voice warns me not to say anything.

When we get back to the table, I toss back the drink Morrie Stempel has finally managed to pour. I wonder whether Mayer might caution me, but he only smiles as if to say keep it up.

Because I do keep it up, I will not be able to recall exactly when or how the easy social dancing of the evening evolved into an outright contest. Had I been more than a week in Hollywood, I would have known that the same thing happened every Tuesday night at the Cocoanut Grove. Had I been more used to the ways of Louis Mayer, I would have known that in taking me to the Grove he was not only giving me a kind of live screen test as Norma, but was also policing the behaviour of his other stars.

This week it is Joan Crawford who is to reap the boss's wrath. Was she targeted by Mayer and Thalberg before they ever arrived at the club? It would make sense, given what I heard on the dance floor about how Joan was behaving about Norma.

The band is playing a Charleston when it happens. The judges

have begun to tap some of the dancers on the shoulder to eliminate them, but there are still a good dozen in contention. None
of the contestants wear a number. Louis Mayer is in the process
of explaining that this is because everybody knows everybody
out here in this town, when suddenly he stops mid-sentence and
leaps up from the table. Thalberg follows.

Joan Crawford is dancing up a storm. She is a flurry of elbows
and knees and thighs. It is easy to see how she caught Al Altman's
eye in that speakeasy in New York in the first place. Mayer and
Thalberg approach her from behind — not that she would
see them; she is so caught up in her dancing. Mayer stands by
while Thalberg taps Joan on the shoulder. She winds down like
a gramophone, taking almost a full minute before she is completely still. Only when she has stopped entirely does she look
around for the judge who has tapped her. It is easy to see that she
is acutely disappointed to have been eliminated when there are
half a dozen others who are still dancing. The disappointment
turns instantly to fury when she recognizes Thalberg. She raises
a hand. Thalberg steps aside. And Louis Mayer catches the hand
as smoothly as if the whole thing has been rehearsed. He draws
it to his mouth and kisses it, and then, without loosening his
grip, guides it back down to the star's side. Finally, he spins on
the balls of his feet so that he is hip to hip with her, tucks the
hand through his crooked elbow, and escorts her from the club.

"Too much flesh. Showing too much flesh. She'll never learn,"
Morrie Stempel is saying when Thalberg rejoins us at the table.
"Louis never gave away anything for free." He downs the contents
of Mayer's cup, says something about going to the bathroom, and
staggers off.

"Just exactly what was that?"

Thalberg smiles. "Call it a demonstration of Louis's Law."

"Louis's Law?"

"It's a special branch of contract law, I guess you could say. L.B. Mayer made Joan Crawford. The studio owns her, lock, stock and caboose."

Like he owns me now, I think. "So she can only shake that caboose when Mr. Mayer says so."

"Something like that. It's not quite as crude as you think."

"What you mean is it's not quite like he's her pimp? Or like she's his slave." This is not me talking. It must be the effect of Stempel's bootlegged booze. Or maybe Thalberg is just one of those people I feel I can say whatever I want to.

"The movies are all about desire. Get it? Wanting something you can't quite touch. Something you can't quite reach. And you only have the barest hint that it's even out there. The industry is all about controlling that desire, keeping it piqued. That's what Louis Mayer is a genius at."

"So you think it's all right for him to own her body?"

"He doesn't give a damn about Joan Crawford's body. He owns her mystique. He owns the promise of Joan Crawford's body, that's what. And that's what he won't let her louse up by showing her body itself off to any Tom, Dick or Harry."

"Unless they pay to see her in a movie."

"Now you're catching on. C'mon, I'll take you home. I know how to order a trip around the block as well as Louis does."

On the street outside the Ambassador there is a man whom I recognize from the papers as an Italian opera star who has been lured by Louis Mayer to Hollywood to appear in pictures. He stands there unapologetically peeing into a potted palm. Thalberg does not even look twice. Someone will have to explain to me how this man urinating in a flamboyant arc on a public street is more acceptable than Joan Crawford wearing a dress that is too small. But the car draws up, and by the time it has circled the block I am almost asleep.

"Goodnight, Miss Shearer," the smiling manager says as Thalberg guides me up the back stairs. I repeat the phrase to myself as I drift off to sleep in the gorgeous bed. It's not what I came for, but it will have to do for now.

6

Hollywoodland

Fade in on a well-known hillside.

"DON'T YOU EVEN think about it."

"What?"

"What you're thinking about. Don't even think it."

Lillie has not heard the man come up behind her. His voice has startled her, and she supposes she must have made a little squawk that might have sounded guilty. But guilty of what, she wonders. She decides to go on the offensive.

"What do you think you're doing, sneaking up on a person like that?"

"I didn't sneak up. I ... I work here."

"Sure, and I'm Joan Crawford."

"No you're not, but you look like somebody. Anyway, it isn't worth it. He isn't worth it. Whatever it is isn't worth it."

"I don't think I'm following you."

"You're young. You have your whole life ahead of you."

"You don't know anything about me."

"I know, but it's what you say."

"What you say?"

"You know."

"Remind me."

"To jumpers. It's what you say to people like you."

Lillie begins to laugh. "Is that what you thought?"

"Well, weren't you?"

"I came up here for the view. And to think." She wants to tell him that if she were the jumping kind, she would have jumped long ago, years before she ever dreamed of coming out here; but he is a stranger, and what good could come of it? "So, is that your job, keeping disappointed young actresses from jumping off the sign or something? Is it bad for real-estate sales?" The man's jaw drops. "Sorry, that wasn't very sensitive, was it? I'm kind of working on this fast-talking, hard-boiled character right now and things just slip out."

"You're in the pictures, then?"

"Not exactly. Sort of. It's beautiful, isn't it? The view from up here."

"I don't get much chance to look."

"Right. So busy with ... what did you say?"

"I didn't."

"But you were going to."

"I change the light bulbs."

"What?"

"The light bulbs, I change them."

"On the sign?"

"The sign. And the dot."

"There must be ..."

"Four thousand light bulbs. It's a full-time job. They never thought of that when they put the thing up. Thirteen letters and a big dot, all picked out in light bulbs that burn out and have to be changed. To try to sell land. Imagine if you did actually build a house up here; the light from the sign would drive you crazy. Some plan."

"Why don't you let them burn out?"

"What?"

"The lights. Why don't you just let them burn out if you think it's so stupid."

"It's a job, isn't it?" She thinks of her father and the street railway.

They are standing dead centre, under the first "O" of the sign. The man offers Lillie a cigarette, which she refuses.

"This is my break," the man explains.

"When you rescue suicidal damsels and get a smoke. Has anybody ever jumped? How high are they, the letters?"

"Fifty feet."

"Would that kill a person?"

"I don't know."

"Some day somebody will find out."

"Not while I'm working here."

"I'm Lillie," she says. The name tastes strange in her mouth. She hasn't used it for weeks. Just saying it makes her feel dangerous. Louis Mayer would fire her on the spot if he heard her using it now.

"Um. Homer," the man says, extending a hand.

"After the blind poet. I like it." Frank has been careful with parts of Lillie's education.

"After baseball. My folks are from Iowa, like most people around here. Till you people came along."

"'You people?'"

"Movie people."

Lillie finds that she likes being thought of as a movie person. She decides not to tell him she is from Canada. He has probably never heard of it anyway.

"I'd better get back to work, Lillie." He throws his cigarette on the rocky ground and treads on it with his boot.

"They should have called you Sisyphus." Lillie regrets showing off the minute she has said it.

"Pushing that rock up the hill all the time? Light bulbs are a lot less heavy." Lillie gains a new respect for Midwest schooling. "Nice to meet you, Lillie."

"Nice to meet you, Homer." As she begins her descent, she hears the *squeak-squeak-squeak* of metal on metal as he unscrews a light bulb and replaces it with another.

The studio car is waiting where she has left it. The driver, who knows her secret, addresses her as Miss Shearer anyway, and says he hoped she enjoyed her walk. Then, shutting her door and jumping behind the wheel, he speeds off for Madam Sylvia's.

"YOU ARE LATE today, my dear," Madam Sylvia purrs, once Lillie has undressed and is lying on the table. The softness of the voice, Lillie has learned, is usually a reliable indicator of the roughness of the treatment that will follow. It's an inverse proportion. She has been to Madam Sylvia's three times already, on days when Norma is indisposed or can't be found. With each new visit, the voice has grown softer and the pummelling harder. Today, she really has to strain to hear Madam Sylvia at all, and all down her back her muscles tighten in anticipation.

What she has not yet been able to figure out is how Madam Sylvia manages to hit her so hard and so long without leaving a mark. Though Lillie is quick to heal, she has always bruised very easily — she imagines Norma does too — but when she checks in the bathroom mirror after her sessions at Madam Sylvia's, there is only a healthy pinkish glow to the skin. Easier to figure out is that the so-called treatment is not in the least effective. The goal, Norma has told Lillie, is to reduce the size of thighs and buttocks. Although Madam Sylvia faithfully reports reductions to the studio every week, Norma says she has never once measured her, so Norma has taken to checking herself. There is no change, she has reported to Lillie. If anything, her bottom is spreading. Lillie wonders whether she should pass this information on to Louis Mayer or Mr. Thalberg, who are paying huge sums for the treatment. In the end, she has decided to keep the information in reserve for the day when the beatings become unbearable and she needs a bargaining chip.

As Madam Sylvia begins chopping at her right thigh, Lillie tries to make herself go limp, tries to leave her body behind, but it is no good. The reflexes are too strong.

"You are very tense today, my dear." Madam Sylvia always calls her simply "my dear." She has never once called her Norma or Miss Shearer. Lillie wonders now whether that means she is in on the secret too. But if she is, Lillie can't see a point to her visits. As long as she is impersonating Norma and keeping up the illusion that everything is all right in Norma's life by keeping Norma's appointments and making Norma's appearances, the whole thing makes sense. But if Madam Sylvia knows she is not Norma, then the treatments that she insists on inflicting must be for her. And that does not make sense.

Her right thigh feels like it must be glowing white hot. That is the theory behind the therapy, Lillie supposes, that the fat deposits will become superheated and melt away.

Madam Sylvia begins on the left thigh. Lillie remembers how she watched Norma, this very morning, operating on her own left thigh. That procedure involved a safety pin, a medicine dropper and a patch of skin high enough up on the leg that even an unexpected gust of wind would not reveal what had gone on. Lillie wonders whether Madam Sylvia notices the absence of the tell-tale prick marks on her thighs — not on the backs, you didn't do it on the backs, but on the inner surface.

When the left thigh has reached the melting point of fat, the strong hands set about the buttocks. In preparing her for the sessions, Norma confessed to Lillie that this part could be fun if you let it. Lillie has not let it. She does not clench her muscles there. She has learned that only makes the pain greater. But she does tauten her stomach in an effort to keep her pelvic bones from being hammered against the cold marble slab. Madam Sylvia's conversation at this point in the ritual always makes her even more uncomfortable than the pounding.

"The young man's ass, this is what they are all after. This is what they want. The young man must have a taut backside, and the women now too. That is what they all like to look at, these wealthy men, the young man's ass. But in America they like to pretend, so they give these asses to their women. This makes it all right, they think. This makes them men still. Now, Madam Sylvia, she likes the woman's ass on the woman. The boy's ass she does not care about at all, but still she works to make the boy's ass. It is a living. There, my dear. Please to turn over."

Lillie's sense of dread at this command is barely balanced by the joy of knowing it means the session is drawing to a close. The first time, she had wriggled around on the table, trying to turn in a way that the sheet that was always draped across her back might serve to preserve her modesty up front. She had tucked a corner of the cool fabric between her thighs, and held an edge tight to her breasts just as she flipped over. Madam Sylvia had clucked and tutted and snatched the covering away. "You must not be so shy, my dear. We are all women here, yes?" Lillie did not mention that that was what made her so nervous. She only nodded and closed her eyes, praying that Madam Sylvia would be contented just to look without touching. It was at that same moment that she had remembered seeing the word "therapist" etched on a copper plate on Madam Sylvia's door, and realized that if you only inserted one space it would read "the rapist."

WHATEVER PUNISHMENTS L.B. pays for for Lillie's body, he appears to take equal care for her soul. Almost from the day she signed her life over to him, he arranged for her to start going to church. This is on Wednesday evenings, with the heat of Madam Sylvia still smoldering on her skin.

As a rule, the studio does nothing to highlight the fact that Norma is by birth a Canadian. It may be a function of their perpetual efforts to cover up the fact that Mayer was once one too. But there are some convenient coincidences that they do exploit. Aimee Semple MacPherson is one of them. Born Aimee Kennedy on a small farm in Ontario, Sister Aimee lives off the proceeds of her International Church of the Foursquare Gospel in a mansion very near the studio gates in Culver City. In the early years of her ministry at the Angelus Temple, she and the studios had steered well clear of one another, but a scandal in 1926 had convinced both parties that they were in the same business after all. Sister Aimee had disappeared one day and was presumed dead. No amount of searching could locate the body, but her flock went into mourning until a month later when she turned up, dishevelled and a little beaten up. She claimed she had been kidnapped and held prisoner in Mexico. The story soon came out, though, that she was simply shacked up down the coast with a man who was not her husband. It was about that time that the alliance between Sister Aimee and Louis Mayer's studio took shape, and not very long after that, Louis Mayer started planning for Norma to attend the Angelus Temple.

Norma has outlined all of this to Lillie in one of her more lucid spells. She went on to explain the strategy.

"There are two kinds of women they've created for the pictures. You will have figured that out, Lil. There's the Lillian Gishes and the Mary Pickfords. They can't ever grow old. They're all about innocence, and all that hair. If anybody ever thought of them having sex, that would be the end of them. Then there's the Joan

Crawfords and the Blondells ... and the Shearers. We're the bad girls. We have all the fun, and eventually, if this talking thing ever works out, we'll get all the best lines. Like the devil. Now that Sister Aimee has been discovered to have a little of the bad girl in her, they've decided she's a good playmate for me. Louis actually hopes to use the Canadian angle to create a whole new category — the bad girl who is part saint at the same time. He thinks he can sell it because nobody knows what Canadians are really like, and they'll swallow anything he feeds them about us. And I guess that includes you now, too."

From the beginning, Lillie has felt especially uncomfortable about the hypocrisy of her visits to Sister Aimee's church; more uncomfortable than when she is impersonating Norma dancing at the Cocoanut Grove or playing Norma naked on Madam Sylvia's slab. She supposes it is because there is an extra layer here. She is Lillie pretending to be Norma pretending to be devout, faithful or whatever these rip-snorting fundamentalists like to call it. And ordinary people — the rubes, she has heard people at the studio call them — are not the only ones being deceived. God is the butt of this one too. Although Lillie has never been a religious person, the dimensions of this deception somehow make her nervous.

Ordinarily, she tries to arrive quite late in the service. The photographers only show up, if they show up at all, at the end of the evening, as the stars are pouring out of the church, so she can be late without missing the photo opportunities. Louis Mayer would never forgive her that. But she hopes that maybe God takes roll call in the opening moments, so her double hypocrisy might go unnoticed. Usually, she can time her entrance for the offertory hymn, just when Sister Aimee makes her perennial plea. "Sister has a headache tonight," she always says, "Just quiet money please." The bills flutter into the plate like the Holy Ghost flapping around the Virgin Mary.

This Wednesday night, the studio car is really late. God might be fooled, but Louis Mayer will be furious. Lillie pleads with the driver to go as fast as he can, but there has been a colossal rain late in the afternoon — pounding on the dry earth like Madam Sylvia pounds on Lillie — and the roads are in awful shape. They arrive just as church is getting out. Lillie, who is getting quite good at the game of sneaking in back doors, beats it up an alley where she finds a side entrance. As long as she issues forth out the front doors so she can, depending on the emotional temperature of the service, be seen pumping Sister Aimee's hand, or tearfully embracing her fellow Canadian saint-sinner, everything should be fine.

"I wondered what had happened to you tonight."

The voice comes from halfway down the church. Lillie thinks it might be God. Then she recognizes it from earlier in the day. It is the man from the Hollywoodland sign.

"The car was late. What do you mean you wondered?"

"This morning, when we met, I knew you looked familiar."

"I should look familiar. You've probably seen my pictures." Lillie thinks she had better go one step further. "What do you mean this morning? Have we met? I'm sorry I don't ..."

"I knew you looked familiar from around here. I see you here a lot. Lillie, that's what you said, isn't it? Lillie, you told me your name was."

Lillie does Norma looking blank.

"Homer. Remember? With the light bulbs."

"Miss Shearer?" A tiny dapper man from the studio, whom Lillie has often suspected of spying on her for Louis Mayer, appears as if from nowhere. "Sister Aimee is about to get into her car. I'm sure you want to thank her for the service." He sweeps Lillie off up the aisle — like the bride of what? — leaving Homer gazing up at the old rugged cross.

They catch the great evangelist just as her uniformed body-guards are opening the rear door of the Locomobile she uses on Wednesday evenings.

"Norma, my dear."

For an instant, Lillie imagines that Madam Sylvia has possessed Sister Aimee.

"Sister Aimee." Lillie thinks they had better hug, though she hasn't been able to gauge the mood of the stragglers still on the church steps. "What a lovely service. So moving."

"Don't bullshit me," the other whispers in her ear while they embrace. "You missed the whole thing. I hope he was good. I'm going home now to get me a little of that." The hug ends, the flashes stop going off and Sister Aimee climbs into the Locomobile and speeds off.

"She got that car from Cecil B. DeMille, you know," says the dapper man from the studio.

"Everybody gets everything from somebody out here," Lillie says as he helps her into the studio car.

EACH MORNING FOR the next week, Lillie visits the Hollywood-land sign, hoping to see Homer. She knows she mustn't explain, but she feels she might help matters by confusing him further. Her plan is to be Lillie for him once again, and to deny ever having darkened the doors of the Church of the Foursquare Gospel. But Homer doesn't turn up. Each night, she makes a point of looking up at the sign to see the toll his absence is taking. From a distance, though, you can't really tell whether the odd bulb has burned out.

It isn't until the following Wednesday that a voice breaks into her reverie as she sits at the base of the second "O."

"Lady, you can't be up here. This is private property. You're in the way; I got work to do."

"Where's Homer?"

"Who?"

"The man who usually changes the bulbs. Homer. It's his job. He's here every day, you know, changing the bulbs."

"I don't know nothing about that. I come up here once a week, check out the bulbs, see if there's any needs replacing. That's my job."

"But I talked to him last week. He tried to keep me from jumping."

"You were going to jump?"

"He thought I was."

"Who?"

"Homer."

"Lady, you can't be up here no more. I got work to do." His face is very close to Lillie's. "Say, don't I know you?"

"No," she says, and hurries down the hill to where the car is waiting to take her to Madam Sylvia's.

7

Betrothal

We cut immediately to a montage — Irving and Lillie-as-Norma dining and dancing in a series of smart restaurants, inter-cut with neon signs and sunset walks. Finally, freeze on a very close shot of a diamond ring. Then dissolve to a close-up of Lillie-Norma, smiling broadly, though a tear trickles down her cheek.

NORMA'S ENGAGEMENT TO Irving Thalberg comes as no surprise to the Hollywood community. Lillie has not been in California six months when it is announced. The news follows hard on a period of eight weeks when Norma has appeared never to leave Thalberg's side. People do marvel at how the star has been able to maintain her rigorous shooting schedule and such an active social life, but they are prepared to believe anything of their idols these days. If they only knew all, they would be even more impressed that Norma has been able to manage her all-consuming courtship with Thalberg at the same time as she has carried on a full-time affair with the former opera star Lillie had seen peeing in the potted palm outside the Ambassador Hotel.

LILLIE IS IN her room at the Ambassador when Norma comes to tell her the news. She is doing the Dr. Bates eye exercises she has been taught. They are supposed to help keep her lazy eye from straying. Norma has recently managed to master them and is now having considerable success even through long shoots, so it has become necessary for Lillie to begin too.

"You'll never guess."

"Probably right."

"He's asked me."

"Who? What?"

"Irving. He's asked me to marry him."

"When did you see Irving?" Lillie hears the tinge of jealousy in her own voice, corrects. "That's terrific, Norma. Congratulations."

"I could never have done it without you."

This is undeniably true, but Lillie does not bother to agree.

"Give me a hug."

Hugging Norma always sends a shiver down Lillie's back, but she does as she is asked. This is, after all, quite an occasion. She can't resist asking, "What does Mario think?"

"Mario can think?" Norma laughs.

"You haven't told him."

"You're the first person I've told. Except Louis, of course. He already knew, as it turns out. I'm so excited. What a break this will be. I wish I could ask you to be a bridesmaid."

"When will you tell Mario?"

"He'll find out soon enough. It's not like we were ever going to, you know, marry. The thing is, I'm going to be so busy the next couple of days. The engagement party, you know."

"Oh no you don't."

"What?"

"I'm not telling Mario for you, if that's what you think." Lillie loathes Mario, the sight of him, the smell of him. He is the one audience in all of Southern California for whom she has refused to play Norma, and she is absolutely intent on keeping it that way.

"You might like him. He's really rather sweet, and he's great in the sack. You wouldn't have to tell him about Irving right away. You could have a little —"

"No, Norma."

"Okay, okay. I was just trying to do you a good turn. Um. Lillie?"

"What?"

"About Irving. You and Irving, us and Irving. We haven't, um, slept with him, have we?"

"No, Norma, we haven't slept with him."

"Okay, great. I just thought I'd better know before the party and everything."

"There are probably a few more things I should tell you about Irving."

Norma curls up in a tub chair to listen, and is fast asleep by the time Lillie is onto his favourite colours.

IN ANY EVENT, Norma decides that Lillie had better make the engagement party appearance after all. There is so much to learn in so short a time, none of it of much real interest to Norma; and Mario proves more of a problem than she has foreseen. He throws a vase at her when she finally tells him the news. While it isn't a direct hit, one of the shards bounces off the wall and Norma requires four stitches in her left buttock — she was naked at the time. That same night, after Norma gets home from having her behind sewn up, Mario shows up outside her bungalow — it must be 3 a.m. — serenading her with selections from Puccini. It isn't that the residents of the Garden of Allah aren't used to wild behaviour in the wee hours, but they do object to looking out their windows onto a weeping Italian tenor behaving like a fountain cherub in their swimming pool. The following day, Norma is having lunch with Irving in the Dining Room of the Stars — her star is up there on the ceiling and she likes to check on it weekly — when Mario bursts in with a stick of dynamite he has stolen from the contractor who is building him a home in one of the hills. At first, he threatens — in Italian, so most of the diners have no idea what he is saying — to do with the dynamite what he has done so many times with his manhood. Norma, whose affair with Mario has taught her several Italian words for select anatomical areas, squirms uncomfortably in the seat that is already painful for her wounded backside. Then, for a minute, it looks as though he might eat the dynamite himself. Finally, he waves it in Irving's face, lets out a demonic laugh and flees out onto Hollywood Boulevard. It takes all of Norma's resources to concoct a story that will hold water with Irving. She tells him that Lillie was unhappily involved with Mario back in New York, and he frequently mistakes her (Norma) for her look-alike and makes these wild displays.

Lillie is not in the least anxious about the engagement party. It will be a large affair, bustling with people she has fooled from her very first day in California, as well as people she has only more recently taken to deceiving. She has discovered that the more she makes appearances for Norma, the more she assumes control of Norma's public persona. She doubts whether even Louis Mayer really fathoms the slow but enormous shift that has taken place. As for Thalberg, he has been wooing Lillie-as-Norma for more than half the courtship, ever since he mistook her for the genuine article one night and she neglected to correct him. So it is only natural that the Norma he loves, the Norma he wants to marry, is at least one part Lillie.

Handing off the ring poses the biggest challenge. Lillie and Norma can never be seen in public together, and neither of them is sure about what kind of watch is being kept on the back stair-case at the Ambassador. Lillie offers to try to sneak into the Garden of Allah early on the night of the party, but Norma vetoes that idea. Lillie suspects that she has plans with Mario. Instead, Norma contrives to pretend to injure her left hand so severely that it will have to stay wrapped up in gauze bandages for several days before and after the party. Lillie has only to wrap her own hand and no one will be the wiser. She resents the plan because she is sure Norma's real concern is to keep the ring off of her finger at any cost, but it does have the virtue of simplicity. So she goes along with it.

She realizes after she has bandaged her hand that she should have waited until she was dressed. Norma has arranged that she should meet Thalberg at the studio, rather than having him pick her up at home, which would obviously cause problems. When Lillie arrives in Irving's office, she has not been able to manipu-late the buttons on her dress. The first thing she has to do is ask the groom-to-be to do her up.

"I could just shut the door and we could ..."

"Just a few more weeks, baby. I promise it'll be worth it." This is the line Lillie and Norma have agreed upon. Lillie has used it so many times in the past weeks she has almost begun to believe it. But worth it for whom? She imagines Norma, no doubt already making some kind of new and unusual love to Mario in her snug little bungalow at the Garden of Allah. Will Irving Thalberg's famously weak heart be up to the kind of strains that lie ahead for him?

"You drive me wild," says Irving, but he has already begun to button up the dress. "Let's get to that party."

The party is on Palisades Beach Road, in the Santa Monica neighbourhood where Irving and Lillie-as-Norma have already planned to build themselves a love nest. Since he arrived in California, Irving has been kept too busy to learn to drive, so they take a studio car. Lillie catches the driver looking at them twice in his rearview mirror before they have even left the studio. She wonders whether he has detected the substitution. Knowing they are being watched makes her bolder than usual with Irving. Really, she tells herself, she is only doing her job. She cannot think of a better way of convincing the driver she really is Norma Shearer, the fiancée of Irving Thalberg, than to be seen shamelessly spooning with him in the back of his studio car.

By the time they reach Santa Monica, she has had to repeat three more times her mantra about the waiting being worth it, each time with less conviction. When the car doors open, both passengers are flushed and a little out of breath. What little wind they have left is knocked completely out when they pass through the doors of Ocean House.

It is a costume party, although no one has taken the trouble to tell the guests of honour. There was no real need, and the joke would have been spoiled. All of the men have dressed up as Irving Thalberg, and all of the women as Norma Shearer. Under other circumstances the joke would be terrific. As it is, Irving seems to think it's mildly amusing. Lillie swallows back a wave of vomit and hopes that the tears that have rushed into her eyes will be taken as tokens of joy.

The first to greet them is Louis Mayer. He is one of several fat Irvings. There are also thin Irvings, tall ones, short ones, even some daring cross-dressed ones, their hair plastered flat, their breasts even flatter beneath the smart double-breasted jackets. The range of Normas is much less broad — a testament to the Hollywood ideal for women. None of them comes close to Lillie's own virtuosic performance of Norma, but then, each of them has the luxury of having somebody else to be when they go home that night.

"What a clever idea," Irving is saying to Marion Davies who, although it wasn't her idea, is happy to take credit. "Can I get you a drink, darling?"

"The usual, thanks." Lillie cannot for a moment remember what that is.

"You look beautiful, Norma. Not as good as me, of course." Marion Davies has an annoying laugh, but a good heart. "How's the hand?"

"Just a few more days," Lillie begins, and has to stop herself before she adds that it will be worth the wait. She waves to half-a-dozen Normas, and makes for a chair. She is sitting, ankles crossed, feet a little behind to give shape to the legs just as she has been taught, when Irving delivers her drink.

"Are you all right, darling?"

"It's just a little overwhelming, that's all."

"Happy?"

"Blissfully."

Across the room, Marion Davies and two other stars are looking Lillie's way. They do nothing to lower their voices.

"See how she had to find a chair? Look at the way Irving's waiting on her. She's up the spout, you mark my words. Mark your calendars, even better," says one.

"That's an appalling thing to say. Norma Shearer is one of the most wholesome, moral girls I know," snaps Marion Davies, but she still joins in the harsh laughter that follows.

After a couple of drinks, Lillie begins to feel better. The campiness of the fake Normas makes it easy to screen out the disguises and see their wearers for themselves. Irving is most solicitous, asking repeatedly whether she is having a good time. She supposes he is still excited from the car ride and hoping for more on the way home. Although she is tempted, she does not suggest that he could probably have his pick of the would-be Normas in the room to take to bed that night.

Like all Hollywood parties, except those on a Saturday night, this one begins to wind down before ten, but not before Lillie has been called upon to do Norma's famous water-glass trick. This involves balancing a glass of water on her head, easing to the floor in a cross-legged sitting position, and then rising again, without spilling a drop. It took Lillie weeks to master, and cost endless embarrassment over what the chamber maids at the Ambassador must think about all the wet patches on her carpet.

"Oh, I don't think I could tonight. Jitters and everything," she says.

"We'll make allowances. Leave an inch empty at the top."

"I'd really rather not. My hand ..." But then the chanting starts, and several Normas appear around her, each with a glass of water of her own. It is to be a contest.

"C'mon Norma, it'll be fun," whispers Irving, and Lillie knows she must.

Her mind races. Doing the trick perfectly could confirm her as the one and only Norma, which is more at issue than anyone else in the room imagines. Failing, though, could also be turned to advantage if one were to accept the premise that a nervous Norma might not be able to pull the trick off with her usual poise. In this light, it seems a safe enough thing to do.

The glass feels cool on her scalp. She wonders, not for the first time, whether her hair may be thinner than the real Norma's. Her mother, she remembers, used to worry about thinning hair. She closes her eyes and focuses on the idea of the glass on top of her head, the idea of the glass staying on top of her head. She begins to lower herself, imagines all the other Normas in the contest at the same time lowering themselves. How low will they go, she thinks, how low will I? Keeping her spine straight, she crosses her ankles to allow her knees to bend deeper. Her hips and thighs feel as hot as when Madam Sylvia pounds them. Then she feels the floor under her behind. She sits still for a moment, listening to shrieks of laughter as glasses plummet to the floor all around her. Finally, she begins her ascent. The room is silent now. She opens her eyes. She is up. Irving reaches over and takes the glass off her head. He kisses her on the forehead. The fairy-tale prince. She is suddenly glad she is not the trained monkey that Norma has turned herself into.

Suddenly, as Lillie and Irving are smiling at one another as lovers, there is an abrupt cut. No iris-out, no gentle, romantic fade. The film has snapped off in the mechanism the way it does when there is too much stress on it. The screen goes black.

NORMA SHEARER MARRIED Irving Thalberg early in the fall of 1927. It was a huge affair with two dance bands and real champagne smuggled from France. Rabbi Magnin officiated, and Norma was given away by her brother Douglas. I was there, in a huge hat and coloured glasses. If Mr. Mayer found out, I would have been on the next train back to Saint John. Fortunately, he never looks past the front few rows.

8

"___"

MARION DAVIES THROWS a party to mourn the imminent death
of the silent pictures. To a casual observer, it might appear as one
more crazy masquerade ball on Palisades Beach Road, with the
bootleggers' cars there most of the morning and the caterer's
most of the afternoon. The two dance bands began setting up at
four. At five, a truck arrived with the giant ice sculpture, a nude
man proportioned like the Hermes of Praxiteles. He was holding
a dripping megaphone. Man and megaphone will gradually melt
all evening long, in what Marion will repeatedly call a poignant
metaphor — she pronounces the "g."

It may look like a regular costume party, but at this one the
stars come as themselves — the titans of the silent screen; now,
overnight, outdated relics of a bygone era, laughable, pathetic,
still much larger than life, but suddenly ungainly too. Jack Gilbert
is there, tripping over his own feet and slurring what little speech
he can squeeze out. Clara Bow, looking "it" and not "it" at all,

passes out beside the swimming pool and is almost knocked in by the staggering Gilbert. Chaplin holds his hands over his mouth like the speak-no-evil monkey when he isn't sipping or puffing or having something irrepressibly witty to say.

I am appearing frequently for Norma at this time. As soon as the morning sickness began, she went completely underground to everyone but Irving, Louis Mayer and, of course, her trusty double. It is not that the studio has any problem with her appearing pregnant in public; the publicity department leapt on the news. It is the kind of good family story that Hollywood needs that year. Norma herself, though, cannot bear the idea of people getting a look at her distended belly. Irving has tried to persuade her to make an exception for Marion Davies's party. She owes it to all those fading stars, he has said. She is one of the lucky ones who is making the transition easily and naturally. It helps having a producer for a husband and a sound-recording genius for a brother, though he doesn't say these things. Instead, he tells her it is important for morale that she be there, socializing with those less fortunate.

"Lillie doesn't mind, do you Lillie?" was Mrs. Thalberg's response. I do. I hate playing the pregnant Norma like this, but I have chosen one of the trick dresses from my new wardrobe, and made sure I was ready well before the studio car called for me at six. I am living right in the house with Norma and Irving by this time. It eliminates all the subterfuge that used to be necessary in the business of pick-ups and drop-offs. I could easily walk to Marion Davies's, just as I could walk to Louis Mayer's or any one of half a dozen of Norma's friends' and associates' places along that stretch of Santa Monica coast. But now I am supposed to be pregnant and delicate, and for that reason I am driven in a studio car. Anyway, stars don't walk.

Despite Irving's argument about team morale, the guests at Marion's party quickly divide themselves into two distinct and hostile camps. I, as Norma, am lumped with the talkers, standing beside Garbo, who keeps glancing wistfully over to the other camp where Jack Gilbert is becoming more and more vocal, if less and less articulate.

"It's th' goddamn machinery," we can hear him say. "Built to do his dirty work."

An obliging nobody, who, with frightening ease, has penetrated the silents' camp, asks him whose dirty work he means.

"Fuckin' Louis fuckin' Mayer, that's who. Him and that bastard Canadian who he's got running the soun'."

I look away, pretending not to listen, since the bastard Canadian is supposed to be my brother.

"It's all set up for baritones. Who ever set anything up for goddamned baritones?" Gilbert's voice has risen almost to counter-tenor heights. "Sonuvabitch's had it in for me ever since I called my mother a whore. He's got some unnatural thing about mothers, that's what."

I remember the Jewish Burying Ground all those years ago, but Gilbert is not talking to me, so I say nothing. Garbo shakes her head, whispers her excuses, and heads off in search of a drink.

"How's the little mama?"

I turn to see Marie Dressler, whose membership in the talkie club seems daily to be more secure.

"Fine. I'm fine. We're fine." I rest my hands on the pillow that has been sewn into my dress. I've seen Norma do this move a hundred times. Every time I imitate it, my palms prickle and my throat burns. I wish so hard there was something there.

"We're just all so happy for you and Irving. There is nothing like parenthood. Having a little life to mould and shape."

I can't help thinking about my father and our walking trips all over the city for his wrestling matches, moulding a little life. I know I will do better, hope I will.

"Norma and I are very excited." Irving has joined us and managed not to tell a lie, all in one move. It's not technically a lie, at least. I remain silent.

"Think of all the wonders she will know. I know it's a girl because you're carrying so low. And what a beauty she will be. The image of her mother."

Fortunately, Miss Dressler is getting on in years and has always had a rotten memory. A week ago, when she met me at the studio when I was wearing a different dress stuffed with a different pillow, she told me she was sure I would deliver a boy — I was carrying so high.

"The world is changing so fast. You young people and your children will have so much to deal with, so many adjustments to make." She looks longingly over at all the silent stars, so rapidly being left behind, as if she is almost jealous of their fossilization. For them, change is at an end.

"As long as our values stay the same, everything will be all right." Irving has taken more and more in recent days to using words like values and morality, especially in places where people can hear him. "Mr. Hays says ..." I can't bear to hear again what Will Hays says, so I pat Irving's arm in a way I hope might read as wifely and I set off in the direction I saw Garbo go. I remember just in time to turn my feet out a little and slow my walk to the hesitant waddle of an expectant mother.

I find Ramon Novarro sitting on a teak bench in a clump of bushes.

"What is the count tonight, my darling?"

This means not how many days until the blessed event, as it would with ordinary mortals, but how many days before we will have to suspend shooting until after the delivery.

"I think we can manage a few more weeks. Maybe we'll get it all in the can."

"You are an amazing woman, Norma. You seem to have as much energy as you did before all this," he points at my belly. "And fit. You are so fit that you do not balloon out like the others. But you eat enough, yes?"

"I eat like a horse, yes," I lie, making a note to get a pillow that is at least one size larger for next week.

"Sit beside me."

I exaggerate the effort it takes to lower myself to the bench, forearms crossed over stomach as much to conceal the unnatural movement of the padding as to complete the illusion of careful madonna. It is an excellent performance. It makes me sick.

"I am thinking of Rudy tonight." Novarro is never quite able to forget that he replaced Valentino as the Latin lover when Rudy died suddenly and left the position vacant. "Do you remember? When they brought his body back across the country by train? How the women lined up along the tracks?"

This was before my time in Hollywood, but not before Norma's. "I remember."

"But who thinks about him now? Nobody! Me, I think about him, but not even every day anymore. It is the same with all of these. Gilbert, Bow, Chaplin — they will be forgotten by next year. Because they would not speak."

"Or because they could not." I cannot forgive Jack Gilbert for repeatedly blaming his failure on our brother Douglas.

"You are a fan of Mr. Darwin, I see. It is your northern blood."

"Jack Gilbert is a drunk with a sissy's voice. Clara Bow is a dope-head who sounds like a steam whistle going off." I am not being cruel. It's Norma. I have heard her say both of these things.

"So we should run right over them. That's progress, isn't it so? Survival of the fittest."

"Not necessarily the fittest. Chaplin will survive. And Marie Dressler, I think."

"And you, my darling, with your sleek tummy and your lioness's haunches, you who are the fittest of us all, carrying your young so fiercely there beneath your Chanel gown. You will not only survive but you will fuck like a rabbit, peopling our waiting world with many little Normas." He plants a kiss on my neck.

"You're drunk." Only that and the fact, widely known in the film community but not outside it, that Novarro is a man who only fancies other men keeps me from fleeing back to hear the rest of Irving's lecture on morality in the movies.

The movie Norma is supposed to be making with Ramon calls for two scenes that involve swimming and diving. In light of that, Irving and Louis Mayer knew from the moment they went into production they would need me to stand in for Norma. Her years by the coast have done nothing to cure her fear of the water. A few days into production, the throwing up in the morning started. They considered shutting down production and picking up again in nine or ten or eleven months, whenever Norma was up to it. It was Mayer who made the initial suggestion to keep on.

"Are you nuts?" Irving asked. "This is a talking picture. It was different when all they were doing was looking at her, but Lillie and Norma don't exactly sound the same."

"It's not all that much talking. And I've got news for you. Most of them, they're still just looking at her. As long as two lips they believe are Norma's are moving, they'll swear they are hearing Norma's voice."

"Norma will never go for it."

"She'll go for it if her husband tells her."

"I'm not like you, L.B."

"Then she'll go for it when her boss tells her to. I'll tell her ... if you don't have the stones."

I waited for one of them to ask me whether I was willing to do a whole movie without any credit. A talking picture, too. Neither did.

"It will keep Norma in front of her adoring public."

"That's right."

"Too bad we already gave out the story about her being pregnant."

"That's the beauty, don't you see? We get to have her pregnant and working. What an angle."

Norma was furious at first, as I could have told them she would be. She threw a vase at Irving, called me an opportunistic little whore. Irving said it wasn't my idea. I didn't say anything. At about that point, Mayer joined us and offered to double her salary in the picture and give her a small percentage. After that, she began to see the advantages of the scheme.

The bathing scenes were pushed forward in the schedule to minimize the risk of detection. Since the set was closed for these, it was really only the cameraman, the director and a wardrobe girl who might have noticed the flatness of my belly anyway. None of them commented. Whether that was natural reserve or extra pay, I never asked. By the time the picture was in release and they were seeing me frolicking in that swimsuit, Norma's fans would never stop to question how she had looked so slim. And if they did, it would only be more of the stuff that myths are made of.

On dry land, the wardrobe department was challenged "to dress Miss Shearer in a way to minimize the effects of her pregnancy." That was what the official directive from Mayer read. I had to stage a series of tantrums to be allowed to dress myself so neither the hollowness of that challenge or the hollowness of my tummy would be revealed. The director and cameraman were instructed to shoot only from angles that would make the least of the burgeoning belly of the star. Fortunately, both Norma and I had been successful with Dr. Bates's eye exercises. That meant the cameraman's hand was not further tied by the "from-one-side-only" directive that had prevailed in her earlier films.

Posing as the producer Irving Thalberg's wife, I was a perfectly plausible figure at the screenings of the dailies. Common studio policy is to exclude actors from these affairs. The dailies are a time to look hard and critically at what has been shot and to begin to develop ideas of how it can be integrated with what has been shot on previous days. The last thing anybody needs is an actor's ego gumming up the works, begging for retakes. But an actress who is also the producer's wife may claim special privileges. For me, for this film, the dailies presented an opportunity to check my performance — not only of the character, but of Norma. I could then adjust my next day's work to both. It became a delicate negotiation between fidelity in representing Norma herself on the one hand, and accuracy of re-representing a performance of her, on the other. As time went on, the latter began to overshadow the former, as I knew it might.

Amazingly, nobody else seems to notice the shift. This probably has something to do with the fact that the earliest dailies are exclusively silent shots of me in a very clinging bathing costume, swimming, diving and splashing. Not since *Blue Water* has Norma appeared so thoroughly wet on screen, and I can easily estimate how many people saw that. And it wasn't Norma they were seeing then, either. So there exists absolutely nothing in the original's work to compare the imposter's to. What Louis Mayer and Irving Thalberg see on the screen as they watch those dailies is a woman who looks strikingly like Norma Shearer, half-naked and cavorting in the waves. What the half-dozen others who sit in the same smoke-filled room see is simply Norma Shearer as they have never seen her before. From there, it is a small step for them to believe the woman they see the next day flirting with Ramon Novarro is also Norma Shearer, the voice they hear is Norma's voice, and so on. Even Louis and Irving seem to lose sight of the line.

"This picture is going to make Norma's career," L.B. says one evening when he and Irving are having dinner with me.

"I think you're right," Irving answers. Only then do they realize what they have said. They desperately backpedal to qualify the statement.

"Being able to keep up production while she's pregnant has been great. We can keep her in front of the public without a break." Mayer pauses before looking at me. "Thanks, kid."

It is the first time he has expressed any kind of gratitude for what I have done. It also marks the moment when he begins to treat me with the kind of caution you might exercise with a stray cat you have taken in, fed and groomed. A cat you fear might still one day be capable of scratching your eyes out.

The day the final cut is ready to go to Pasadena for a trial run, I wear the largest cushion I can find. The press snaps photo after photo of an immensely pregnant, but still working, Norma Shearer climbing out of Louis Mayer's Packard at the cinema. I sit between the two studio bosses. Each holds one of my hands. Mayer does it in case I should try to make a spectacle of myself, but Irving does it out of real affection I think.

None of us knows until hours later that at precisely the moment we were watching me emerge dripping and svelte from the surf, Norma's water broke and she went into labour.

THE BABY CHANGES everything for Irving and Norma, as babies usually do. We had expected that, of course. I understand it much better now.

Their baby also changes everything for me, as it turns out. Public appearances by me as the new mother quickly prove impossible. The baby will not stop crying from the moment I touch it, and Norma, to my surprise, is reluctant to let it out of her sight anyway. She poses for the press with her tiny bundle of joy. One time, I am sure it is only a bunch of towels wrapped in a receiving blanket, but who am I to cast stones? She even walks a huge-wheeled perambulator around the studio lot on fine afternoons.

With her (my) latest picture going into release, and no projects planned for the immediate future — outside of being a mother, that is — Norma's screen career is on hold. As a result, I find I cease to exist. I sleep late, sneak swims when I am sure nobody is around to see. I keep doing Dr. Bates's eye exercises, though, and I start working on my voice.

One day, Norma catches me at the piano, singing along with a G-Major scale.

"What are you doing?"

"I can't be seen. I thought I might as well work on what I sound like."

"Well don't."

"I beg your pardon?"

"I know what you are doing."

"It's G-Major."

"They should never have let you speak."

"My parents?"

"You know damned well who. I warned them. I told them it would be just like *Blue Water*."

"You quit *Blue Water*. You needed a favour, remember? I gave you your break. You wouldn't be here without —"

"Don't you think I know they reshot half of it? With you? Wasn't that what you wanted all along? Cozying up to Uncle Ernie? Gobbling my leftovers even then."

"I never ... the picture was a flop."

"And so you had to follow me out here."

"How many years later? I did a screen test for Al Altman. L.B. invited me. I thought I was going to have a career of my own, not some —"

"Irving loves me."

I finally twig that this is not only about talking in a movie.

"He gave me a baby. I am the mother of his child. Do you know what that means? Pathetic, second-hand Lillie! You couldn't possibly know what it feels like, but do you know what it means?"

I think of a dirty stairwell a long time ago. The smell of cabbage. A feeling. A fall. But no, I can't know what it means to be a mother.

"It means that you are over, sister. I want you out of here by the end of the week." She slams the piano lid shut.

I pull my fingers away just in time. I want to ask her how she even knows the baby is actually Irving's, but I don't have the energy to play that scene. I know she'll relent before the end of the week — when she starts thinking about how good she's had it with me around. Besides, I have a contract.

Norma does not relent. Louis Mayer opts out of my contract, even though the six-month clause has long since expired. It seems there is other fine print that his lawyers can show me if I really want. Or I can take a large cheque. Irving is at the meeting and says nothing. I decide to take the cheque.

When the car comes to pick me up to take me to the station in Pasadena, the driver is holding a telegram.

"This arrived at the studio for you this morning." He knows my real name but is discrete enough not to use it. I put the telegram in my purse, to read later on the train. It can't be urgent. I know it cannot be from Irving, and his are the only words I want.

As the train pulls out of the station, I spy the man who introduced himself to me by the Hollywoodland sign all those months ago. Homer, he said his name was. He is talking on a pay phone, looking sideways in my direction and nodding his head vigorously. I don't need to hear him to know what he is saying into the phone. He is confirming my departure. Louis B. Mayer is a very thorough man.

The telegram is from Percy. It's funny to think of a deaf man sending a telegram. Frank is dead.

REEL FIVE

Silver
Nitrate

1

Mourning

PERCY MEETS ME at Union Station. He looks older than he should.

"Where's Nathan?" It's not that I've been expecting a crowd or a brass band, but Percy is easier when there's an interpreter around. I try to mime Nathan — his posture, hair, glasses come to mind. Percy looks blank. I mouth the name once again, so broadly this time I can feel the dry corners of my mouth cracking.

Percy's face shows he understands, but he simply shakes his head, which doesn't help much. I have only one bag. Most of my clothes I left in Frank's apartment. I knew they would never work in California. What I wore out there mainly belonged to the studio. Percy's way of offering to carry my bag is to snatch it out of my hand. What does he have to be so angry about? Frank was closer to me than he ever could have been to him. I am the widow, or the heir, the nearest possible mourner. Even with the long train ride I have not worked out exactly what I am, what I feel. Besides, if either of us should be angry, I am the one. As far as he knows, I have never forgiven him for knocking off all those paintings of me and getting rich selling them as portraits of Norma.

In the cab, after I have told the driver the address, Percy hands me a cocoa tin.

"Um. Thanks."

Percy shakes his head, and motions that I should open it.

It makes sense, with the heat and the time it has taken me to get across the continent, that Frank should have been cremated already. But I would have liked to see him just one more time, to say goodbye properly to his shape, his face. A tear runs down my cheek, plops into the dust in the can. I push the lid back on. Percy puts a hand over mine as it clutches all that appears to be left of Frank. There are traces of paint under his nails and in the cracks of his knuckles. Looking at them, I can almost believe I have never been away.

The apartment is locked. Percy shakes his head and starts again for the stairs. There must have been a mix up. Nathan must have the key. I reach up over the door frame. My finger catches on a nail. The spare is still there. I shove it in the lock and let us both in. The curtains are pulled and there is the throat-closing smell of dust as soon as I open the door. I look at the cocoa tin I am still holding in my left hand. The place always smelled a little like Frank. And now it does too.

"Just put the bag anywhere, Percy." It is stupid to speak, I know, but I feel even more stupid just gesticulating silently. I have been planning to stay at the Dufferin until I can find someplace else, but suddenly I think I will have to stay here after all. There will be so much to do, so many things to forget. I wonder whether the rent has been paid.

"Let's get these curtains opened up and let a little air in." The window sticks and I have to use a dirty kitchen knife to pry it open. "If I open the window in Frank's room, we can get a draft going."

Percy just looks at me dumbly. I brush past him to open the bedroom door. It won't budge. How many times did I stand at this door in the months before I went away, trying to open it, while Frank sat, lay, crouched, cowered behind it, refusing to let me in. Sometimes I spent whole nights outside the door, ear to the wood, trying to hear whether he would choke on his own vomit, planning how, if he did, I would splinter the door with the fire axe from the stairwell. But now he is not in there. He is in a cocoa tin on the table. The strange thing is that the lock was a barrel bolt that could only be worked from the inside. So I put my shoulder to the door and push — nothing but the slightest bit of play. Again. Nothing. I look at Percy, who looks away.

There is a knock. For an instant, I think it is coming from the other side of the bedroom door, but then a voice calls out behind me.

"Hello?" I know that I know this man, but I can't place him. "Lillie? Well, well, Hollywood certainly agrees with you."

"Hello."

"Mike. Mike Steeves. I used to play the piano —"

"At the Gem, of course. I remember. For Trifts."

"I'm so sorry for your loss."

"Thank you."

"Percy and I would be happy for you to stay with us at our place while you're in town."

At "our" place? Where's Nathan? But I don't ask. And how has Mike ended up with Percy? Mike, who wouldn't play the piano in the same room where they showed pictures of a naked lady swimming. But this isn't the time to figure that one out. "Thanks, I think I'll stay right here. There's probably quite a lot to do." We both look at the door to Frank's bedroom.

"Percy and I, we went through things pretty thoroughly with the landlord. We took most of Frank's things to the Sally Ann.

There are a few of his things we thought you might want to keep. We have them at our place, for safekeeping."

"What about my things?" I ask, heading for my own room.

"Didn't you take ...? We thought you had ..."

Everything is gone. It is as though I never lived here. The nails that I used for hanging my clothes are bare. Only the worn arcs on the wallpaper, where the clothes hangers rubbed when they swung, hint at what the nails used to be for. My dresser is still there, but the drawers are hanging out, empty. There are no sheets on the bed, and the mattress has been folded over, the more sinister of its stains lost in shadow. I look for a long time at the place in the bedspring where the wad of money should be. Of course we must have spent it all long ago, I think.

"My things. All my things."

"I'm sorry, Lillie. We just thought you must have them. Frank wasn't ... Frank wasn't very well the last few ..."

But I'm not listening. I run for the kitchen, grab the cocoa tin and tug at its lid. I am about to empty the ashes down the sink when Mike catches hold of me.

"What are you doing? How did you get these? Lillie, stop! Stop!" His voice is overtaken by a high-pitched squeal, a sound I have heard once before in my life — the unearthly sound of Percy's pain. "These are Nathan's ashes. Percy carries them around with him. I tell him it's morbid, but he doesn't seem to care."

"He handed them to me in the cab." I am shaking. "I thought they were ..."

"It was his way of trying to tell you about Nathan, I guess."

"When did he ...?"

"At Christmas. He shot himself. It was a Sunday; there weren't any shows at the Imperial. Percy found him. It was awful for him. Obviously."

Should I try to sweep up the tiny mounds of ashes that have fallen on the scrub-top beside the sink, or should I try to comfort

Percy first? Mike takes the cocoa tin from me and pushes on the lid. Then he hugs Percy.

"I hope you'll stay with us," he says.

"Thank you."

"We'll take you and get you settled in. Then we can go see Frank. He's resting at Campbell's. The funeral's tomorrow; that's as long as they would allow. The heat."

When Mike pulls the door shut behind us, I start to reach reflexively to return the key to its usual place, but I stop myself and let it drop instead into my purse.

"Why is Frank's room locked?" I ask.

"The landlord said something about falling plaster from the ceiling, I think. Something like that."

Percy suddenly clasps my hand in his as we start down the stairs.

THE FUNERAL IS thinly attended, which does not surprise me. I wondered whether Faith might make the trip, but I'm not surprised she hasn't. She wrote to me in the summer to say that things were pretty bad with Frank. I suppose she gave up on him. There are some people from the newspaper there, Percy and Mike, and Walter Golding, who tells me on the way into the chapel that he wants to hear all about Hollywood later. Mr. Campbell has discouraged me from viewing "the departed," as he put it. "Better to remember him in life, my dear," he said. So that's what I try to do all through the service. I find it's not very easy. Scenes come back for a moment and I think, yes, I've seen this picture, and then the film breaks and neither of us is there on the screen anymore.

Interment is at Fern Hill. Frank arranged for that, and paid for it too. Just this summer. I do as I am instructed and crumble a clod of earth in my hand before dropping it on top of the wooden box. There will be no quicklime here. As we turn to walk back to the undertaker's car, I hear the gravedigger's shovel start in on the real work. A cocoa tin suddenly seems much more sensible.

Fade in again. There are some things that are too hard to tell any other way. A shadowy streetscape cuts to the hallway outside the apartment, where Lillie stands.

SHE'S GLAD SHE didn't put the key back over the door. Something tells her Percy or Mike would have gone back to claim it. They don't want her in there; that much is clear. She supposes it's out of concern for her feelings. She has to admit she is glad not to be sleeping there after all, on the stained mattress in the airless room, heavy with dust, memories. But she does need to visit once more, to say goodbye to the place, to Frank. To lay some ghosts to rest. So immediately after the funeral, she lies to the boys, says she is going to see Golding with some messages from L.B. Mayer, and heads straight for the old place.

The cabbage smell hits her like a wall when she opens the street door. Some things never change, she thinks, no matter how many times you move. She counts the stairs. The light is burned out on the landing, but she can feel the lock easily enough, and the key slides in. Cabbage gives way to dust. She hears a mouse — no, bigger than a mouse — scutter across the floor. The electric power has been cut off, but the windows are not so dirty as to block out all light. Lillie tries the bedroom door. It still won't open. How, she wonders, could it possibly be locked from the inside? Someone would have to be in there. Is that what Percy and Mike are trying to keep from her, that the place has been rented already? Why would they think she'd care, especially after all her things have disappeared anyway? She pushes at the door again. She has remembered a barrel bolt, but now she is not so sure. There may be a little more play to the door than that would allow. She kneels on the dusty floor, feels the grit through her stockings. With one eye cocked a few inches above the doorknob, she pushes on the door once more. The thin crack of light is broken by a narrow line. She fumbles in her purse and produces a card Louis Mayer gave her before she left for the train. It has his office telephone number, as well as the name of a banker in Saint John he says she can draw on if she's caught short. Pushing the card into the crack between the door and the casing, she slides it up. The hook latch — not a barrel bolt — lifts out of its eye, and she falls forward into the room.

The heels of her hands shriek with pain as they catch her, keep her from landing on her nose. The floor is covered with jagged chunks of plaster. That much of Mike's story appears to be true. Lillie looks up and can see where the ceiling has fallen away around the medallion the gaslight would have hung from when the building was new. Keeping her eyes on the ceiling, worried about fresh-falling plaster, she gets slowly to her feet.

There is no furniture in the room. Frank's bed, the chair, the table he sometimes used as a desk, all have been removed, each leaving four small indentations in the wood where it once stood. There's also a fresher scrape on the floor, directly below the spot where the ceiling is the most damaged. Looking up, Lillie can see the beam through the broken plaster. In the dust that coats its sides, she sees the line of clean wood. They took the rope down, she thinks after a minute of staring at the beam.

She backs out of the room, rewinding the film to the moment before she flipped the latch, wanting to forget everything after that moment. In front of the door, she kneels again, carefully balancing the latch on the card from Mayer while her left hand closes the door. She lets the card slip down the crack and hears the hook fall into its eye. She hasn't decided yet whether to tell Percy and Mike that she knows. She decides to stay kneeling, feeling the pull in her thighs, the bite in the small of her back.

It's a pitiful attempt to match the pain Frank must have felt, she knows, but nevertheless an attempt. An atonement. Why should she atone? It's stupid, but there it is.

Through the apartment door she can hear someone on the stairs. That's when she realizes she has left it open. Whoever is out there might see her here on the floor and think she is praying. That would not do. She gets up quickly, turning as she does. She hears a door somewhere else in the building. No one. Just in case, she shuts the apartment door. Then she sits on the bed. Her bed. She has to unfold the mattress first. That's when her fingers discover the loose basting along one of its seams. She knows this mattress intimately, she laughs to herself, though it isn't funny. The stitching is new. Once more she sinks to the floor, thinking she has made up in this one afternoon for decades of not kneeling. The stitching gives easily, opening a gap she can work both hands into. From the moment she saw the rope mark on that beam, she knew there must be a piece of paper somewhere.

It is several pieces of paper, folded together in half and then again in thirds. Before she unfolds them and smoothes them in her lap, she holds them to her nose. They smell of Frank. Or is it mattress? She has no way of being sure. She is surprised to find the smell comforting.

The note says he has confidence she will find it, that she'll know where to look for it. He apologizes for spending what money he had left on the plot in Fern Hill, but calls it blood money and says she'll be better off without any of it. Then he goes all the way back to the war.

"*It was supposed to be over by Christmas. That's what they said at first. The battles were to be over in hours or days. It's what we printed. But the battles dragged into weeks and then months. For a lot of the soldiers, it was over pretty quick. I don't know why I expect you to believe that actually made it longer for us here at home. But it did. We began to think it would never end. Boat load after boat load of young men had been fed to it, and still it was hungry. But you know that. You lost Patrick and Mike. People lost heart. The newspapers had to try to keep them from doing that. It was our duty. We had to write the stories that kept their spirits up. But at the same time, we couldn't say too much. There was a lot we couldn't print for fear it would give Fritz the advantage. So we printed good-news stories without many details. And we stayed silent on the bad-news ones. I was actually happy to do it. It seemed like the right thing, under the circumstances. It was a way I could help, even if I was not over there fighting. Then came 1918, in what seemed the darkest days of the war, and the Spanish Flu. Here was a bad-news story that the public really needed to hear. People needed to know what to look for, what to do if they got sick. People needed to know not to gather together in crowds. But the problem was that we couldn't let Fritz know that it was happening to us. For him to know might have given him an advantage that we would never be able to win back. So in the spring, we told ourselves there was a high incidence of pneumonia; nothing to write about. Nothing to worry people about. In the summer, the numbers went way down. It looked like it had passed. As long as nobody read the Spanish newspapers and made connections, everything would be all right. The Spanish were non-combatants, so their newspapers printed whatever was actually happening. Eight million Spanish people had the flu in the spring of 1918. But as far as the public was concerned, nobody had it here. That was my work, keeping it out of the paper. When it hit again in the fall, I knew about it before most people. It was my job to know and not to tell. Not even the people I loved. Your parents were some of those people, Lillie. I couldn't tell them. No, that's wrong. I did not tell them. And so you got sick. But you were young and strong and you recovered. Then they got sick and we had to watch them die."*

She turns the page and reads how Frank has come to believe that he is guilty of murdering her parents. But not for the obvious reason; not because he followed the censorship rules and did not warn them. It's for what happened night after night in their first apartment. The thing that Lillie came to tell herself was the price of belonging.

"Their deaths gave you to me, you see. And I think that was what I wanted all along. What I wished for. Of course, I told myself at the time that I would raise you like my own child, that I would be the father you had lost, an even better father, all of that. But you weren't a child. Not really. At least, I couldn't see it after a few days. I suppose losing them like that made you grow up very fast. Which was how I told myself that it wasn't so bad. We both needed to belong to someone. I loved you always. That's what I told myself. That's how I explained it to myself every night I left you shivering in your bed. 'Influenza' — I think I told you what it means in Italian. Not warning your parents was nothing in itself, relatively speaking. But not warning your parents so that I could have you, that was the crime. That was murder. And that is the offence I stand at the bar to answer. And may God have mercy on my soul."

Lillie folds the note up again. For a moment she thinks about stuffing the bundle back inside the mattress, but she realizes that would be as useless as walking backwards out of Frank's room. She pushes the papers into her purse instead. Maybe later she will burn them. Then — she doesn't know why — she lies down on the bed. Her hand finds its way inside the ticking once again, and she brings out a dog-eared square of cardboard. "Miss Lillian Dempster," it reads, in fancy script. It is the presentation card for the gala screening of *Blue Water*. She lies there for a long time, staring at the words and thinking about what they mean.

We iris-out slowly. Afraid of the black screen.

THE NIGHT AFTER we bury Frank, I go with Percy to the Imperial. Mike is working there now. The orchestra has been replaced with a Wurlitzer. Mike plays the organ like he played the piano at the Gem, responding deftly to every subtle shift in mood. He also controls the machine's dozens of traps with his feet. He has a pedal for a car horn, a pedal for a steamship whistle, one for bugles, even one that does footsteps. He still prefers the music, but Golding insists that audiences want the effects — it makes it more real for them to hear birds twittering in a country scene, even when there are no birds anywhere in sight on the screen. The main feature is a movie called *Love* that is supposed to be a rewrite of a Russian novel. Percy is enthralled by Garbo, and even more fascinated by Jack Gilbert. I wonder what he would think if he could hear Jack Gilbert's whiny nasal tenor. After the third reel, I get bored and go to find Golding.

"When will we be seeing you up there, Lillie? Or are you waiting for these confounded talkies to really take hold before you make your debut?"

"Oh, I'm not in Hollywood to act, Mr. Golding, I'm more of an office clerk out there." I have not told anyone that Louis Mayer sent me packing and ordered me not to come back. I let them think I came back for Frank.

"Personal assistant to Norma Shearer is what I heard. That's better than some old office clerk. How is she, anyway, Norma? She's tried one of those talkies, hasn't she? She was quite a gal."

I realize then how long I have been away from Saint John. When I left, nobody who had been involved in the failure of N.B. Films Ltd. could bring themselves to name any of the people Ernie Shipman had brought to town. Not even Norma. Golding had shown some of her films, of course, but nobody, from newspaper reporters to ushers, had been permitted so much as a whispered acknowledgment that she was the one-time star of *Blue Water*.

"She still is quite a gal, Mr. Golding. She's married to her producer. They have a baby."

"I read that. They say the christening's next week. I bet you can't wait to get back there for that. Oh. Sorry, I didn't mean —"

"Any disrespect to Frank, I know. Don't worry, Mr. Golding, I know you didn't. Truth is, I've never been much of one for weddings and christenings and all that anyway." I think about that for a few minutes. "Mr. Golding? I have a favour to ask."

2

Cut

IT IS DAMP in the basement room where I go to work each day in the months that follow, splicing film for Walter Golding. There is a natural spring they discovered in excavating for the building fifteen years ago. The builders drilled a well to tap it for utility water in the theatre, but that didn't eliminate the creeping damp. In winter, I imagine I am in a lonely Scottish castle like the ones my mother used to read about. In summer, it becomes the steam room I visited once or twice after Madam Sylvia's.

Mostly, I work alone, doing routine repairs, preparing the latest films for showing on the Imperial's equipment, preparing them for return to the distributor. I find I like the monotony of it. And I love working with the film so directly, feeling it as a material, tangible thing I can actually run between my fingers. A thing I can control. It reminds me of learning about the glass plates with Isaac Erb. In time, I stop missing being out in front of the camera.

On Saturday mornings, my solitary routine is interrupted when Mr. Golding and I put in several hours with a stolid, pearl-necklaced woman who seems to have an endless collection of mannish hats. Mrs. A.C.D. Watson. First thing, Golding will screen the coming week's centrepiece film. The theatre is empty of all but the three of us. I am usually dying for coffee, but Golding doesn't hold with caffeine, and the doyenne doesn't seem to need any kind of fuel whatsoever. Mrs. A.C.D. — I never found out her real first name — makes notes as the film runs, asking Golding from time to time to give her readings from his watch. Then we move to the basement where I hand crank the film from supply reel to pick-up, trying to find the sequences that correspond to Mrs. A.C.D.'s annotations. When I find one, Mrs. A.C.D. has me make two marks with a wax pencil. Then I'm told to cut out whatever is in-between, splic- ing the ends back together once I have performed the surgery. The excised strips are clipped and hung, carefully marked. At the end of the week, I will be expected to insert them back into the film before it is sent back to the distributor.

The first Saturday of this strange procedure, I must have looked at Golding for approval with every cut. It wasn't long, though, before I learned that whatever Mrs. Watson said was as good as law. At least while she was in the room. Golding told me, after we'd been at it for a couple of weeks, that it simply wasn't worth arguing. Mrs. Watson was part of the Catholic League of Decency and very well-connected in the city. If she said a bit had to go, then it simply had to go.

This particular day we are cleaning up a film called *The Girl from Rio*. I have a hunch that this could be really interesting because the picture features Walter Pidgeon, and Mrs. Watson was Pidgeon's first childhood drama coach. I dare to hope that the crusader, faced with a choice between cutting her beloved Pidgeon and for once leaving a piece of questionable morality in a film, might do the right thing and leave the film alone.

"He was a lovely young man, Walter," the old teacher has told me repeatedly while I was setting the film up on the projector. "An upright, moral young man. And such a voice."

I didn't bother announcing that I had heard him sing the national anthem once at the Opera House on a night when the electricity failed. I knew I could not pretend to be in the same league as she was.

"I wrote to the New England Conservatory when he went, you know, I wrote them that they were getting the finest young talent to pass through my hands. They knew me in those days; that counted for something."

"I'm sure they know you still," Golding crooned.

"I saw him on Broadway a few years ago. *The Puzzles of 1925*. Silly stuff, really, but I enjoyed it. And Walter invited us for supper afterwards. Mr. Watson insisted on paying, of course. Imagine the boy inviting us for supper on an actor's salary. He was always unselfish like that."

"Ready when you are, Mr. Golding, ma'am," I call out, anxious to stop the gush.

"Roll it!" Mrs. A.C.D. intones.

Every time I hear her say it I have to suppress a giggle.

The opening sequence has been made in full colour — very expensive, Golding has been quick to tell me, as if I don't already know. I have never actually seen what all the fuss is about, though. If movies were meant to be in full colour they would be stage plays is what I think. I feel sure that other people will see this eventually. Maybe for musical pictures the colour might be an idea, but not for serious films.

Mrs. A.C.D. is scribbling furiously throughout the opening sequence. The attractions of Rio de Janeiro, especially in full living colour, are obviously deemed unsuitable for a pious Saint John audience. Even after the film descends to black and white,

Golding is being asked for time readings every few minutes. In Mrs. Watson's world, it seems, women like Lola the cabaret dancer mustn't exist. Or if they do, they are certainly not the kept woman of the most powerful man in Rio. I think for a minute about how simple such a world must be.

In addition to being the kept woman, Lola is lusted after by her dancing partner, a greasy man named Raoul. Mrs. Watson breaks her pencil and has to fish another one out of her reticule. There are moments when the dancing surprises even me, in spite of my not-exactly-sheltered experience of the Cocoanut Grove. It makes me wonder how much longer Will Hays will be able to keep up the charade of protecting public morality when his office is letting films like this through its net in return for a fistful of dollars stuffed into the right hands. Even the studio bosses' pockets can't be that deep.

When Pidgeon finally appears on screen it is like a cold shower. The English coffee trader he is playing, with his stiff upper lip, opens Lola to a whole new way of conceiving of relations between men and women. Mrs. Watson's hand is stone-still for nearly twenty minutes. She starts to write something at the moment when we learn that Pidgeon's character has a fiancée back home, a fiancée he is obviously betraying as he befriends Lola; but she apparently thinks better of it after a moment, and she sits back to watch the picture through to its smug conclusion in the triumph of true love over the evils of abused power, lust, envy and sexual dancing.

In the basement after the screening, I wonder just how rich that triumph will appear to be by the time I have finished making all of Mrs. Watson's cuts. Rio will seem like Sunday school. However, I don't even bother to look over at Golding as I locate the bits as instructed, mark them, cut and splice.

Mrs. Watson chatters on about her beloved protege as we work. How he worked so hard at his paper route and at his father's store in Indiantown as a boy. How he flourished at Saint John High School, which wasn't easy, following in his brother's footsteps. How it was as a singer that everybody thought he showed most promise, but how she, Mrs. A.C.D., had seen something more in him. How he had not been happy at the university, and had enlisted. How he had been pinned between a pair of gun carriages during training and spent most of the war in an infirmary. I think of Patrick and Mike, pinned between heaven and earth somewhere in Flanders, their graves never properly identified. As the crone drones on about how Walter remembers to send his old teacher a card every Christmas, I am suddenly struck. Who in the world would have been able to wax this eloquently about my childhood, about Lillie Dempster's childhood? Who could have gone on in this "I knew her when" kind of way if I had managed to make it on my own in the pictures? And what would they have said? Or would the studio have had to make it all up? Luckily, it no longer matters.

By noon we are finished. Twenty-five strips of film dangle from the wire that I have run across the room. Dead birds.

"It's all right, Mr. Golding," I say as the boss reaches for the freshly cut print. "I'll see that it's all ready for Monte in the booth."

Mrs. A.C.D. always shakes my hand when we have finished our butchering. I always wipe it once the woman is out of the room.

"Till next week, my dear."

"Yes ma'am."

As soon as I hear the door at the top of the stairs swing to, I go to work. I know that Golding must be aware of what I do, what I have been doing now for weeks. We never talk about it, but he sees the results on the screen. I am always very careful to keep the wire festooned with the right number of strips of film, to preserve the illusion, just in case we have a surprise mid-week visit from Mrs. Watson.

In a steel cupboard in the southwest corner of the room —
symbolically pointing towards Hollywood, I like to think — is
a stack of canisters containing old films in various stages of
decay. Some are stray reels from multi-reel features that apparently nobody ever missed when the rest were sent on to their next
engagement. Some are prints that Golding was left holding when
their distributors went out of business or decided to pull the film
and didn't want the expense of its return. This graveyard provides
me with the dummy strips I need to undo the brutal excisions of
our Saturday mornings.

The Girl from Rio presents a special problem because of its
early coloured sequences. I know that all of the canisters on top
contain ordinary black and white footage. Probably, it doesn't
matter. Probably, Mrs. Watson will not happen by through the
week to check on the dead birds. She never has. And I know that
Golding won't care. But I have come to take pride in my work,
even in its more deceptive aspects, so this particular day I decide
to dig a little farther down in the pile, hoping to find some tinted
prints. Anything more than a few years old is almost certain to
have used tinted stock at least somewhere. It's not true colour,
but it will pass. I only hope that the film won't have started to go
gummy the way it eventually does.

That is when I find the canister.

3

Not Kosher

THE INVITATION TO dinner at Walter Golding's flat comes as a surprise. I have, of course, met Mrs. Golding on several occasions, even carried on whole conversations with her, but I have never thought of my relationship with her or her husband as anything that you would call social. I would hesitate and make up an excuse, only I do not think that bosses usually invite their workers over for supper in order to fire them, so I accept, and, for the occasion, I even break out one of the Norma dresses I stole from the studio.

The surprise at being invited is nothing compared to the shock when Golding opens the door and ushers me into his parlour. There, perched on the upright Victorian furniture, are two men I never expected to see again except in the newsreels.

Mayer is the first to greet me. "Lillie, my dear, it has been too long." Hardly what I would expect, given the final exchange we had when he cancelled my contract, but there isn't time to think much about that because now Irving is on his feet too.

"Lillie." And he takes my hand between both of his. His eyes look wet, I think, but then I recall that he suffers from allergies.

"Mr. Thalberg," I say. He goes on holding my hand. I want him to stop. I hope he never stops.

I'm dying for a drink, but I know I will be out of luck here. Baptists. Now I am sorry I decided not to take a drop of Dutch courage before coming over. I was afraid Golding would smell it on me. And I wasn't expecting the ambush from Hollywood.

We go in to supper almost immediately. Golding insists that Mayer sit at the head of the table. Why do I feel sorry for him? I end up beside Irving. Good. We won't have to make eye contact.

Mrs. Golding takes the lid off a tureen of soup and that is when I begin to relax. I will not be the only one in agony tonight.

"It's clam chowder. I make it with milk, the New England way. I hope you like clam chowder. Walt and I thought we should have something local."

Both Irving and L.B. mutter that they are very fond of clam chowder. I can see the tiny beads of sweat forming on Irving's brow. Milk and shellfish. Ouch.

I ask Mrs. Golding where the clams are from.

"Mispec, dear. I always get the Mispec ones when I can."

"That's out the other side of the harbour," Golding supplies, for Irving's benefit, I suppose. Mayer, as a local boy, might reasonably be expected to know the geography.

"Near St. Martin's?" Irving asks.

"Not very. Well, along the way. If you went along the coast. St. Martin's isn't for clamming. Rocky." Golding's sentences grow shorter as he gets increasingly involved with his soup.

"Do you know St. Martin's, Mr. Thalberg?" says Mrs. Golding, who has put her spoon down. Her people must be from there, I think.

"Just the name. Louis tells me there's salmon fishing. A brook or something."

"Are you a fisherman?"

"No."

"Irving likes the idea of it," says Mayer. "There's not much fly-fishing where he grew up, eh Irving?"

"I know a fellow with a cabin out there. If you're interested."

"You sure do like your saints up here." Does Irving know what a funny thing this is to say to these Baptists? "St. Stephen, Saint John, St. Martin's."

"Who was St. Martin anyway?" This is Mayer, joining Irving in a desperate effort to divert attention from the mounting piles of wizened clams they are leaving at the bottoms of their bowls.

"I actually read up about him, if you can believe it. I was curious too," Irving carries on. "He is supposed to have been a Roman soldier who divided his cloak in two to clothe a stranger." Why is he looking at me when he says this?

"On the farm, when I was a girl," says Mrs. Golding, "St. Martin's Day was the day we slaughtered the livestock we weren't going to keep over the winter."

"You grew up on a farm?" asks Irving, the same way he might ask someone if she was from Mars.

"Yes, but you needn't worry, Mr. Thalberg, the pork we're about to eat came from the City Market. From McArthur's. Walter, would you help me clear?"

"I'll help, Mrs. Golding." I leap to my feet and grab Irving's and L.B.'s bowls, holding them close to my belly so the Goldings can't see the remains. In the kitchen, I quickly scrape the colonies of clams into the garbage and shut the lid. Mrs. Golding does not comment. Perhaps she is more sensitive than I imagined. Or more blind.

Over the main course, Golding regales us with the story of how he persuaded the Keith-Albee chain to let him put an orchestra into the Imperial when it opened.

"I tried it at the Nickel first, of course. That was the old

Mechanics' Institute up on Carleton. We'd been presenting a vaudeville slate, with the pictures between the acts, and something struck me as wrong when the pictures came on."

"It was the silence," Mrs. Golding chimes in. She has performed this story with him hundreds of times, I expect.

"Exactly. The silence. One tinny piano — when we could even find somebody to play along. It was no match for the scale of the pictures. So I hired an orchestra."

"And when the Keith-Albee folks wanted Walter to run their new house, he said he would, on condition they'd let him have an orchestra there too."

"They said they'd let me try it out. Now they have house orchestras in all their theatres."

"They were never meant to be silent, the pictures, that's what Walter says."

"And that's exactly what we're thinking in Hollywood more and more," Mayer says. "Warner's got the jump on us, but we're catching up pretty fast, aren't we Irving?" And he tells them about the latest experiments with matching sound to picture. It's definitely the way of the future. They have an engineer at the studio, he tells them, a man called Doug Shearer. He's a Canadian too.

From there, the conversation inevitably shifts to Norma.

"It's a shame you couldn't have brought her, Mr. Thalberg," coos Mrs. Golding, oblivious to her husband's tiny shakes of the head. "What a wonderful career she has made for herself. And to think that we had her here all to ourselves that summer they made that picture out of Mr. Wallace's story. If only we had known."

Neither man takes the bait, and it looks as though the subject will drop.

"*Blue Water*, the picture was called. I don't suppose you've even heard of it. It never really took off. The producer was a man called Shipman. You probably don't know him. He did quite a lot of work in Canada. He wasn't a very nice man, as it turned out. Not a very nice man at all."

I wonder whether the Goldings are still hurting from the loss on their investment.

"You were involved in that picture, too, weren't you my dear? I'm sure I saw your name on the list of stockholders. Along with that Mr. Rhodes from the paper. A shame about Mr. Rhodes. How did he pass away again, Walter?"

Golding offers to help his wife in the kitchen. He is a good-hearted man. Merciful. While they are gone, I make myself look directly at Irving for the first time. He looks down at his plate. All three of us laugh. I pile their uneaten pork beside the potato I have barely touched.

When the Goldings return, they talk about the weather while I cut, shovel and chew pork.

Dessert is an apple pie, to just about everyone's relief. Although there is no coffee to retire to, the three men and I nevertheless repair to the parlour while Mrs. Golding finishes up in the kitchen. She says I can't help her. I wasn't going to offer.

"Speaking of *Blue Water*..."

I am surprised that we still are, and I wonder why Mayer, who so obviously did not want to discuss it at supper, would bring it up again now.

"Yes, right," Golding begins. "Lillie, Mr. Mayer and Mr. Thalberg are on a bit of a hunting expedition."

"Not fishing after all?"

"We're looking for prints. We're looking for prints of *Blue Water*."

"You're thinking of re-releasing? Have you seen it? It's not very —"

"We want to destroy them." Mayer's voice is a little loud. We all pause to listen for Mrs. Golding's reaction out in the kitchen. Nothing. She has not heard. I am not sure why that is so important.

"What makes you think there are prints here?"

"Just one. We have traced every last one of the others, we think."

"And looked after them."

"It has been quite a job."

"I bet it has."

"We think there's one that never left Saint John after it was shown here back in '24."

"But what about ...?"

"Norma wants the picture gone. This was her idea in the first place."

I can't completely believe that, though I bet she is on board now.

"The thing is," says Golding, "I just can't recall what happened to that print. I kind of thought it hung around in the basement at the Imperial. A reel or two anyway. I thought I remembered seeing it there a couple of years ago. But I guess I must have been imagining things. Were you there in '24 for the screening?"

I say I think I must have been there. I don't add that I was unannounced.

"I was in shock at the time," says Golding. "We all were, I think. I know I wanted to bury the picture as deep as I could. But I simply can't remember what I actually did with that print."

"You've checked the boneyard?" This is our name for the pile of rotting films in the cabinet in my workroom. I want to be sure.

"Just this morning. Not a trace."

"Then I guess you're out of luck, aren't you Mr. Mayer?" I say. "Or in luck. But I'm not quite clear about one thing."

"What's that?"

"The question of ... ownership. You tell us you want to destroy all traces of a film that doesn't really, in fact, belong to you. Is that right?"

"It was Norma's film. She starred."

"It was Ernie Shipman's film." I can barely bring myself to utter his name, all these years later. In my head, of course, I am saying it was my film.

"Technically, I suppose it really belonged to N.B. Films Limited," notes Golding, though he does not follow up after Mayer sends him a withering look.

"Quite a lot of people gave quite a lot of themselves for that picture. I'm not so sure Norma has the right to just ..." I am in fact damned sure she doesn't.

"But Norma's career. Think what it could do to her. L.B. needs to know that there are no prints remaining out there in circulation anywhere. Nothing that could embarrass the studio." Irving looks down as he says it, unwilling to meet my gaze. Coward.

"I'm not sure I understand why you're telling me all this."

"We thought you might know if there's a print somewhere. You and some of your friends were stockholders, Walter tells us. You don't know if any of the men might have, perhaps ...?"

"Frank and Nathan are dead, and I never heard Percy say one word about it."

"Well that is that, then. We just thought we should ask, didn't we Irving?"

I can't believe how quickly the matter is resolved in Mayer's mind. That is what makes him so successful in the business. It is how the industry works too, I suppose, erasing its memory as it goes. I think for the first time in years about how quickly a little white dog was replaced after David Hartford ran it over.

4

Damsel

WHEN IRVING THALBERG appears the next day in the low door-way of my basement workroom I almost slice my finger off.

"Sorry," he says.

"No, I just wasn't expecting ... I don't get that many ..."

"I can't imagine why," Irving says as he looks around. "So this is the dungeon you have consigned yourself to."

"I like to think of it as a lonely tower. That makes me a princess, in case you were wondering. And I don't think of it as having consigned myself."

"Then who's the ogre? Louis? It certainly can't be that sweet Mr. Golding."

I bite my tongue to keep from saying Norma. "Sometimes, I think it's Mrs. A.C.D."

"Who?"

"A worthy lady in town. Wears big hats. Protects the public morals."

"Sounds like Will Hays."

"No, she's actually serious about it. We spend Saturday mornings down here, bowdlerizing people's work."

"'Bowdlerizing'? Wow."

"I have a lot of time to read. What else am I going to do?"

"Come fishing."

"Right."

"I'm serious. To St. Martin's. Golding has spoken to that friend of his."

"You don't fish."

"I do scout locations. I hear it's breathtaking."

"You don't drive."

"That's where you come in." Why am I hurt by this? "I know that Dieter let you drive sometimes out on the coast." Dieter was my regular driver. Sometimes, he would let me take the wheel out on Pacific Palisades. I liked to keep in practice. The big studio limousine was much more fun to drive than Isaac Erb's little jalopy.

"What about L.B.?"

"He's going out to some burying ground. His mother."

I hear the *chuff-chuff-chuff* of a gramophone. "I don't work tomorrow. I guess we could go. I could pack a lunch."

THE CAR IS a fairly old McLaughlin. Irving has arranged to hire it from a place on Waterloo. It may even be the place Fred Trifts used to run. He picks me up in a cab before nine. The man at the livery looks skeptical when Irving announces that I will be driving, but the wad of bills Irving waves at him seems to calm him. I am glad the city part of the drive is mainly downhill. I could never completely get the hang of the clutch going uphill.

On the way, we try to talk about the scenery. Irving laughs when I point out that it's mostly trees. We avoid talking about Hollywood, the studio or Norma for nearly an hour. Then I make a comment on how loud the car is, and Irving launches into a speech about sound.

"It's opening up whole new horizons, Lil. Not only dialogue. Imagine being able to watch a car drive across the screen and hear it at the same time. Not just some klaxon from a trap on a Wurlitzer. It puts you right there, doesn't it? It is just like being there."

"I still prefer to make up the dialogue in my head. I even feel a little sorry for Jack Gilbert lately."

"I'm not saying that some people aren't going to be left behind. But you know, that's business." He looks pained the minute this escapes his lips. I remember this is one of the things I like about him: the way he always thinks about what he says, even if it is after he has said it.

"Norma is fully talking now?"

"It's funny. She has come to sound just like you."

"She couldn't." Then I realize she has probably had to. I got in there early enough.

"I wasn't always so sure about your faces at first, you know, but the voices, I always knew your voices apart right from the start. Now I can see how different the two faces really are, of course ..."

We come up over a hill and the Bay of Fundy fills the windscreen, glittering blue to the horizon.

THE CABIN IS perched well above the road, and we have to scramble up over loose shale that breaks off and scutters down in our wake. Irving is no help carrying the picnic as he insists on bringing his over-sized briefcase out of the car, even though I tell him it will be perfectly safe. I have packed devilled eggs, bread and some cold corned beef I was able to get at the market. I have even made a chocolate cake, which almost joins the shale in its suicidal path downhill.

We sit, winded, on the edge of a little porch that surrounds the building. I have had to pull Irving up the last few feet. His heart. He takes off his hat. I love the wave of his hair as it mounts backwards from his forehead. The view is spectacular.

Irving says the corned beef is very good. I have no real basis for judging. I know the eggs are just right — the whites slide easily across the lower lip, the mashed yolks like velvet. The bread is not as fresh as I would have liked, but Irving cuts himself several pieces for his makeshift sandwich. I did not think to bring anything to drink, but we find the pump and a bucket that looks fairly clean and a couple of glasses in a cupboard inside the cabin. Irving calls it Chateau St. Martin's, and we laugh, but we stop short of making a toast. What would it be?

The icing on the chocolate cake is soft, and a large smear ends up on Irving's cheek. I dip my handkerchief in my water glass and wipe him off. I won't look at his eyes, though. I know they are gazing unblinkingly at me.

"So what would this be a location for, Mr. Producer? A sailor picture? The sea-captain's widow who watches from the hillside for the ship that is never coming back?" I try not to sound bitter.

"I had thought something a little happier."

"A tale of growing up wild in the countryside, fishing and hunting and walking that long stone beach?"

"A little bit of a love story, maybe."

I don't remember his lips being this warm. And I don't tell him this time about how waiting will be worth it.

AS I AM fixing my hair with the help of a little frameless mirror on the cabin wall, Irving comes up behind me. He is still naked although I have put my slip back on. His chin fits neatly on my shoulder. How great we look together in the reflection. When I start to pull away, he holds on.

"What do you see?"

"You know damn well what I see."

"Tell me."

"Irving and Norma. Hollywood's sweethearts."

Still, he won't let me go.

"I see that Thalberg fella, but who's that gorgeous dame with him?"

"Nice try."

"I could tell the two of you apart after a week. You never fooled me, you know. I knew what was going on. I always knew."

My eyes blur and my cheeks burn.

"And you were right all those times. It was worth waiting for. Say something."

"What?"

"Look in the mirror and say something. Move your lips. Watch. Ir-ving." He repeats it, "Irving."

"Nor-ma," I whisper finally, and slip out of his embrace.

When I come back from the outhouse, he has dressed and is buckling up his briefcase. I suppose that he carries an extra pair of shorts in there. In case.

"We should get back. I don't like to drive in the dark."

"We'll go back then."

5

Lillie

I DO NOT go to see Louis and Irving off on the train, though that's what I let Walter Golding think when I ask him for the day off. Instead, I take the street railway all the way out to Glen Falls, where I know I can meet a man who has a kind of bus service to St. Martin's. It's really nothing more than a truck bed fitted with wooden benches from an old sleigh. The sides are open except for a few braces that support a wooden roof that groans at every bump and turn in the road. The bus leaves when there are enough people for it to be worth the man's while, or when he feels like it. Luckily for me, he feels like it quite soon after I get off the tram.

The seat beside me is empty, which means I could set down the enormous bag I have packed for the trip. I choose instead to balance it on my lap. The contents are too precious to risk an upset, and the pain to my thighs is probably good for me. It's not just the weight of the film canister, though that alone would be enough to print deep red welts through my skirt. It's all the other mementoes too. By Loch Lomond I am sweating rivers. When I reach the cabin in St. Martin's, I am drenched.

I HAVE BROUGHT a thermometer with me, and once I have the fire kindled, I unpack it. It advertises motor oil in letters long since faded by the sun. I found it in the trash, but there's nothing wrong with the tube, and you can read the calibrations if you squint hard. Eighty-five. A good head start.

The windows in the cabin are not tight. I knew this from before; they rattle when there's a wind. I have brought rags to wedge in the gaps between sash and frame. I tear them in strips, dip them in the galvanized bucket filled from the well, twist them, and use a kitchen knife to drive them home. Then back to the stove to add wood. Something catches in my throat; the burning dust and mouse shit, the smell of hot metal. A drop of sweat races between my breasts, my armpits give off a tang like dulse. I wonder about stripping down to my slip. But how would that look? Not that I am expecting an audience, but in the larger sense, how would it look? I take one of the rags I couldn't find a place for, dab at my temples. Then I move the bucket away from the stove, thinking the water will stay cooler longer that way.

The canister is on the table. I like the contrast of its cold metallic glint with the warm pine. In it is the only reel I could find, though I scoured the Imperial's basement after I discovered it. From what Mayer and Irving have said, I think that this is all that remains anywhere in the world. What luck it should have come to me. Luck is not the word.

The nail on my right index finger breaks as I pry the tin open. No loss; it was a stupid piece of vanity trying to keep them so long.

I have had the film out of the canister before to be sure it is actually what the label promises. The first two or three feet are very faded, the amber discolouration of the stock beginning to efface the images that were printed; but it's still recognizable. Not everyone would be able to identify it, but I know every shot by heart. The emulsion is a little sticky, and the base is beginning to become brittle. I've seen this before, I know what it means. I have also witnessed the later stages of disintegration — the gas bubbles and the noxious smell, the viscous froth, the brownish acrid powder that marks the final state. Cellulose nitrate film. In the basement at the theatre, there are dozens of reels of the stuff decomposing, still-living bodies in lime. If you look at it that way, what I have planned is a form of mercy killing. Above a temperature of one hundred and twenty degrees, the film will spontaneously combust, burning fast, fuelled by its own released oxygen. Better than the slow journey to brown powder. There will be fumes and by-products, that's what the safety manuals at the theatre warn — nitric oxide (laughing gas), nitrous oxide, nitrous dioxide, and (the *coup de grâce*) nitric acid.

I pull a couple of yards of film off the spool and let them coil in my lap. The images are clearer here. I shiver as I hold a strip up to the light from the window and check the thermometer. The figures printed on the film don't seem to feel the heat. The silver dust they're made of, though, is beginning to react, the odour creeping up over the smell of my armpits and the stove's hot metal. I scrape at the emulsion with my broken nail. At work, in the theatre basement, I use a special stone to sand this layer away before making a splice. It's amazing how well I can manage without. I think about the newer films, with the sound recorded right onto them. What effect is that going to have on the craft of splicing? I am glad I will not have to worry about it. I am glad, too, that the images I am looking at are not crowded over to one side by the ghosts of the sounds they made.

Two more logs in the stove. I push the table closer to the heat, scratching tracks in the linoleum. From the bag, I fish the odd collection of objects, line them up beside the film canister. A shard of mirror glass, a piece of tinfoil, a cracked glass negative, a dogeared presentation card. One hundred and five degrees. Nearly there.

As I cross the room to pick up two more sticks of wood, something catches my eye in the mirror. I go to investigate, but see nothing unusual. The same old face with the lazy eye, the face that could launch a thousand ships when it is worn by Norma Shearer. My hair is plastered to my brow. "Oh, Lillie," I say and I reach to push it away. Then I watch my lips in the mirror as the face says it again. "Lillie." I try it slower "Lillie." Yes. It all fits. My voice. My face. My name. Together. Sound and sight reunited in one single frame.

My toe brushes against something hard under a blanket that lies on the floor.

It looks identical to the canister laid out on the table. They all look alike. Grey in the dark or the light. This one happens to be stamped with the name of a movie house in New Jersey. I break another nail opening it. A piece of paper falls to the floor. As I pull off the first few feet and hold them up to the light I know I have been here before.

The piece of paper is a note. To accompany the first of Irving's gifts to me. It did not strike me at the time how light his briefcase seemed as we clambered back down the hill to the car. He has saved another reel of *Blue Water* from Mayer's slaughter. Has he watched it? He claimed he could tell us apart. Has he seen me in it? The note is only one line. "What will you do with it?" And his initial.

I throw open the windows and the door. The cooler air rushes in. The fog bank has begun to roll towards the shore again.

For a long time, I sit watching the mercury drop on the thermometer. Every now and again, I go back to the mirror and mouth my name. I will stay the night. Tomorrow I will pack everything up into my bag and try to find the man who runs the jitney so I can go back home. Maybe I will stash the film reels in the boneyard, where they can decay at a natural rate. Or maybe I should keep one of them for a rainy day. For now, it is enough to know that Irving saw me in it and thought to give it back.

6

Iris Out

AS IT TURNS out, I carry out both plans, one after the other. For three months, I hide the reels in the boneyard at the Imperial. When my belly begins to threaten to show, I resign. I tell Walter Gold-ing I am going back to Hollywood. Norma needs me, I say. Now that she's a widow, I say. I sneak the two canisters out on my last day.

Of course, I don't go to Hollywood. I move in with Percy and Mike — Percy who will never tell anyone where I have gone, and Mike, who has obviously had plenty of practice at keeping a secret. I cut my hair and colour it, wear loose clothes — black, out of respect for Irving, his poor heart. No one would ever take me for Lillie Dempster. No one will ever again take me for Norma Shearer. Mostly, I stay in the apartment.

I write to Louis Mayer and he sends money from time to time. It's just good business, I tell myself whenever I feel a pang of conscience. I never get so much as an acknowledgement of the sympathy card I send to Norma. Maybe it's because I send it so late that it gets lost in an avalanche of sympathetic fan mail. I doubt it. I don't send her a birth announcement.

FAITH WRITES TO me the summer after you are born. It is the second summer she has not come north, and she is feeling ... well, it's so hard to tell what other people are feeling, don't you think? It's hard enough most of the time to know what you feel yourself.

She writes that the talkies have changed the motion picture business for a lot more than just the actors. Faith was a continuity writer. That meant she took the story — literally took it from a book or a magazine — and made a list of the shots they would need to tell it. Then they shot it. She worked in images, in pictures, though when she got really stuck, she could always write a title card. If they wanted to, the actors could improvise little speeches to fit with the situations they found themselves in, but nobody ever heard them. With the talkies, a writer on a picture has to come up with the dialogue, too. Words for the dummies to speak. That's what Faith writes to me about. She knows I have been around the studio, have even watched some talkies being made. She thinks I must know what L.B. Mayer likes. Would I consider working on a screenplay or two with her, just on spec, just to see how things went? We could do it through the mail, and she could hop on a train if we absolutely needed to meet.

Percy and Mike encourage me to say yes, to give it a try. Coming from one guy who used to play piano in a silent movie house and another who is a deaf painter, this advice is hard to discount. Where could you find more disinterested counsellors?

It turns out I like working with words. Pretty soon I am not just writing the dialogue, I'm also helping with the story, choosing the scenes that will tell it best, putting them in order. I don't have to be anywhere near the actors, or the directors, or even the men who run the theatres. If I don't want to, I don't have to be very near myself. But my words, in sharp black type bitten into fresh white paper and mailed to Hollywood through New York, make them see the pictures and hear the sounds and tell the stories.

The most magical thing of all is that I can do it all from right here while I look after you and watch you grow, every day amazed to find my reflection reproduced once again in your tiny face.

Acknowledgements

This book is indebted to the patience of the reference staff at the Saint John Free Public Library as well as to David Wallace's *Lost Hollywood*, Thomas Doherty's *Pre-Code Hollywood*, Samuel Marx's *Mayer and Thalberg*, Diana Altman's *Hollywood East*, and Sue McLuskey and Grant Kelly's, *Saint John at Work and Play: Photographs by Isaac Erb, 1904–1924*. I am also grateful to all of those biographers of Mayer and Shearer who are silent on the subject of *Blue Water*, as it was their silence that originally piqued my interest, and led me to invent Lillie.

For Arthur Motyer's constant encouragement and example, and for Marc Côté's keen sense of story, endlessly challenging questions and kind support I will never stop being thankful.

ENVIRONMENTAL BENEFITS STATEMENT

Cormorant Books saved the following resources by printing the pages of this book on chlorine-free paper made with 100% post-consumer waste.

. TREES	WATER	ENERGY	SOLID WASTE	GREENHOUSE GASES
16	**5,828**	**11**	**748**	**1,404**
FULLY GROWN	GALLONS	MILLION BTUs	POUNDS	POUNDS

Calculations based on research by Environmental Defense and the Paper Task Force.
Manufactured at Friesens Corporation

Recycled
Supporting responsible use
of forest resources

FSC

www.fsc.org Cert no. SW-COC-1271
© 1996 Forest Stewardship Council

100%